ROCK ME TWO TIMES

DAWN RYDER

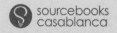

Copyright © 2015 by Dawn Ryder
Cover and internal design © 2015 by Sourcebooks, Inc.
Cover art by Blake Morrow

Sourcebooks and the colophon are registered trademarks of Sourcebooks, Inc.

All rights reserved. No part of this book may be reproduced in any form or by any electronic or mechanical means including information storage and retrieval systems—except in the case of brief quotations embodied in critical articles or reviews—without permission in writing from its publisher, Sourcebooks, Inc.

The characters and events portrayed in this book are fictitious or are used fictitiously. Any similarity to real persons, living or dead, is purely coincidental and not intended by the author.

Published by Sourcebooks Casablanca, an imprint of Sourcebooks, Inc.
P.O. Box 4410, Naperville, Illinois 60567-4410
(630) 961-3900
Fax: (630) 961-2168
www.sourcebooks.com

Printed and bound in Canada.
MBP 10 9 8 7 6 5 4 3 2 1

Chapter 1

"KATIE...SWEETIE..."

Kate Napier raised her head, shifting her focus from the strips of leather she had pushed under the industrial sewing machine she was using. Her partner only called her sweetie when he was nervous about something.

One look at Percy Lynwood confirmed it. All six foot four of him hovered in the doorway between the machine shop and the cutting room of their design studio. He was pulling on the measuring tape draped around his neck, looking at her with pleading eyes. She looked past him to find that their staff members had suspiciously disappeared into the prep room at the back of the building.

"This is part of the Stanton order, Percy," she warned him. "He wants it for Sturgis in two weeks."

Percy wrung his hands, looking like a gigantic teddy bear with his naturally curly hair framing his forehead. He shifted from side to side before taking a stiff breath and stepping onto the concrete floor of the machine shop.

"I know, *sweetie*..."

Kate flattened her hands on the edge of the sewing machine table and narrowed her eyes. Percy grimaced and lifted his hands to keep her from arguing further.

"I'll put Paula on it," he said in a rush. "Giles just called with an emergency."

She took the opportunity to stand up and stretch her lower back, arching all the way until her neck popped.

"Leather is my department. No offense to Paula, but she doesn't fit ass like I do," Kate said.

"Definitely not," Percy agreed. "But this is an emergency on an epic scale," he finished with a flurry of his hands.

Kate lowered her chin and locked gazes with Percy. His tone was downright miserable. "Okay, so what is stressing you out so bad?"

"It's the Toxsin account."

Kate lifted her hand and pointed to the wall behind Percy. Her personal operating rules were on a corkboard. Number one: no cuts to the front of the line.

"I know about your rules, Kate, but this is urgent!" Percy was back to wringing his hands. "Toxsin is going on stage in four hours, and there is some sort of problem with the lead singer's leather pants."

"As in Syon Braden?" Kate asked.

Percy nodded. "The Marquis." He supplied the stage name of the man currently topping preeminent entertainer lists around the globe with a breathless sigh.

She moved around the large industrial sewing machine and jabbed her finger again at the corkboard on the wall that had her name on it. "Rule number two: I don't do rock stars. Besides, are you really telling me that you don't want to get your hands on the Marquis?"

Percy cracked a saucy grin through his worried expression. "You know I do, and I think even Steve will forgive me for it as long as I share every last succulent detail. That Syon is an animal." Percy made a soft sound that was a cross between a moan and a growl.

"Glad we got that squared away." Kate turned and headed for the leather pants destined for the biker paradise known as Sturgis. The end-of-summer rally held in Sturgis, South Dakota, drew bikers from all over the world. Making leatherwear for attendees was her bread and butter. "Have a blast with the Marquis."

"But, Kate," Percy whimpered again. "Showtime is seven, and they are playing the Staples Center downtown."

"Ahhh…" Kate turned to look at the large clock on the wall next to her corkboard. Every staff member had a corkboard. Schedules were posted there, along with any rule anyone felt they couldn't live with being violated. The boards kept the peace pretty well, but the clock read three sharp.

"With afternoon traffic, which will be even worse than usual with Toxsin playing, I'll never make it down there in time. They've been sold out for months," Percy explained.

"So why did Giles call us? It's his account, his premiere account. Why isn't he flying out to defend his turf?" Percy's costume college buddy had jumped through flaming hoops to score the account with Toxsin.

Percy spread his hands in a pleading gesture. "Because he's in New York, and it's an emergency. They need something fixed immediately. He wouldn't trust just anyone to deal with them. That's why he called us."

"Giles called you, not us." Kate propped her hand on her hip. "I'm still a little sketchy on why you need me for this, Percy. I don't drive any faster than you do."

"They're sending a helicopter from the Staples Center. That's how desperate they are." Percy looked miserable again. "You know I can't stand heights."

Kate's stomach knotted. Percy could get woozy on the third story of their building if he got too close to a window. He'd turn green just looking at a helicopter.

Shit.

"Wear a blindfold and think about what you'll get for your courage," she said.

Percy gave a sigh, which was pitiful until she coupled it with his overall size. He had the body of a linebacker and the heart of a 1950s suburban housewife. A mouse sighting would send him screaming. When it came to his marriage with his husband, Steve, Percy was the wife all the way.

"I tried the blindfold in Alaska, but I still threw up all over Steve before we finished the helicopter tour of the glacier. And it was his birthday present too. I tried so hard." He shook his head sadly.

The knot in her stomach was tightening with the help of guilt. She did love Percy, but rock stars drove her insane. She chewed on her lower lip as her partner looked at her pleadingly. *Yup, hungry, starving baby bear.*

"Take a bucket," she suggested.

"I'll arrive as weak as an infant and light-headed. Definitely not professional." He pointed at the three phrases posted above everyone's corkboards. They were the operating foundation of their business, Timeless Custom Creations:

Always push the creative boundaries.

Always wow the customer.

Always be professional.

"Shit," she cussed as the word *professional* cut through her personal phobias. "Just...craptastic!"

Percy sent her a relieved look. She was folding,

and he knew it. "I always fucking cave in when it's our image on the line," she said. "Giles is so going to owe me."

Percy tried to soothe her. "You'll be just fine, sweetie."

"Don't 'sweetie' me." She pointed at him. "You'd better tell them I'm a lesbian, because if even one of those arrogant asshats pinches my butt, I'm going warrior princess on them."

Percy rolled his eyes. "Hardly. You're so strictly dick, I get jealous when you sit next to Steve at lunch."

"I'm not a home wrecker," she defended herself.

"But you are a little uptight lately…maybe it will be good for you." Percy was back to being saucy. "Find out if they know how to use those succulent bodies for more than dancing. You know, just 'cause you got great buns doesn't mean you know how to fuck worth—"

He ducked when Kate chucked a chair cushion at him. It collided with the wall, making a soft, unsatisfying sound before sliding to the floor.

Percy was laughing when he peeked between his hands at her. "Is that a definite no? Because the Marquis does have a whole lot of yumminess going on. I bet he could make you forget all about Todd—"

"Rule number five, no kissing on the first date," Kate reminded him.

"Technically, it's not a date," Percy pointed out with a smirk. "You should exploit that loophole darling, or let it exploit you!"

Kate groaned and stomped off to take a shower. Working with leather was a sweaty business. The water restored her confidence in her appearance, but she was still chewing on her discontentment when she heard the helicopter landing in the back parking lot.

Rock stars. Geez. Just what she didn't need. Todd and his two-timing had been more than enough.

But at least she could dress how she liked. She pulled on a pair of leather pants and tightened the laces that ran up their sides from ankle to hip. They fit her like a second skin, and she admired the way the blood-orange leather cupped her ass.

No one fit leather like she did. She couldn't help it. She loved the stuff—the scent, the feel, and most especially, the look. She added a thin silk tank top that fluttered over her buns like a teasing veil, ending right at the curve of her butt, and shrugged into a leather corset top with brass closures. Once it was tight, her cleavage was halfway to her chin.

Perfect. At least she had one good thing to say about rock stars: they had good taste in clothing.

———— ∿∿∿ ————

"You've got a full set kit." Percy pointed at the black cases being loaded into the helicopter. "So no matter what the issue is, you should be fine."

Kate wasn't sure what she'd expected, but the sleek black aircraft in her parking lot wasn't it. The thing was plenty big enough for the eight heavy-duty traveling cases that made up their "on set" kit. The pilot hadn't even needed to disembark, because he had two burly assistants to help him load everything. They were outfitted in tuxes, and *not* the off-the-rack variety. She knew a custom job when she saw one. They kept those suit jackets on even as they lifted and stowed her gear, which meant only one thing: they were bodyguards too. Had to have something to hide their chest harnesses.

"I am so jealous," Percy whined. "These guys are premium…"

Kate rolled her eyes. "There will be at least a hundred starstruck fangirls willing to grease their poles just for the chance to get near the band."

"I know, Katie girl, but I have to admit that I wouldn't mind playing games with any of them." He made a sound of enjoyment and smacked his lips.

"You're married," she reminded him.

"But not dead." Percy batted his eyelashes at her. "You look like a blood orange. Sweeten up a little and stop letting Todd make you into such a bitch. It's his loss."

Kate offered him a genuine smile. She felt a little tug on her heart, because she did love Percy, quivering insides and all. He had an unparalleled eye for color and could draft a pattern like a fairy godmother.

"Todd who?" she purred.

"There's my girl." He reached out and patted her hair. Newly washed, it was rising up into a cloud of tiny copper curls. She had it clipped back, but there was no way it was going to lay flat. "I think they're ready for you."

Kate looked up to see one of the private security men moving toward her.

"Be careful with the warrior-princess thing. I hear the Marquis likes his women wild," Percy added with a suggestive grin.

Kate stuck out her tongue at him before striding toward the sleek aircraft. One of the security men

opened the sliding door behind the copilot seat and
offered her a hand as she stepped up into the cabin. The
seats were plush and covered in black leather. The security guy waited while she pulled the seat straps over her
shoulders and secured the chest harness. He pointed to a
set of earphones hanging from the ceiling. The rotor was
beginning to spin, filling the cabin with noise.

She pulled the earphones off the hook and fussed
with them until she adjusted them small enough to sit
on her head. They were the sort that covered each ear
completely, and a microphone stuck out in front of
her face.

"Once I take off, I'll turn on your feed, Ms. Napier.
Push the button on the side of your headset before you
talk." The pilot's voice had an electronic quality to
it through the headphones, and there was a click the
moment he finished talking. The helicopter shuddered
as the rotor reached full speed. They began to lift
off the ground, Kate's belly doing a tiny flop at the
sudden weightlessness.

She leaned forward to look out the window. There
was something thrilling about being able to lift up and
over the afternoon traffic. They flew over the freeway,
confirming her suspicion that there was no way she
would have made it by car. It was bumper-to-bumper
rush hour in the Los Angeles basin. No one was going
anywhere fast.

Unless they were in a helicopter. She smiled, enjoying the moment of being someone important. Because it
sure wouldn't last. There was a pile of leather waiting
for her back at the shop and a line of impatient bikers
to deal with.

In the distance, the towers of downtown Los Angeles rose up. The air was surprisingly clear, and the sun sparkled off the glass-sided skyscrapers. The pilot was talking to some air-control personnel as he made a wide circle around the Staples Center. It sure was a different picture from the air. She'd been to the huge arena plenty of times, but she'd never seen the top of it.

There were three helicopter-landing circles, complete with blinking lights set into the concrete. There was also a ramp that had two black SUVs parked on it, facing away from a glass entry into the arena. A burly bodyguard was standing near the driver's door, watching the helicopter hover over one of the landing circles.

What a different world.

"They are waiting for you, Ms. Napier. We'll get your gear unloaded and down to you."

Someone opened the side door before the pilot stopped talking. The rotor was still winding down, and air rushed inside. The suit jacket on the guy at the door flipped up, giving her a peek at a shoulder holster and the butt of a pistol.

Yeah, different world completely.

She pressed the release buttons on the latch holding her harness and managed her way to the open door. The wind and noise were dying down, allowing her to hear something else: the unmistakable sound of people cheering from the street. It was like a roar coming over the top of the building.

It sent a tingle along her spine.

"Don't mind them. They just think you're part of the band arriving."

The bodyguard offered her a hand, but she grabbed

the handle on the ceiling of the aircraft. He cupped her elbow the moment her feet hit the pavement and guided her toward the glass entry port from the roof. Now that she'd landed, she could see painted walkways leading toward two huge double doors.

"You don't need to hold on to me." She lifted her arm, earning a stern look from the bodyguard.

"Let's go over the rules." He kept hold of her elbow as someone inside opened the door for them. "No touching the performers."

"That's going to make fixing a costume issue challenging," she remarked.

He lifted a finger into the air. "Unless they give you permission."

Once inside, she had more space and stepped away from the guy. He was burly enough to maintain his hold on her if he wanted to, but he only sent her a annoyed look before holding out his hand.

"I'll need your cell phone before you go any farther. No backstage pictures," the bodyguard continued.

"Oh…" That made sense. She started to dig it out of her purse.

"The whole purse," he insisted.

She froze and studied the look on the guy's face. He wasn't kidding. She handed it over. "That's a one-of-a-kind bag; don't let it get punctured."

He gave it to a man standing behind him and gestured her toward a security-screening machine, just like one she'd find in an airport.

Rule number two wasn't changing.

—⁓—

"Mmm… The candy is arriving. Ginger candy too." Ramsey pointed at the glass of a two-way mirror that allowed the members of the band to see beyond their private dressing room.

"Don't make that sound this close to showtime, Ramsey," Drake said. "I don't have time to redo my makeup."

"There's no makeup on your cock," Ramsey shot back.

Drake looked away from the mirror and flipped Ramsey the bird. "I actually like spending more than ten minutes with a girl before getting my load off."

Ramsey let out a whistle. "Syon! Looks like your costume girlie is here. I think I'm going to go rip my pants so she can…fix me."

"Don't you fucking dare," Syon shouted from across the dressing room. "We can buy off-the-rack if you won't take the time to unbutton them before fucking."

"You might be the Marquis on stage, dude, but back here, you're just one of the boys," Ramsey retorted.

"I still outrank you," Syon barked back.

"We're not sitting in Afghanistan anymore. The only way you outrank me is by bringing in more chicks," Ramsey said.

Syon grinned in victory. "She's here to see me."

"Shit." Ramsey threw his hands up in surrender. "She's a ginger too. You know I love a natural redhead."

Syon threw Ramsey a bone of hope. "After the show, dude." There were a few sounds of agreement from the other members of the band. Syon leaned toward the mirror and checked his makeup. He still wasn't quite comfortable wearing it, but he loved being on stage. Fucking loved it more than anything he'd ever done. So

the makeup was like body armor. A necessity, a tool of
the trade.

The doors opened and the Staples Center security
escorted in a lone female. Syon turned his head and
found himself grateful his hands were braced on a
sturdy countertop.

He felt sucker punched.

Yeah, she was a ginger all right.

Light orange hair crowned her head, and she had
delicate eyebrows of the same hue. She could've faked
those, but the fine dusting of body hair on her arms
confirmed that she was pure ginger. The teasing bit of
leather she had covering her tits just made him want to
lick her before he tore the thing off.

His cock hardened painfully; the damned thing was
like granite.

Ramsey let out a whistle, and she sent him a harassed
look. A flicker of flames in her blue eyes struck him
as challenging.

There was nothing he liked better than a challenge.
Especially one with such a great pair of tits.

Ramsey slid across the room with a gait Syon recognized all too well. Ramsey shot her a killer grin before
opening his hand and offering it to her. She cast a quick
glance down at the open palm in front of her before
tucking her hand against the side of her body. She'd
crossed her arms in front of her so Ramsey couldn't kiss
the back of her hand.

Spitfire.

Damned if that didn't make his cock hurt. He was
used to being hard during a show, but the thing was
swollen so stiff, it ached.

"Only have eyes for the Marquis?" Ramsey turned and sent her packing with a quick gesture. "There he is, hoping you'll save him from going on in his jockstrap."

"Screw you, Ramsey," Syon barked. What was normally a good-natured remark suddenly came across his lips as something entirely different. There was a flicker in Ramsey's eyes as he noted it, but Syon realized that he didn't give a crap.

He'd meant it. Completely.

~~~

Kate needed to get a grip on herself.

She drew in a stiff breath and regretted it.

The damned room smelled hot.

And it had nothing to do with the temperature.

Ramsey was a long-legged, lean-hipped animal with dark hair that flowed over his shoulders in unruly waves. It wasn't feminine in the least—just sexy in a savage, no-holds-barred sort of way. To her right were a pair of wide-chested guys spotting each other on a weight-training bench.

But what made her feel dizzy was staring at her from a pair of caramel eyes. The lead singer of Toxsin had a head of dirty-blond hair that was spiked out and falling past his shoulders. His eyebrows were slashes that angled up. His shoulders were wide and cut with hard muscles that his thin T-shirt showed to perfection.

He looked like the Goblin King from *Labyrinth*.

Shit!

Professionalism.

She stepped forward. "Kate Napier."

He moved with a fluidity that bordered on a prowl.

Once he closed the distance between them, she had to tip
her head back to keep her eyes locked on his face. The
guy had to be at least six foot four. His eyes narrowed,
his gaze cutting into hers. Something radiated from
him—a sense of control that reached out and smacked
her. For a moment, she was stunned, trying to decide if
he really was affecting her this strongly or if she was
oxygen deprived from the airlift.

"Napier… Scottish. That suits the ginger hair," he said.

"You know the origin of my name?" Damn, she was
saying stupid things now. Rule number two had obviously saved her from more than oversexed musicians. It
had kept her from making an ass out of herself. His lips
twitched as he read her expression far too easily.

"Am I disappointing you by having intelligence?"
he drawled.

She tried to collect her scattered wits, but the way he
watched her was just too unnerving. His gaze was piercing, and he had a commanding presence that was off the
scale. She felt pinned by his caramel stare.

"*Surprised* would be my word choice." But that was
still slightly insulting. "Not to say I expected you to be
a high school dropout. There aren't many people who
know the origin of my name off the cuff."

Ramsey came up behind her. "The Marquis likes to
read." He scooted right up and draped an arm around
her, letting his fingers splay out over her hip. "His heart
is a deep ocean…"

Kate trailed her fingers up the bare center of his chest
that his leather vest didn't cover and clasped the bar
piercing his nipple.

"Alright…alright…" He backed off with his hands

up in surrender. "At least until after the show," he added with a husky chuckle. "I like rough play."

"In your dreams," she replied.

There was a flash of anticipation in his eyes before he pressed his lips into a silent kiss. "You're going to be fun."

She snapped her head around to find Syon watching her from beneath hooded eyes. There was something ultrasensual about the way he was studying her. Something that sent a jolt of heat through her and left her mouth dry.

There was a rattle behind them as the doors opened wide, and more suit-clad men pushed a flatbed cart into the room. The distraction gave her a chance to get ahold of her racing heart. It was just a job. Tomorrow she'd wake up in her own bed, and the closest she would be able to get to Syon Braden would be a poster or a four-hundred-dollar concert ticket.

Ramsey and the Marquis, on the other hand, would likely wake up in a tangle of limbs belonging to some of the horde of fangirls who idolized Toxsin. Their music was supreme, and so was their reputation for torrid after-concert parties.

For a nanosecond she lingered on the idea of being naked with him.

"Perhaps you might explain the problem?" Kate said, trying to get grip on her professionalism.

Ha! You mean your hormones!

No, she had it under control. Really.

But her heart started racing the moment she locked eyes with the Marquis again. His gaze shifted, and his lips parted, showing her his teeth. Her breath caught.

"Over here."

Kate turned and discovered that the back of the Marquis was just as devastating to her libido as his front. His shoulders were broad and tapered down to a lean waist, and the pair of jeans he was wearing gave her a perfect look at his ass.

Yummy.

"I'm out of pants," he said.

Syon pointed to two long, rolling costume racks. Various pairs of leather pants were hung up. Kate moved closer, spotting problems instantly. She pulled one navy-blue pair out to look at the way the lower half of the leg was shredded.

"Don't ride double with Taz. He'll dump your ass," Syon said.

"You were wasted," the Asian guy on the weight bench yelled across the suite, "and fell off."

She released the blue pants and pulled out another pair, which was covered in what looked like bleach splatters.

"Cleaning ladies don't have a sense of humor." Syon clicked his tongue. "She decided to help me clean up my act."

Kate pulled out another pair and gapped at the missing fly. It was just cut clean away with jagged slices from a pair of scissors.

"Some girls get impatient—"

"I bet," she cut him off. He shrugged and sent her a self-satisfied smirk. "But you let someone cut your custom-made performance wear?"

"Heat of the moment" was his reply.

Arrogant ass. It was on the tip of her tongue to say it too. The part of her that knew how hard it was to make quality pants was itching to take him down a notch.

Professionalism.

She looked back at the rack. There were three pairs on the end of the rack that didn't seem to be damaged.

"They don't fit," Syon informed her. "Giles forgot the special instructions."

A note in his tone warned her against asking. But he also shut his mouth, just daring her to ask. It was a verbal game of cat and mouse.

"Giles doesn't make mistakes that affect fit. Elaborate. I can't fix what I don't understand." There. She hadn't asked.

He straightened up and moved closer, looming over her and sending a trickle of sweat down her back. "There's not enough room for a hard-on," he drawled in a low, sensual tone. "At least, not a really hard one. Understandable really. Giles didn't turn me on during my fitting. I had to improvise." His gaze lowered to her cleavage.

Her nipples twisted into hard little nubs. He was an asshole, but he also oozed sex appeal. She felt like she was going into heat.

"I get hard every show," he continued. "Music is a sexual experience for me."

Oh boy, did she believe him.

Her attention dropped to his package, a split second before her face exploded in flames, and she jerked her head back around to the pants. The blood roared in her ears, but she thought she heard a soft sound of male approval behind her.

She'd looked at his… *Damn it!*

Fangirls gained a smidgen of respect in her book. There was something about rock stars that just scrambled a girl's wits.

He chuckled and reached out to stroke one scarlet cheek.

His touch sent her clit throbbing.

And her tongue felt glued to the roof of her mouth.

It was humiliating.

And exciting on a scale she'd never experienced. Not that she would be admitting it.

But his eyebrow rose. "Any chance you can help?"

"I think so." Provided she could jump-start her brain.

She made her way over to where the polo-shirt-wearing crew was busy opening every single case she'd brought. She stopped after a few steps because her hips felt like they were swaying too much.

Sweat actually beaded on her forehead. The guy was sending her into a sexual frenzy for Christ's sake.

Her vibrator was so getting a workout when she got home.

She bit her lower lip, realizing she needed more information.

"What side do you tuck on?"

He rolled his lips back, baring his teeth at her. "Left, because there is nothing right about me, Ginger."

That was for damned sure!

Problem was, she really liked it.

—⁓—

He was making her nervous.

Ramsey was warming up behind him, and Syon really should have joined him, but Kate had his full attention.

She had a curvy body that fascinated him. The little

edge of her top was flipping around like a fringe scarf on a belly dancer, teasing him all to hell. One moment he could see her cheeks, and the next, that fabric was sweeping across her tight ass. Did she wax or keep a nice little nest of ginger curls between her thighs?

He wanted to bury his face in them.

She was trying not to look at him, apparently attempting to ignore the charge between them. It was thick and heady. He closed his eyes and waited to see if the connection would dull without the sight of her.

It didn't. He could still smell the scent of her skin, and it turned him on to see her working on the crotch of his pants. A clean scent of warm, female flesh with a hint of some sort of bodywash that was just subtle enough not to strike him as fake. He knew when a female was pushing herself into his space, saw it a hundred times a day. Kate was being herself, grooming to her own standards instead of trying to hook his attention. That confidence was sexy. Her determination to remain professional was a serious kick to his libido. It was hitting him out of left field too, because it wasn't like he had a shortage of possible companions. No, it was a little bit more like fate reminding him that some girls were quality, and that beat quantity every time.

She had skilled little fingers too. Long and nimble, they worked on the waistband of his pants with a finesse that mesmerized him. She stroked her fingers across the surface of the leather like she loved it. Well, she had to. The pants she was wearing were perfection. They didn't even have an inseam. She was a fucking goddess of leatherwork. And he could see why. She was so absorbed with her work, he didn't seem to even register in her world as she threaded a machine and started it up. She even ran a loving hand over the thing before beginning to feed his pants under the head.

First time he'd been beaten out by a pair of pants.

Ramsey started in on a solo, turning up the volume. Syon sighed and turned around. The show always came first.

He picked up his guitar and began to let the music take command of his brain. It wasn't a hard switch. Kate had him worked up. Music was an extension of his soul. Lust was just one of several powerful components. There was also aggression and drive. What he put onstage was the inner demon that most people in the civilized world struggled to conceal. His music was a raging of his desires for everything from sex to blood. The song crested, he and Ramsey in perfect unity. They both had their heads thrown back, bodies arched, as they pushed out the last wailing notes.

Satisfaction moved through him, but it was one peak in a chain that he planned to climb that night.

He wanted to lick her...

Syon turned to find Kate watching him. The tip of her tongue passed over her lower lip. She looked back down at what she was doing, but the dark blush on the side of her face was still visible.

"I think she bites..." Ramsey cooed, his fingers moving across the strings.

"She's mine."

"Says who?" Ramsey demanded.

Syon took the lead, feeling the music pulsing through his veins. It was a crazy combination of rhythm and stimulus, pushing him into revealing just exactly what sort of animal he was to the screaming fans waiting to glimpse it. Kate's presence was more potent, more intense than any he'd felt in a long time. It was the unknown factor that was driving him to a fevered pitch—that hint of challenge she presented, and something else that he had no fucking idea what it was, beyond the fact that it made him feel mean.

And made him more determined to get between her thighs than was probably healthy.

Anticipation...

"She's blushing...for me," Syon declared.

"Yeah." Ramsey leaned back, letting the music overwhelm him completely. Taz and Drake joined in, flooding the suite with music that shook the walls. "I still want to taste her."

———

Kate listened to music and even found some of the songs shaking the suite familiar. But she'd never heard it quite the same before.

She could have sworn she could feel it on some level she couldn't really explain. It was just there, inside her, like a second heart. Moving her along with the tempo as she worked with the machines that were so familiar to her hands. The two forces combined, her love of creation with the music. Sweat covered her skin by the time she stood up and pressed the new waistband she'd put on the pants. She shook them out and ran a critical eye over her work as the music died down.

She felt him coming this time, and looked up as he bore down on her. For a moment, she wasn't sure he was going to take the pants from her hand.

Determination blazed in his eyes—and a hunger that matched her own.

But he took them, crumpling the leather in his fist. His attention lowered to her mouth, and she rolled her lower lip in. His eyes narrowed before he ripped open the button fly of his jeans. She had just enough time to turn around before she saw him kick them across the floor.

"Chicken," he whispered.

She heard him stepping into the leather and pulling it up. The sound of a lace sliding through the eyelets of the fly was something she recognized, but tonight, it was far more sensual than usual.

She looked over her shoulder before turning. He was looking at his reflection in the full-length mirrors the suite was furnished with, stretching up and arching his back while watching just how low the waistband dipped on his tight abdomen.

"Hopefully that will do the trick," she offered. "There is only so much I can do with an existing garment. Leather doesn't stretch, so I opened up the crouch and put in a gusset. It's a pretty close color match. Someone would have to be right between your thighs to notice it."

"Fans in the pit pick up on every detail."

He was being serious. Dead, hard serious.

Kate stared at the glimpse of the businessman inside the rock star. Toxsin had come out of nowhere just three years ago and was now on the top of the charts. Rumors varied on the band's origins, and she had the feeling that she was getting a glimpse at a very personal side of Syon Braden, the man under the Marquis. He caught her watching him, their gazes meeting in the polished surface of the mirror. For a moment, she felt a pull toward him so strong it threatened to overwhelm everything else.

Like common sense. Or professionalism.

Or the very blunt reality of knowing she was going to end up like a used condom if she didn't get her sex drive under control.

"Stay for the show—there's a private box up here with all the amenities," Syon told her. "If your work fails, you'll have a good view."

"My work doesn't fail," she said. "And those aren't my work. If they were, they'd fit."

"You're passionate," he said softly.

"Perfectionist," she corrected. "Leather is a...personal experience for me."

He turned around and cupped her cheek before she realized he was in motion. The connection sent a shiver down her spine that traveled all the way to her toes. He leaned down, hovering over her ear. "Passionate," he bit out, slipping his hand back to cup her nape with a grip that twisted her clit.

"I dare you to be here when I'm finished, Kate."

"No problem."

She was a sucker for a dare. Her head was spinning from the mix of pheromones and raw sexual allure bleeding off him, and the words were just out of her mouth before she engaged her brain.

At least the higher functioning parts of it. Animal instinct was working just fine.

He lowered his gaze, targeting her mouth before leaning forward and pressing a kiss against her neck. His grip on her nape was solid, his body hard as stone, but his lips closed over her skin with just enough aggression to throw more fuel on the flames licking her clit. He teased her, stroking and tasting her before licking his way to her collarbone with a delicious stroke that left her knees weak.

The lights in the suite began to flash. He pulled away, leaving her leaning on the wall.

There was a hint of violence in his expression. His eyes narrowed as he pulled away from her, reluctance flickering in his gaze.

She was gasping, so turned-on she was in a daze. She needed to run.

Because she was way out of her depth.

The Staples Center was roaring.

It sounded like a tsunami coming in, or a freight train passing three feet in front of her face. It was more than sound; there was a vibration that traveled through her body, all the way down to her bones. There was a current in the air that practically crackled with excitement.

The bodyguard-slash-security guy showed Kate up to a private box. She followed because she didn't want to squeal like a little girl and ask to be taken home.

She'd never lost her head like this before.

It was embarrassing on an epic scale. She was pissed at herself for rolling over so easily for a man who wouldn't recall her name by the end of the night.

The box had plush seats and an open rail overlooking the stage. The lights went down, and the drummer started up. The beat was infectious, taking over her heart until she was sure the muscle was keeping the same rhythm.

The crowd roared again, thrusting their hands up into the air as two guitars joined the drummer. Her nipples puckered again, her memory offering up an image of Syon arching back as he played those final chords. It was like he was pushing the music out of himself, almost as if he were giving birth.

Onstage, he was just as raw.

Syon took command of the space completely. The audience ate him up.

And were they *screaming*. Syon worked them just as skillfully as he did his guitar. He really was lord of all he surveyed. Kate discovered herself leaning forward, being drawn toward the spellbinding energy pulsing on the stage. Sitting still was impossible; her body wanted to move in time with the notes Syon was wringing out of his instrument. She became fixated on his hands; the way he worked his fingers was downright dominant.

Her teeth were clenched. By the time the last song finished, she was panting softly and felt wrung out.

But it was fucking wonderful. She was drifting on a high and collapsed back into her padded chair, her composure scattered around her like fall leaves. She felt spent but amped up at the same time.

Fangirls were definitely climbing the respect ladder in her book.

Okay, so she was drooling over a rock star like some high schooler, but at least B.O.B.—her battery-operated boyfriend—was waiting for her at home. All in all, the buzz was worth the slightly stinging blow to her pride, because in some corner of her mind, she believed she should be grown-up enough to realize fantasies weren't mature. So disappointment wouldn't stalk her in the wee hours of the night.

A hollow feeling in her gut warned her she was hoping in vain.

As Syon and the rest of the band left the stage, Kate indulged herself in a long moment of reflection. Syon had worked that guitar until it wailed. He had to be hell in bed if he applied even half that effort to pleasing his partner.

"So, what'd you think?"

She jumped, grabbing the armrests of the movie theater–style chair. Her eyes popped open wide, and her belly did a triple flip when she found Syon watching her.

"Ah…" Her tongue suddenly felt like a wad of cotton in her mouth as she scrambled to stand up and turn around to face him. "It was fantastic…"

He grinned at her, a huge, arrogantly pleased expression that showed off his perfect teeth.

God, she wondered if he knew how to bite…

There was a curtain in the doorway that she'd never closed. Syon reached over and tugged it off the hook that held it back. The velvet shimmered as it swung down to give them privacy, adding a dose of intimacy that was spine tingling.

"Why did you do that?" she asked.

He shrugged, drawing her attention to the tightly corded muscles of his forearms. "I don't want to get jumped."

"Oh." She took a quick look down at the fans still crowded into the seating below. Now that the house lights were on, she could see people sitting in the private boxes that lined the second and third stories of the arena.

Syon was hanging back, staying behind the seats where there was still some shadow.

"Shouldn't you be backstage somewhere…with those security guys?" Kate asked.

He bared his teeth at her. "Maybe in forty years. Their job is to protect the fans from me."

"Yeah, I can see that side of your personality." Hell, she could have sworn she could feel it.

"I earned it," he answered with a confidence that was admirable.

He opened his arms. "Want to take a measurement? So you can make me a pair that fit…perfectly?"

"I get a hard-on when I play…"

"Oh…" *Damn it.* That was the third time she'd done nothing but answer in monosyllables.

She wasn't sure it was healthy for her to be taking a good look at him, but her costumer's eye switched on as she scanned his groin, tracing the bulge straining the leather.

Oh…yeah…serious package.

"It's Giles's account. I just stepped in because of the timing issue." There. At last. A perfect, professional deflection.

Syon's grin widened.

"Giles is in New York. You're here. I can't play 'Insatiable Craving' without this pair pinching."

She had to swallow the lump forming in her throat. "Insatiable Craving" was one hot song.

And she looked back down to find the leather straining.

Kate's breath froze for an instant as a bolt of excitement tore through her. "We're not going there. I'm not measuring you."

He looked down at her left hand and raised one of his perfectly groomed eyebrows. "Husband?"

"No," she admitted. He was stripping away her defenses like a kid pulling the petals off a daisy.

His attention returned to her face. There was a flash of determination in his eyes that made her quiver.

"Boyfriend?" He stepped toward her. "Girlfriend?"

She shook her head, the feeling of being overly exposed trying to drown her. "Just not going there. I'm way past the age of impulsive behavior. Got a business to run."

He bared his teeth again and moved in closer. "But it feels like it would be so much fun if you...*came*..."

She lifted her hands to ward him off and felt ridiculous, because what she really wanted to do was grab a handful of his chest hair. He smelled male, and some part of her was insanely turned-on by it. She was ready to claw him. His eyes were slightly dilated, like he was on the edge, and it excited her wildly.

Well, he was hard.

And she was wet.

"I have rules," she sputtered. "You don't look like the type who follows rules. So, good night. Nice to meet you and all. I doubt you'll miss me. Giles is likely working up more wardrobe for you as we speak. You're his premier account."

She expected him to recoil from the mention of rules. Instead he crossed his arms over his chest and cocked his head to one side. "Lay 'em on me."

"Excuse me?" she asked.

He flashed a grin at her. "The rules. Let's hear them."

She was back to feeling like her personal space was

being invaded. "I'm not interested in amusing you. I'm sure you won't have to go far to find that sort of companionship though."

"I won't," he confirmed, his tone deeper, serious. "And I'm standing here. You have discipline. So do I."

Of course he did. Beneath the makeup and the lights, there had still been some serious music. No one got that good without self-control.

"Your rules, Kate." She was pretty sure he wasn't asking. There was a flicker in his eyes that looked a lot more like a demand.

Well, he'd asked for it. Part of her wanted to see what he did when she laid it down. Straight out. Her fingers were closed into fists with anticipation, her head spinning just a bit at the idea of someone like him being willing to please her.

"No married men, no rock stars or celebrities, no drugs, no kissing on the first date, and no men still living with their parents."

She finished in a rush, feeling like she was trying to hold him off with a slingshot and a marshmallow instead of the well-thought-out rules she lived by. He was going to eat her ammo and lick his lips afterward.

"I rank below drugs?" he growled. "That's harsh. I've been studying guitar since I was four."

That was impressive. But she couldn't say so, because then she'd be right back to thinking about getting her hands on him. He smelled hot and ultra-male.

"It's just that I've done my share of movie costumes, and rock stars and celebrities, well, they don't really"— she found herself searching for some way to put it that wouldn't offend him—"do relationships."

"I don't do anything in half measures," he assured her.

"You asked," she said, trying to swallow her disappointment. Like there had been a chance in hell of them ever connecting beyond impulsive sex. "And now you know why I'm telling you to call Giles. It's been great meeting you."

"You haven't given me a chance to meet your demands." Syon chuckled softly, menacingly, and closed the last pace between them.

"You rejected them," she said.

"Relationships require negotiation. I can't change what I am, so number two needs to be struck from the list," he said.

"Maybe I don't negotiate."

"Maybe you need incentive," he offered in a raspy whisper.

They were toe to toe, the scent of his skin wrapping around her. He reached up and opened the clip she had holding her hair back. She heard it drop to the floor as he threaded his fingers through the strands, sending a torrent of sensation through her. It was bold and aggressive and presumptuous. She should have protested, but her eyes closed as waves of enjoyment rushed through her. All she wanted to do was arch and purr.

"You're ginger." He leaned over and buried his face in her hair. She heard him draw in a deep breath before exhaling next to her ear. "Spicy and sweet... I wanted to know what you tasted like the moment I saw you."

"Really?"

He closed his hand in her hair, pulling it tight but stopping shy of hurting her. "Yeah...really."

The hold sent her over the edge into some alternate dimension, where instinct ruled.

He hovered over her lips, almost touching them until she stretched toward him.

"Wait for it…" he growled softly, holding her back.

"Like hell." She smoothed her hands back until she found the opening of his vest. He'd never closed more than a few buttons, just enough to cover his navel. She slid her hands inside, needing to touch his bare skin.

But she closed her fingers, trapping a handful of his chest hair.

He stiffened, surprised. His chest rumbled with something that sounded a lot like a growl.

"Ginger all the way through…" He smothered her retort beneath his lips, kissing her with a force that left her breathless. He commanded every motion, moving her head to suit his whim. But she wasn't going to submit. She slid her hands up, over his collarbones until she found the corded muscles running along his neck. She threaded her fingers through his hair and grabbed him.

He pressed her mouth open, demanding complete surrender, but she still didn't give it to him. She teased the tip of his tongue with hers and then licked along his lower lip as he shuddered and pressed up against her.

His cock was rock hard.

And huge.

She shivered with need so sharp, she was half-afraid she might climax just from being against him. The need to lift her thigh and rub against him was insane.

"I thought you'd be up here, trying to beat me to the punch."

Kate jumped and would have fallen over the back of the chair if Syon hadn't slid his arm around her waist to hold her.

Ramsey grinned at her without a shred of shame on his face and flicked the curtain closed behind him. Syon let Kate push free of his embrace and offered his bandmate a shrug. "I waited until after the show, didn't I?"

"Barely," Ramsey griped. "You skipped out on that reporter and dropped her in my path like a land mine."

"Doesn't look like she exploded on you."

Ramsey leaned against the wall, pinning Kate between them. "She latched on."

"But you're still here," Kate observed. She probably shouldn't have spoken. It was a weird enough conversation and an even weirder situation. Things like "making sense" just didn't belong at all.

Kind of like herself. She was so far out of her element, she wasn't sure she knew how to make it back to reality.

Ramsey grinned, giving off a bad-boy vibe that had her teetering between the urge to smack him or bite. "I promised her an interview later." His eyes narrowed seductively at Kate. "Unless we're too busy."

"Excuse me?" Kate looked back at Syon, but all he did was frown and shrug. *Rule number two.* "Seriously, I'm leaving."

Kate made it two steps toward the curtain before Syon clamped his hand on her wrist and stopped her.

"Ramsey, get the fuck out. I told you, she's mine."

"Yeah...yeah..." Ramsey grumbled as he pushed off the wall and headed back for the curtain. Syon pulled her against him as his bandmate passed by.

But Ramsey paused next to her, giving her a look at his dark eyes. They paired with his black hair perfectly, completing his lone-wolf persona. "Maybe next time."

Syon extended his hand past her with his middle finger raised right beneath Ramsey's nose. With a snort, the other guitarist was gone, the curtain shimmering again as it settled back into place.

"Do you guys actually go in for threesomes?" Kate pulled away from Syon, stunned to hear her own question. Who asked stuff like that anyway?

Duh…rock stars.

"Don't knock it if you haven't tried it, Ginger," Syon said.

"Enough of the redhead references."

"I'm talking about your nature." He started after her, and she propped her hand onto her hip.

"Hold it right there." She stuck her finger out at him.

"Here?" he asked innocently. "Or…" He moved forward, jabbing her finger into his chest and pushing her into the wall at the same time. "Here?"

"Just…back off," she snapped. "I am not into group sex."

He flattened his hands on the wall next to her head. There was a mere inch between them, and her heart started accelerating again.

"Ramsey is just pumped up from the show," Syon offered in a low tone. "We have to put a lot of ourselves out there on the stage, and sex is the smartest way to blow off steam when we're done."

"What's smart about random sexual encounters?" Kate asked.

"No hangovers, and no chance of overdosing." He

leaned down and inhaled the scent of her hair again. "Although, overdosing on your sweet body sounds like a great idea. I'm willing to take the risk."

Oh hell...

She felt like her insides were vibrating. The level of excitement was so off the scale, she was tempted to give in just for the sake of not missing out on a once-in-a-lifetime experience.

But it would be giving in. Compromising. Something she didn't go for.

"This is not my thing."

"I can make it your thing." His caramel eyes were full of a promise that made her shiver.

"Yeah *right*." She ducked under his arm and swept the curtain aside. "I am not falling for that line." But it just might come back to haunt her when she was playing with B.O.B. "I'm leaving now." With what was left of her pride.

Which wasn't much. Her hair was floating around her shoulders, and she had a nightmarish mental image of what she must look like—wet lips, smudged lipstick, and hungry eyes.

"I'm sure you'll find someone to deal with your...desire to overdose..."

There was a grunt behind her. Kate didn't wait to see if it was an agreement or further argument. She took off down the hallway and headed for a door marked *restricted access*.

The moment she pushed through it, a dark-suited guy stepped into her path. He was a mountain of muscle and scowling.

"Call your goon off," she snapped back at Syon, who had appeared right behind her.

"She's with me," Syon said right on cue.

Kate turned and pointed her finger at Syon as the door closed with a snap. "I'm not 'with' you."

His eyes narrowed. "I liked our communication better before we broke off the lip-lock."

"Yeah? Well—"

He leaned right down and smothered her retort. His mouth was just as hot as a few minutes ago, and he really did know how to use it. He teased her lips, sucking on them before biting her lower lip gently. He closed his arms around her and cupped both sides of her ass before pulling her into contact with his erection.

She gasped, the feeling making her insides twist. Her entire core yearned to toss her rules aside. She was aching for him.

Syon tightened his grip on her ass, setting fire to her senses. Her clit was throbbing painfully, and she just couldn't take it anymore.

She reached for him, pulling the buttons on his vest open. There was a pop as a button went flying and bounced off the floor. The costumer in her would have cringed, but right now it pleased her on some base, primitive level. She wanted to eat him alive.

"Oh, God, yeah…run your claws down me."

He arched back, offering the wide expanse of his bare chest to her. But it also allowed her to see the security guy still standing at his post near the door. He was doing a pristine job of looking straight ahead, but Kate's jaw dropped in horror.

Syon straightened up, looking disappointed before turning his head to see what she was looking at. "Fuck. Forgot about him."

"You mean, you usually don't worry about anyone watching." She tried to push him away, becoming frustrated when he stood still, defying her efforts. "Because you're pumped up, right? Sex in the hallway is no big deal around here. I get it."

And it pissed her off, but for an entirely different reason than she'd anticipated having to face. She didn't want him to be so shallow.

But he was.

"I really…really…can't…" She was sputtering, losing it completely as disappointment stung her eyes with unshed tears. "I've never behaved so…slutty…"

"Don't insult yourself." He opened his hands and wiped away one of the tears. "I'm being an asshole."

Syon caught her hand and started to lead her through the maze of hallways. He took her up a flight of stairs and then another before she recognized the landing port. Someone opened the door for them, and she saw the pilot sitting in the helicopter, waiting for her.

The landing lights were on, spilling over them as the ocean breeze blew through her loose hair. He reached out and smoothed it back, cradling the side of her head.

"I'm going to kiss you good-bye, Kate."

"Okay."

She wasn't sure what she was saying, only that she wanted one last taste of him.

Syon didn't disappoint her. He leaned down and closed his lips over hers. It was a sweet meeting of their mouths this time. He pressed short little kisses against her lips before deepening the pressure and slipping and sliding his way across her mouth. He massaged her head, sending little ripples of delight through her.

But he lifted his head away too soon.

Or maybe not soon enough.

"It was a pleasure to meet you, Kate."

He watched her climb aboard and stood there with the wind of the rotor fluttering the open sides of his vest while they lifted off the rooftop. Below him, the area surrounding the Staples Center was teeming with fans still pumped with energy. The restaurants surrounding the auditorium were filled to the brim, customers spilling out onto the pavement as music blared and alcohol flowed.

Syon Braden stood above them, looking like he belonged right there. Up high. Unreachable.

Yeah, rule number two. She needed to follow it, or she was going to have a long, hard fall when the god of music finished with her.

—⁕—

Ramsey walked out onto the roof as the helicopter headed off into the night. "I didn't mean to screw it up for you."

"You didn't." Syon sighed. "I don't hide who I am from chicks."

"Weren't you even tempted?"

"Maybe this time." Syon shot his buddy a smirk. "She needs to know who I am, or there are going to be hurt feelings. I'm not a complete asshole."

Ramsey crossed his arms over his chest, which was bare except for an open black leather jacket that exposed his nipple piercing. "Yes, you are."

"Takes one to know one," Syon shot back at his bandmate.

Ramsey curled his hand into a fist and smacked it into his opposite palm, but Syon shook his head. "Save your energy for the girls," Syon said, heading back into the building.

"Got some cuties up in the penthouse suite over at the Ritz," Ramsey said. "Plenty to go around. Big tits, little tits… I think Drake might have brought a drag queen back, but I don't want to ruin the surprise when the skirt drops. I'm betting his cool, crisp Brit demeanor will finally fail."

Ramsey yanked open the door to the first of the SUVs waiting to take them to their after party. Syon slid in beside Ramsey and pulled the door closed.

"Keep poking Drake with a stick, and he's going to kick your ass one of these nights," Syon predicted.

"Can't help it," Ramsey replied. "He's like Data from *Star Trek*. No emotions. Only, I've seen him bleed, so I know he's human…hence…"

"You won't stop dicking with him," Syon finished off.

Ramsey nodded.

The interior of the SUV was decked out in party lights and long bench seats terminating at a minibar. Their music was playing. There was a sea of flashing cameras as they passed the press, but security staff did a good job of keeping them on the sidewalk so the driver could thread his way down the ramp and into traffic.

"You could have had the bird drop us off before taking her home," Ramsey complained.

"I think she might have jumped out if we'd climbed in after her."

Ramsey selected one of the single-serve bottles of

whiskey and popped the top loose. "That would have given me an excuse to hold her down."

Syon picked up another whiskey and toasted with it before taking a swig. "I'm looking forward to her sitting on top of me."

Ramsey lowered his empty bottle and tossed it into a cup holder. "Looking forward?"

Syon nodded and took another slow sip of his drink.

"You're actually plotting about how to get her?" Ramsey exclaimed, turning to stare at him. "Let the chick go. Those *ladies* don't cross the tracks very well."

Syon shrugged as they pulled up in front of the Ritz. There was a mob of fans waiting, cameras going off the moment they stepped out. Ramsey reached out, stroking some of the hands thrust toward him. Girls squealed and did their best to snatch a feel of his bare chest. One leaned all the way forward and pulled her top down. Ramsey took a good long look before offering her his hand. The security men holding the mob back let her duck beneath their spread arms. She nestled up against Ramsey with a huge smile on her lips.

Once inside, they made their way to an open elevator and punched the button for the top floor.

"Oh my God!" Ramsey's new pet gushed. *"I so can't believe I'm here!"*

"Are we sharing?" Ramsey asked Syon over the top of her blond head.

"Sharing?" The girl squealed again, louder. "Oh. My. God! I gotta text everyone!"

Ramsey grabbed the phone the girl pulled out of her purse, earning a squawk of frustration from his newest plaything. He cupped her chin and fixed her with his best attempt at a serious expression.

"Here's the thing, sweetheart. No phone, and I'll make sure you don't have any time to miss your cyber buddies."

"Alright," she cooed.

Ramsey tucked the phone into the inside pocket of his leather jacket before the girl turned to give Syon a naughty look. She reached for his open vest, boldly running her fingers down his chest.

He caught her hand and lifted it to his lips before handing it off to Ramsey.

"Really, dude?" The elevator chimed as it arrived, and the doors slid open.

Syon offered him a two-finger mock salute before striding down the hallway away from the blaring music. There was no missing where the other members of the band were partying, but he turned and went down the hall toward his room and slid his key card into the door.

"Wait up, Syon," Ramsey called. "I'll be right back," he said close to the girl's ear as he opened the door and the music poured out like a tidal wave. He swatted the girl on her backside, and she giggled as she jumped forward to join the after-concert excess.

Ramsey made it down the hall just before Syon's door closed all the way, bouncing it off his shoulder and pushing his way into the room.

"Fuck," Ramsey growled. "You on the rag or something?"

Syon went toward the vanity where his makeup remover was already laid out.

"Orgies get old after about two hundred of them," Syon answered.

"Like hell they do." Ramsey opened the fridge and selected a beer. "She really got to you. Un-fucking-believable." He yanked the cap off and took a long drink. "Is your pride really that tender? So she turned you down. There's plenty of tail for the asking."

"I want to see her again," Syon said. "And it's Kate. Her name is Kate."

Ramsey started to say something, but he snapped his jaw shut, leaned back against the wall, and took another drink from his beer. Syon sat down and began yanking off one of his boots.

"Whatever," Ramsey said at last. "The last time you got hung up on a girl, you wrote 'Insatiable Craving,' so go chase her ass for all I care. Just don't forget I warned you where it was heading."

Syon dropped his second boot onto the floor. "I think you just said it would take us to another double platinum record, so quit whining."

Ramsey still hesitated before pushing himself away from the wall. "Yeah, I guess that's what I said. Come on down if you change your mind."

Ramsey stopped with his hand on the door. "Why are you such a romantic?"

"I said I wanted to see her again, not hit my knee and propose," Syon shot back. "Sometimes, I even get to know a girl's middle name before I take her to bed. You might try it once in a while. You know, to shake things up."

Ramsey snorted. "We've got everything we ever wanted, so don't let some chick convince you you're not happy."

Syon leaned back and closed his eyes the moment the door closed behind Ramsey.

He should go blow his load.

Find someone that looked like Kate and fuck her out of his system.

Instead, he removed his makeup and showered. The suite had three rooms, but Syon felt like a canned vegetable without a balcony. Most of the upscale hotels were going without balconies because of lawsuits over drunken falls. He could still hear the steady beat vibrating down the hallway from where the rest of the band was decompressing.

He pulled on a pair of jeans and wandered over to where his guitar had been set up. Only the bathroom light was on, letting him sink into the shadows as he fingered the strings, letting a melody flow from his mind to his fingers. The concert had taken the edge off his passion, allowing him enough patience to toy with a new rhythm.

———ᴡᴡ———

"Overdosing on your sweet body sounds like a great idea."

Kate growled and looked at her bedside clock... again. She needed sleep, but every time she closed her eyes, she heard Syon's raspy voice. B.O.B. was sitting on her bedside table, charging away. She'd moved her trusty vibrator onto the table the moment she found out her boyfriend Todd had been two-timing her. She gave a little snort and turned over, because what she craved was hard, body-to-body contact. Bare skin, raspy breath—in short, the whole enchilada. B.O.B. couldn't deliver that. The moment she closed her eyes, all she saw was the way Syon's eyes had narrowed before he kissed her.

Damn, the man could kiss.

"Oh, God, yeah…run your claws down me."

Maybe she should have, because she wouldn't be getting a second opportunity.

Chapter 2

A HARLEY SAT OUTSIDE THE COSTUME SHOP THE NEXT morning. It was brand-new, the chrome shining in the morning sun. Kate paused for a moment to admire the custom work on the machine. It was definitely not factory specs.

Shit.

Sturgis was three weeks away. She didn't have a second to spare for the boys who hadn't gotten their orders in. But bikers didn't tend to take "no" very well, and Percy would be the first one to run screaming, leaving her to face whatever growling grizzly bear of a disgruntled customer was waiting inside. The guy clearly had money and would expect a cut to the front of the line with a click of his checkbook pen. He wouldn't want to hear that there were just so many hours in a day and she was maxed out. She took another swing of her coffee and squared her shoulders.

"Kate...*darling*..."

Kate froze on her way into the shop. She tugged off her sunglasses and leveled a hard look at Percy. He had a measuring tape draped around his neck and stood in the doorway between the machine shop and the cutting area.

He was beaming, smiling from ear to ear with his hazel eyes sparkling. *Darling* was worse than sweetie when it came to getting worked over by her partner. If

there was an asshole in the shop, Percy wouldn't be calling her *darling*. Nope. *Darling* meant Percy was licking
whipped cream off his fingers and fully expecting her to
join the party.

"I'm going home," Kate declared preemptively. "I
didn't get enough sleep to deal with an ambush."

Percy rubbed his hands together gleefully and walked
up to her with an unmistakably giddy look in his eyes.
He leaned in close, clasped her wrists with a death grip
fueled by excitement, and whispered, "I could *kiss* you
for being late. You're too good to me." He backed up and
cleared his throat. "So I started the basic measurements,
and you're right on time to get going with design."

"Design of what…?" Her jaw hung open as her gaze
fell on the person leaning against the door frame behind
Percy. Syon Braden was just as deadly without his
makeup. More so. There was a raw power in his face.

And he was grinning with victory.

Total ambush!

"Mr. Braden—" Kate started.

"As I told Percy, call me Syon," he drawled in a deep
voice that sent a tingle through her.

Her partner shivered and rolled his eyes before turning around to face Syon. "You did." Percy trotted off
into the third room, which served as the office, leaving
Kate facing Syon.

Starbucks was *so* not strong enough to help her deal
with her morning. There was a charge in the air, setting
her nerves on edge. It shouldn't have been possible. The
guy's persona was just fucking huge.

"Come on in, everyone!" Percy called.

Syon crooked a finger at her, but there was nothing

playful about it. He was arrogant and damned fucking proud of himself.

She abandoned her coffee cup and forced herself to stride forward with all confidence she could muster. Her system was going haywire again. The fatigue headache she'd woken up with—courtesy of Syon Braden—doing nothing to dull the impact of his presence.

Heat snaked through her, awakening her clit like she hadn't gone three rounds with B.O.B.

She needed to stock up on batteries.

Syon was wearing a faded pair of jeans that looked extra yummy on him, and a button-down khaki shirt that complemented the lighter streaks in his hair. The spikes weren't teased up as much today, but that just gave him a rakish appearance. She felt the attraction bleeding off him, growing stronger with every step she took. She was completely off balance having him here in *her shop*; he'd invaded her safe zone.

He knew it too. There was a look in his eyes that told her how much he enjoyed riling her.

Much as it unsettled and excited her, she knew exactly what he was doing. He was proving how much power he had, and it pissed her off.

"What are you doing here?" she asked when she was close enough to keep her words from traveling to Percy.

Syon pegged her with that intense gaze of his. "Chasing you."

She stumbled past Syon through the doorway to the office, the gruff, sultry sound of his voice completely unhinging her thought process. There was a suspicious chuckle from behind her, but she couldn't turn around to snap at Syon because Percy was watching.

No unprofessional behavior.

"Now, Kate, I've already spoken to Giles, and he's on board with the whole thing," Percy announced with a flourish of his hands.

Kate sat down in one of the chairs in front of Percy's desk. Syon lowered his frame into another one. She cut him a sidelong glance—there were four chairs in the office, but he'd taken the one beside her.

Syon winked at her and pressed his lips into a silent kiss.

Her damned nipples puckered. She needed something a lot harder than Starbucks.

"When Mr—Syon called to confirm his appointment, I made sure to check with Giles so there wouldn't be any tension over jumping his contract," Percy continued.

"Giles is fine with you jumping me," Syon said with a smirk.

Kate's jaw dropped.

Percy let loose a peal of laughter. "You are so naughty." He wagged a finger at Syon. "I love it, but I'm a married man."

"Percy, could you fill in some of the details?" Kate asked as she steeled herself. Syon wasn't a subtle sort of personality.

"Oh yes, sweetie…" Percy laid his hands flat on the desk as he leaned forward. "You're going on tour as personal leather specialist to Toxsin."

Words failed her.

Syon leaned on his armrest and looked at Kate. "I'm not the only member of the band running short on stage wear. We're a little ignorant of what the wardrobe needs as far as maintenance. That's where you come in. The band and I agreed it would be best if you joined us. That way, you can produce what we need, when we need it. No lag time."

Kate's eyes widened, and she started to shake her head. Percy made a low sound in the back of his throat as something crashed in the cutting room, followed by two more loud bangs and a shouted word of profanity.

"I'll be right back." Percy scurried out of the office.

"Bastard," she bit out.

"Brilliant bastard," he corrected.

Her mouth was hanging open again. "Don't fuck with my life," she sputtered. "Percy and I built this place from nothing. I don't have time to be your groupie."

His teasing expression evaporated. "You think I don't understand having a dream? Or what sort of devotion it takes to turn it into reality?"

His tone was a slap in the face. Behind the sex appeal was a hard businessman. As in razor sharp. She drew in a stiff breath to calm herself. "Okay, you're right. I'm insulting you without knowing anything about you, but *you* are messing with my life here. I have commitments, and if I piss off my customers, they won't be back next year when you're history."

He absorbed her words, weighing them. "I only work with the best, and that's you. I checked. You'll do custom work for us that will get worldwide press. That will bring in new clients. Ones with enough money to keep you from working eighty hours a week for guys who want to trade you brake jobs for their pants."

She had nothing to come back at him. He really had done his homework.

She was staring at the business side of his persona

again, and her pride glowed as his word sunk in. Beyond the sex appeal, the guy was a brilliant musician, and it looked like he knew how to market it. No wonder he was swamping her in his sex appeal; he could channel his energy and fire it off like a laser.

"It will also give us time to get to know each other, Kate."

She shivered. "I can't do this." She was chickening out, but it was safer.

"Of course you can," Percy said as he reappeared and patted her on the shoulder before rounding the desk and settling into his padded captain's chair. "I've already juggled the schedule, and the contract Syon is offering even covers designer rights."

Designer rights. The fabled pot of gold at the end of the rainbow for every struggling artist like her and Percy. A band with Toxsin's fame wearing her work would catapult her to the top of the design-label world. Instantly. It was prime bait. Her mouth was watering.

Another thud and shout came from the cutting room. "Can no one get along without me for even five minutes?" Percy wailed before heading back out of the office.

"You sure know how to bait a hook," Kate said.

"Maybe I give credit where credit is due. You're a rare talent, Kate," he said.

His expression became pensive, calculating, and she found it attractive on a whole different level. Some place where she enjoyed the sting of dominance just because it reeked of a level of confidence she couldn't help but admire. Syon was no metalhead getting lucky on the charts due to a kick-ass marketing team pushing his work.

"Your band buddies can't be keen on this idea of attaching me to your baggage train. Won't I throw off the vibe?" she asked.

"Business is always first," Syon informed her, his tone fitting the gleam in his eyes. "You can keep us looking top-notch. Our fans expect a certain image. We plan to give it to them."

"And she will do just that," Percy practically sang on his way back into the office. "When I said I had to juggle her schedule, I wasn't kidding. No one sews leather like Kate. She could fit an angry goat."

"I noticed she's one of a kind," Syon said.

Kate felt that touch on her heartstrings again, but this time, it scared the hell out of her. Syon was perfection: his body drool worthy, and the intensity flowing out of his caramel eyes absolutely mind melting. He was like some kind of drug, and she was afraid of getting addicted.

She was going to end up getting sucker punched straight in her heart if she stayed near him. "Thanks for the praise, but…"

Syon gave his watch a cursory glance. "The truck will be pulling up in front of your place in about an hour." He sent Kate a piercing look. "Just as soon as the guys finish loading up what you need from here."

"I'm packing you a ton of hides to start with, Kate, and I'll ship you some more when I get downtown to shop," Percy informed her like the pro he was.

"You planned all the details, I see," she said, pursing her lips at Syon.

He gave her a stiff nod. "Yes, ma'am." There was something in his formal response that hinted at a big part of him she knew nothing about, some darker portion of his person that scared her even more. She got the feeling she just might end up respecting him.

"This is going to look so good on our résumé, darling," Percy cooed.

Shit.

Shit...double shit.

Custom work had seasons. After Sturgis, there was going to be a long dry spell. She and Percy could tighten their belts, but it sucked when they had to let their staff go because there wasn't enough business. Designer rights would change all of that. Just one tour, and Timeless Creations would blossom into the business she and Percy had dreamed of.

"It sure will," Kate agreed. She was folding but also taking a chance. Seizing the opportunity she'd been longing for. As a partner, she'd be a real deadbeat not to step up.

Percy threw his arms around her and squeezed.

"Have *fun*," he said suggestivly in her ear. When he released her, he smirked. "Oh, and Todd called this morning, since you aren't returning his messages. I told him you were going on tour with Toxsin and didn't have time for him."

She grinned, unable to control herself. "Awesome."

Syon's eyes narrowed. The little hint of jealousy pleased her. Maybe it was an irrational, immature feeling, but it gave her the leverage she needed to break away from Syon's powerful persona. There were more hugs and squeals from the other members of the team before she walked out of the door and toward her car.

When it came to ambushes, Syon did them just as big as he did everything else.

———∿∿∿———

Syon had said truck.

She hadn't expected a semi, much less four mega-bus-style motor homes clogging the street in front of her house. They were all covered in images of the band members from past concerts. Not exactly subtle. The neighbors started coming out as Syon appeared with a grin that grated on Kate's nerves.

A drab-colored sedan squeezed its way into her drive-way as a team of movers strode through her open door to take charge of the suitcases she'd haphazardly tossed the majority of her possessions into. She had no idea if she even had a complete matching outfit at this point.

Syon introduced the portly, balding man who got out of the sedan. "This is Karl. He's a property manage-ment representative."

Karl offered her his hand. "Pleasure to be working with you." She shook it before he held out his other hand for her house keys. "We'll make sure everything is kept in order while you're away, including your car."

It was the smart thing to do, but she still had trouble handing over the keys. But the idea of what the tour was going to look like on her résumé helped her move into action.

"Hey, Ginger. Nice to see you again."

Kate turned to see Ramsey coming out of one of the buses.

"You know Ramsey," Syon said as the two other members of the band made their way over to her. They didn't seem to notice that their motorcade was causing traffic to drive on the wrong side of the road. A few squeals came from open car windows as people realized who was standing in the street.

"This is Taz," Syon said, introducing a black-haired Asian guy with amazing dark eyes. "Bassist and backup vocals."

"Drake." Another dark-haired guy but with ocean-blue eyes. "He keeps us all on beat on the drums."

The last guy looked at her with a stony expression.

"Drake is still getting used to the idea of having you along," Syon said with reluctance.

"Thanks, Syon," Drake growled. "Now I'm the band asshole."

"Is that news to you?" Ramsey chirped with a smirk on his lips. "I knew it the moment you reported for duty."

"Reported for duty?" Kate asked, perplexed by the formal term coming out of Ramsey, with his shoulder-length hair, nipple piercing, and leather pants.

"Yeah, Ramsey and I have been playing together since grade school, but the rest of the band connected with us in EOD," Syon supplied.

"What's EOD?" Kate asked.

"Explosive Ordinance Disposal."

"No way." Kate turned with a disbelieving look. "Bomb patrol? That's one elite unit."

"Got my honorable discharge papers to prove it," he assured her.

It was stunning and impressive and fit perfectly with the expertly performed ambush she'd just been party to. "No wonder no one really knows where you guys came from."

Syon shrugged and pointed Kate toward the lead motor home. They had to climb several large steps before ducking inside. A tinted glass wall separated the driver from the rest of the interior, leaving Kate alone with Syon.

Kate stared at him, drinking in the details of his amazing physique. Without the screaming fans and the guitars, she could see the hard body that must have served him well in the service. The length of his hair suddenly drew her attention.

"You've been growing your hair out since you left the service." She stepped close enough to reach out and finger it without thinking about what she was doing. Instinct was taking charge again. She was drawn to him, the urge so strong, she couldn't seem to control it. Sharing air with him was apparently enough to intoxicate her.

"Yeah…" he drawled, his voice turning husky.

He reached up and grabbed her hair clip again. There was a click, and her hair fell around her face.

"I love your hair." He shoved his hand into it and captured a handful. "I can't stop thinking about how it smells."

He buried his face in the cloud of her hair. A little moan escaped her lips as he tightened his hold. Just enough. It was just the perfect amount of pressure on her scalp to send a jolt of red-hot desire through her.

"I like that little, sexy sound you make too," he rasped.

"You totally ambushed me, Syon." She tried to pull away, tried to recall just how much she didn't like anyone rearranging the details of her life. The least she could do was chastise him.

He leaned forward and caught her waist again. He hauled her against his body and pressed a hard kiss against her mouth. "You bet I did. Invested time in planning it too."

She pressed a hand against his chest. "I don't like controlling men."

"You haven't had a sample of my type of control." There was a dark promise in his tone.

"Arranging for me to come along changes nothing," she warned him.

"During work hours, it means my band has what it needs to stay at the top, and that is very important to me, Kate." His attention dropped to her mouth. "On personal time, it means we can explore the buzz between us."

"Maybe we should stick to business." She said it, but she didn't mean it. Not really.

"Let's put that to the test," he said.

His lips thinned, and a moment later he was kissing her breathless. It was hard and scorching hot.

She moaned again, but this time, the sound was hungry. She threaded her hands through his hair and held his head as she angled hers to fit their mouths together. He reached around and gripped both sides of her bottom, lifting her up. He moved back and ended up on a sofa that she had only a dim memory of seeing. He sat down, and when he lowered her, she ended up spreading her legs to accommodate him. Her clit throbbed insanely as he pressed her right down onto his erection.

"Oh shit," she cussed as she arched. It felt good. Incredibly good.

He stretched up and kissed the side of her neck. Her skin was hypersensitive, and she jerked, but he tightened his hold, keeping her prisoner for another kiss and a long lap from his velvet tongue. She jerked again, grinding her clit against his crotch. It was almost enough.

"Well, I know you said you wanted her here to get into our pants, but I guess this works too."

Kate squealed, trying to scramble off Syon's lap as Ramsey walked right up behind her. But Syon locked an arm around her and kept his hand in her hair to keep her exactly where she was. His cock was hardening even more, making her breath catch in the back of her throat.

And her face went up in flames as Ramsey sat right down beside Syon with a lazy grin on his lips.

"Should have started with the other RV," Ramsey suggested. "It's got a bedroom. Not that this sofa hasn't seen its share of action."

Kate gathered up some of her scattered wits and tried to push against Syon's chest. "Let go."

Syon responded by sliding his arm lower around her waist and grabbing one side of her butt before lifting his hips. She gasped. She couldn't help it. The moment he moved against her clit, pleasure went shooting through her.

"I'm not into sharing," she hissed.

"This isn't sharing," Syon said as he massaged her scalp again.

"Nope," Ramsey said, lifting his hands and wiggling his fingers at her. "Don't have a finger on you."

Nothing made sense. Kate struggled to form a complete sentence, but it was almost impossible with Syon's hard cock pressed against her open slit with just a couple of layers of cotton denim separating them. She could feel the heat of his skin burning through that fabric, promising her relief if she just ground herself against him a few times. Her nipples were already tightening.

"But I'd like to," Ramsey added. "Put my fingers— and other body parts—on you."

Kate was going to die of mortification. Ramsey was calmly observing them without even a hint of reservation. He dropped an arm along the back of the sofa and leaned back so he had a good view of them.

He was enjoying every second of it.

"Okay...I'm not into voyeurism either," Kate clarified.

"I thought there were only five rules," Syon grumbled. "You're complicated."

"And you're presumptuous," she countered. "Let me off your lap *now*!"

Syon's eyes narrowed, a promise of retribution flickering in them before he released her. She scrambled off his lap as Ramsey made a sound that too closely resembled a muffled chuckle for her fraying composure.

"It's *not funny*." Kate lashed out at him. "If that's what you're into, get yourselves another costumer. Rule number two is in place for this very reason."

"Rule number two?" Ramsey asked.

"No rock stars," Syon filled him in. "We rank just below 'no drugs.'"

Ramsey frowned. "That's low." His voice had deepened, turning cold. He pushed off the sofa and jumped down the steps, disappearing outside.

Syon wasn't happy either. She could see the injured pride in his eyes.

"I wasn't the one out of line here," Kate defended. "I'm not going to say I'm sorry for pissing off your band buddy when he just sat down and asked to join in. Maybe you don't like my rules, but at least I have some standards."

"You were just as hot for me." Syon drew a deep breath. "Claim you weren't and what you are is a liar."

"I didn't say I wasn't hot." The words were past her lips before she realized she was making an admission. His lips thinned with renewed hunger before he came up off the sofa after her.

"No." She jumped down the hallway to get out of his reach and had to quell the urge not to turn and run. "If I'm here as a team member, fine, but I am not going to be your sex pet."

He captured her wrist and tugged her to him. She ended up smacking into his chest. He closed his arms around her, imprisoning her, the feeling of his hard body threatening to make her senseless again.

"You haven't tried being mine," he growled against her ear before he nipped the lobe.

She was losing her wits again. Heat surged through her, overpowering everything else. She ached for him. Her body was liquefying into a molten pool of need.

"Do you even recall the name of the last woman you kissed?" she demanded. "Before me? Or is it all a blur?" She was lashing out, flailing in an attempt to regain control. Under different circumstances, she would have been mortified.

He lifted his head, locking gazes with her. There was something in his eyes that chilled her. It was hard and wounded.

"Yes." His tone was clipped and subarctic. "It's been two years since I kissed another woman. Her name was Jen."

"Yeah, right," Kate scoffed, but she wanted to believe him. She had no business being possessive. No reason to notice the sincerity in his eyes.

He released her, backing away, and it felt like he was emotionally pulling away from her too. Almost as if he was wounded by her disbelief.

"Come on. Your buddy is all ready to jump into a ménage with us twenty minutes after I show up, but you expect me to believe you haven't had sex in two years?" she asked.

"I didn't say I haven't had sex. I said I haven't kissed a woman in two years," he said. "I can't risk getting cold sores or some other shit in my throat. I don't put my vocal cords in jeopardy. Especially when I'm on a tour that I've put up half the money for."

"Oh." She felt a ridiculous little zip of excitement go through her. "I guess that holds water."

A whole lot of it. It gave him layers. Made him less two-dimensional.

His attention lowered to her lips. "You're trouble."

"You kicked in my door, dude." The excitement died. Why in the hell did it hurt to hear him rejecting her? She wanted to reject him, so what did it matter?

His expression changed, became more distant, more professional. All business again.

"We need a leather specialist. When it comes to the show, there is nothing I won't go after if it is the best. I checked around; there's a reason you don't have an assistant. You can't find one with your talent." His gaze settled on her mouth again. "So I want you."

She ended up nodding and conceding the point. There was a standing opening at the shop, and a whole lot of people had tried to fill it. None of them had the touch.

"Ramsey is just about the only human being on this planet who understands me. We've bled together. So telling him he's lower than a drug addict is pretty harsh. Keep that sort of shit to yourself."

"Rule number three is 'no drugs,' not 'no drug addicts,'" she said. "There's a big difference there. I'm not willing to compromise on something that has such a potential to blossom into addiction. I don't work as hard as I do to end up in a relationship where I could lose everything, or end up having my car seized by the state because I made a bad choice on my date night."

He weighed her answer for a long moment. "Fair enough. As you put it, that holds water. As for Ramsey walking in on us, we live on top of one another when we're on tour. Privacy can become a casualty from time to time."

"That was more than a walk-in oops," she snapped. "He sat right down and asked to join."

And she really wished her knees didn't go weak over that idea. But they turned to jelly when Syon's lips thinned and his eyes flickered with something very wicked. He closed in on her again, hooking her around the waist and turning her around, away from the stairs. He cupped her nape and buried his head in her hair.

"Sex is better when it's more than fucking," he rasped next to her ear.

She stiffened, but he held her still, his warm breath brushing her ear.

"There are a thousand different ways to experience pleasure." He teased the shell of her ear with the tip of his tongue. "If you're honest, you'll admit he turned you on."

"Oh…damn." She wiggled as he traced the entire outside of her ear until he closed his lips around the lobe.

She ended up gripping his shirt.

"I want to know what you like, everything you crave." He trailed kisses down her neck before lifting his head and making eye contact with her. "I want to know that I satisfy every fantasy you have, so you don't go looking for it without me."

"That's nuts…" she whispered.

"So is the pull between us," he said.

"Does that line really work?"

His face tightened, irritation flickering in his eyes.

"Who's Todd?" Syon demanded.

Her wits were dulled by the idea that she'd insulted his cheesy line. "What?"

"Todd." Syon massaged her neck. "Percy said Todd called looking for you."

She pushed against his chest, but he didn't budge. "Are you actually jealous of an ex-boyfriend?"

"Not if he's an ex."

He leaned over and teased her neck with a flick of his tongue. She stretched away from him.

"But it's just fine if your buddy Ramsey is sitting next to us while we make out or more?" Kate asked.

"Mmmmm…I like the idea of more."

He was going for her neck again, and she was sure she was going to combust if he succeeded. So she flattened her hand over his mouth, but it backfired. He captured her wrist and turned it up so he could tease the sensitive skin on the underside with a kiss. She shuddered, the sensation rocking her to her core. She was fixated on his mouth against her skin. He rolled back his lips and bit her gently.

She felt like she was flying apart.

"I can't do this…"

He locked gazes with her but maintained his grip on her wrist, and his thumb stroked the wet spot he'd left.

"He's an ex, so no complication," Syon insisted. "I want to explore why I kissed you. Kisses are intimate for me."

"I guess they would be," she said, recalling his protection plan for his throat.

His tone had deepened. "I don't indulge very often. I've been thinking about the way you taste all night. Should have been focused on the risk I left myself open to."

Two years. It seemed impossible, but there was a little bubble of joy growing inside her as she contemplated having something no one else had from him. "That's hard to believe, Syon."

He stepped up, moving too close again for rational thought. She pressed a hand against his chest, and the connection shocked her with a jolt of lust.

"Believe it and google it, you won't find a single picture of me in a lip-lock with a chick."

He pressed a kiss against her mouth, sucking and teasing her lips with expert motions. He was constantly undermining her ability to form cohesive thoughts. He ripped the very foundation of her world away and left her floundering in a flood of need. She moaned softly and gripped his shirt.

Someone pounded on the door of the RV. "We've got

to roll, Syon!" Ramsey hollered from outside. "Playtime is over."

Syon gave her one last, hard kiss before releasing her. "On my way," he growled. "'Cause I'm sure not coming."

Her jaw dropped, and he chuckled at the look on her face.

"I think I like scandalizing you, Kate."

She snapped her mouth shut and tried not to think about how much she wanted to come too. "I've noticed."

He pointed to the driver's cockpit. "Kenny is driving. He'll switch out in four hours. This coach is the office. A couple of bunks are in the back. Normally Kenny's relief driver beds down there, but he switched over to one of the other RVs so this can be female only. Make yourself at home. There's TV, Internet, shower works while we're moving, pretty much everything. For the price, it better be outfitted right. I'll be in the music coach if you need me. We've got a show in Oakland in two days. It takes a day to build the stage and set up. The crew will have your shop set up by tomorrow morning so you can work while we're rehearsing."

"What's a music coach?" she asked.

"A traveling music room. Costs a bloody fortune, but it's worth it. Gives us the chance to work on new songs while we're moving or parked in back of a convention center."

Ramsey banged his fist on the door again. Syon flashed her a grin before disappearing. The door closed, and she heard the engine start.

"We're going to start moving, Ms. Napier."

She jumped when the driver's voice came over the sound system.

Well hell. Everyone knew who she was and what she was doing.

Except for her.

The coach shuddered as the powerful engine started up. Kate sat down on the sofa, realizing Syon had somehow managed to turn her into his personal pet.

She had her very own luxury pet carrier to prove it.

—⁓—

"She's hard to please," Ramsey fired off the moment Syon climbed into the music room coach.

The rest of the band members were fiddling with their instruments as the drivers began the task of moving Toxsin to its next concert location. Engines turned over, filling the area with a dull roar.

"Having a chick along is going to kill the mood," Taz added as he tuned his guitar.

"She'll have her own space," Syon insisted. "We got another three months on the road. Without her, we're going to look like shit and be reduced to buying off the rack at a Harley Davidson store, because you're all just as hard on your gear as I am. None of you has more than two pairs of pants left either."

There were several reluctant "all rights."

"Why did you have to kiss her?" Ramsey accentuated his question with a squeal from his guitar. "You're a total prick when you're stuck on a girl."

Syon flipped Ramsey the bird as he picked up his guitar and began to tune it.

Kate was making him crazy, but he'd be a liar if he said he wasn't enjoying it. The spark of excitement stirring up his insides made him realize how bored he'd

been. Easy pussy was like junk food, cheap and unsatisfying in the long run.

"She's like a breath of fresh air," he argued.

Drake and Taz groaned.

"I thought the last one cured you of your tender-heart
issues," Drake said from behind a set of drums positioned at the back end of the motor home.

"We did get 'Insatiable Craving' out of it," Taz mused.

"Yeah, but we had to restrain ourselves from putting
the poor bastard out of his misery," Ramsey added. "My
trigger finger is already itching."

Syon pulled on a few of his strings, filling the coach with
noise. "I'll remember all that love coming from you, Drake,
the next time I have to bribe a bouncer to turn a blind eye
when you get too shitfaced to keep your hands off the
strippers, and he wants to have your ass hauled off to jail."

"All right…I guess we need to look good. But I wish
we could have brought the guy along, even if he has
a taste for sausage," Taz grumbled before putting his
energy into the music. He was the only member of the
band without long hair. Instead, he had short spikes that
accentuated his Asian features.

People looked up when they drove past—there was
no way to contain all the sound inside the coach. The
rest of the band was in good form, but Syon caught
Ramsey watching him a few times.

Ramsey knew him too well.

When they broke off, it was Ramsey who put his
guitar on its stand and moved over to sit beside Syon.
Ramsey began nursing a beer. The silence grew between
them while the other members of the band waited to see
what Syon would say.

"The rule is 'no drugs,' not 'no drug addicts,'" Syon clarified. "She's got some good business sense in that pretty head. Can't really blame her for not wanting to lose a chunk of her holdings because the dude was packing a rock of meth."

Ramsey tipped the long neck back before answering. "I guess I can live with that."

Taz and Drake were taking silent notes at the other end of the coach. Syon shared a look with each of them before he drew in a deep breath.

"We need a leather artist, and there aren't a whole lot of choices if we want a good one," Syon continued.

Ramsey's eyes narrowed. "Do you hear how many excuses you're making? We're not playing in piss holes anymore. We get whatever the fuck we want, when we want it, and you sure as shit don't have to put up with a woman playing hard to get."

"She's not playing," Syon shot back.

Ramsey snorted.

"Maybe I like the fact that she doesn't just jump my bones the second she's hot."

"I bet she likes it too, because you're already showering her with stuff. We're stuffed into two coaches so she can have her girly privacy." Ramsey tossed the empty bottle across the coach where a trash can sat.

"What the hell is your problem?" Syon demanded.

"You!" Ramsey yelled. "You're messing up what was working just fine."

"I'm solving our fucking wardrobe problem."

Drake started hammering on the drums, drowning out everything. He kept at it until Ramsey got up and retrieved another beer from the fridge. Syon lifted his leg and laid it across the sofa, making it clear he didn't want company. Taz joined Drake, driving home how much the rest of the band didn't want to hear him and Ramsey going at it.

So Syon got up off the sofa and started playing. Music was the one thing he and Ramsey always agreed on. Fame had been good to them all, but there was still one thing it couldn't deliver: happiness. Ramsey was pissed at the world because he was the same man he'd been before they became megastars. Fame didn't drive their demons away.

As for himself?

Syon wasn't sure. Even with all the fame, he still craved acceptance. And Kate had been so goddamned hot in his arms. His cock hardened just thinking about it.

But she was holding back. Struggling against the tide of desire trying to drag them both out to sea. On one hand, he admired her. But on the other, maybe Ramsey was right. She might just be working him over, holding out just long enough to get the leash around his neck.

He wished to fuck he knew, because he'd spent too much time working to be where he was. It was gonna suck if he ended up like Ramsey: so pissed he couldn't enjoy the success he'd earned.

But Kate didn't want him because of that success. Which made it just a little bit funny.

If he'd had a taste for irony.

The coach was a marvel.

Kate spent a good hour just exploring it. There was a kitchen that someone had stocked with the basics in miniature. Kate lifted the tiny Tabasco bottle, enjoy-ing the fact that it was still made of glass. Beyond the kitchen was a full-size shower. The bathroom was across the hall and had a nice vanity with a marble top. If she hadn't been able to feel the vibration from the road, she would have thought she was in a hotel room. A really nice one. Once they parked, there were sections that would slide out to make it feel very roomy.

Farther back were the two bunks Syon had told her about. Each one had a privacy curtain, flat screen TV, and even an Xbox.

There were also mirrored ceilings, and condoms dis-creetly stored by the pillow.

She suppressed a giggle. Well, at least they weren't shattering her fantasies of how rock stars lived.

The back of the coach was a large office. It contained a full-size desk, computer, and printer all latched down. On all three sides of the office were cleverly designed windows with little half arches on the top to make it feel like an office building.

Kate felt a slight shift as the caravan of coaches began to climb the mountainous stretch of highway in the middle of the state known as the Grapevine, the motor coaches taking surprisingly well to the steep incline of the road. They must have gotten crap for gas mileage though. Once they made it to the other side, the interstate became a straight shot up the state of California. The coach settled into a steady gait as the miles passed.

And boredom set in.

Kate tinkered with her tablet, browsing Toxsin's website to discover where she was going. Oakland,

Portland, and on to Seattle. She'd be a bold-faced liar if she didn't admit that the European stops excited her.

A phone buzzed in the kitchen, but she was too comfortable in the bunk, so she let it ring. It probably wasn't for her anyway.

A few moments later, another phone started buzzing in the bunk. She jumped and looked around for it. The inconspicuous wall mount held a phone so slim, she hadn't seen it until she was lying down in the bunk.

"Hello?"

"What are you wearing?" Syon drawled on the other end of the line.

She laughed. "What are you wearing, pretty ginger lady?" he rasped out again before she could answer. The space between them suddenly empowered her, because he was too far away to overwhelm her.

"A silk corset and a short, flared skirt with a garter belt and hose."

"Hmmm…panties?" He sounded like he was smacking his lips.

Danger…danger…

The warning went unheeded. Syon was sucking her back into that vortex of insanity.

"No panties, 'cause it's an all-girl zone."

There was a groan on the other end of the line. "I guess I started it," Syon came back at her after a long pause. "We're stopping for fuel and grub, if you go for fast food."

"No thanks. I want to live past fifty."

"There's fresh stuff in the fridge." Syon stopped for a moment, and she got the feeling there was something else on his mind.

"And?" she pressed.

"There's going to be a couple of the crew guys standing by the door. Fans can get a little crazy. The guys are
there to protect you, but they're packing heat, legally. So
don't flip out if you see a piece."

"Worried I might jump a Greyhound bus back to Los
Angeles?" she asked.

"Are you thinking you might regret it if you did?"
Syon countered.

Her mind froze for a moment, heat licking at her
insides. His tone had dropped to that husky one he used
when he was burying his head in her hair. A tingle went
across her skin at just the memory.

"Touché," she muttered, feeling awkward.

"We'll roll into the Bay Area around ten. Want to go
for a ride with me?"

"Are you asking me on a date?" She toyed with a
lock of her hair, feeling as breathless and awkward as a
seventeen-year-old.

"Are you surprised?"

She clicked her tongue at him. "You keep answering
questions with questions."

"You're the one with a rule about dating rock stars,"
he answered smoothly. "I'm searching for a loophole. Is
a ride on the back of my Harley a date?"

Oh hell, she'd forgotten about the Harley.

"Okay, I'm feeling *mildly* guilty about telling you
rule number two. It might also be—only a slight pos-
sibility, mind you—discriminatory."

"And totally fucking unfair to me," he hammered
home. "You're rock star–phobic."

"In my defense, rule number two was made after

dealings with several of your colleagues who thought fittings included bedside service," Kate said.

"I waited until I was down to my last pair of pants before calling a costumer in, because I'm sick of getting my package grabbed during fittings," he responded.

Touché, again.

And she was starting to like the guy.

"You don't back off, do you?"

There was a very male sounding grunt on the other end of the line. "You don't want me to, Kate."

"You're arrogant," she said, stating the obvious. "Presumptuous."

"I'm taking command of the situation," he countered. "Don't worry, I've been trained."

"I notice you aren't arguing with the arrogant charge."

"You're as turned on as I am."

"That might not be a good thing." As in epic crash and burn on the horizon.

He took a moment to reply. "It might be an explosive thing. Only one way to find out. Take a ride with me."

He *was* arrogant, but there was something sexy about it. They had more in common than she'd realized.

She felt the coach slowing down as it exited the interstate. "You're on."

You're a lunatic...

"Cool."

Kate replaced the slim phone on the wall mount and worried her lower lip for a moment.

A date.

She was so screwed.

And too damned giddy about it.

—᠁—

Showering while rolling down the freeway was going to take a little practice.

Kate yelped as she cut herself with the razor because she'd lost her balance and twisted it.

She knocked her head on the upper bunk when she laid her suitcase out in the lower one and tried to find a matching outfit. Everything was a huge mess, because she'd just thrown things indiscriminately into the case. By the time she got dressed, she was flustered and growling.

At that point they were pulling into the city of Oakland, winding their way through industrial sections of town. Kate saw the concert center in the distance and hurried back to flip her case closed and zip it up. The driver of Kate's coach rolled up behind the semis into the loading area of the Oracle Arena. Air brakes hissed, echoing off the concrete. A loud whoop came from behind Kate as the band spilled out of their mobile music coach, like kids hearing a recess bell.

The sun had set several hours ago, but huge flood-lights illuminated the loading docks. Even at ten at night, teams of dockworkers converged on the semis. Up on the docks, there were supervisors with tablets, holding black radios up to their ears. The backs of the trucks were opened, and cases marked with "Toxsin" were being wheeled inside as team leaders barked orders.

"You really had the corset on?" Kate turned to see Syon coming up behind her.

Syon was staring at her cleavage. There was only a small slice of it on display, because she'd put on a summer cotton top beneath her blouse to act as a chemise. The low, rounded, country girl neckline hugged the tops of her breasts.

"I prefer a corset over a bra any day."

"Your rules suck, but that look rocks," Ramsey hollered on his way over to one of the semis that wasn't backed into the loading docks.

The rest of the band members glanced over at her, curious. A few low whistles came her way, and Syon flipped off the lot of them.

Taz hopped up on a loading ramp attached to the rear of one of the semis. When the lift reached the top, he stepped into the truck and rolled out a shiny mass of black paint and chrome before hitting the button to lower the lift to the ground.

"You guys carry your bikes?"

"Yeah. Beats paying someone else to run up the mileage on them." Syon stepped up closer. "Besides, a wise man never goes on tour without an escape plan."

Syon moved off toward the gate of the semi. As soon as Drake pulled up with his bike, Kate watched Syon jump onto the tailgate ramp.

Leather on that man should have been outlawed. His ass looked damn good in a pair of leather pants.

He'd put on a dark green T-shirt that complemented his eyes. When he came out of the truck, he was rolling another black-and-chrome creation that made her heart race.

On cue, one of the crew members rolled a large black case over to Syon and flipped up the lid. Syon reached down, pulled a leather jacket from it, and shrugged into it. He pulled another one up and whistled at Kate before tossing it to her.

She caught it, the scent of leather filling her nose. Another whistle and a pair of gloves came her way. Kate flexed her fingers into the gloves and noticed there was now a row of Harleys, parked in a neat line as the band members slipped into jackets, gloves, and helmets.

Syon brought her a helmet.

"You weren't kidding me about EOD." She took the helmet from him.

"What brought that comment up?" he asked.

She nodded toward the bikes. "I never would have thought a heavy metal rock band could be capable of such a precision exercise."

"Still can't imagine me with any sort of self-discipline?"

Kate locked gazes with him. "That's a little harsh. I'm not that judgmental."

He looked down at the cleavage peeking through the open front of her leather jacket. "With you, it might just be an accurate account. I'm guilty of losing my perspective due to distractions." His gaze lingered on her cleavage for a long moment.

He reached down and fitted the bottom stop of her zipper into the slider, holding it firmly as he slowly pulled it up. When he passed the area where her breasts were being lifted onto display, he let his knuckles brush her bare skin.

"Really accurate." She tugged the zipper up the rest of the way, and he gave her a disappointed look.

"Damned shame to cover that view," Drake said as he rolled his bike past them and offered her a wink.

The moment for Kate's retort was taken up by the sound of three beefy engines roaring to life, and Syon's eyes filled with excitement. For just a moment, she got a glimpse of the boy he must have been.

The naughty one.

He pulled her over to his bike, lifting one of his legs to mount it.

"Come on, baby…" He patted the seat behind him. "I've been looking forward to telling you to hold on tight, because this ride might just get a little rough."

"Ha…ha…" she responded, but there was still a hint of heat teasing her cheeks. He pointed to his head and then to the helmet in her hand.

She slipped it on before climbing onto the bike, and he captured her wrist and pulled her arm all the way around him. He'd always been the aggressor, but now she was the one scooting up behind him and holding tight to his lean waist.

Geez… The man smelled good.

He felt good too.

The hint of leather from his clothing only intensified the rawness of the moment. Her insides were liquefying again, her thoughts descending into the gutter so fast, she wasn't sure she'd ever left it since the moment she met him.

She realized this "date" setup was just him using a different method of commanding her. The guy was dominant to the core. It pissed her off a little, but at the same time, she couldn't deny the rush of anticipation it fueled inside her.

Syon peeled out first, with Ramsey falling in beside him. The bikes roared, cutting through the night like razor blades. They sped past the entrance to the stadium before spilling out onto the streets. The local nightlife was in full swing, and people dressed in going-out clothes looked up as they passed, some flashing them thumbs-up.

The vibration from the bike turned Kate on, but the feel of clinging to Syon's hard body made her crazy. They drove across the Golden Gate Bridge before pulling into a scenic overlook to take a break.

Kate's legs felt like jelly when she dismounted, but the experience was worth it. She left the helmet on the back of the bike. The wind coming off the ocean whipped her hair about as she climbed up onto a concrete picnic table to get a good view of the bay. Syon wandered over and offered her a beer.

"Where'd you get that?" she asked, taking the bottle and scrunching her eyebrows.

"Drake keeps them in his saddlebag." Syon climbed up beside her with another beer in hand. "His daddy was a Brit, taught him never to drink water."

Kate lifted the beer in a salute to the dark-haired drummer. He wiggled his tongue at her, then turned around to talk with Taz farther out on the overlook. Syon took a swig from his bottle before casually setting it aside and fixing her with a look that sent her heart pounding.

"Now, where were we?"

"Excuse me?" she asked, wincing when she heard her own sultry tone. What was it about the man that instantly reduced her to a cinder?

He reached right over and effortlessly scooped her up. One moment she was sitting on rock-hard concrete, and the next she was straddling his rock-hard cock.

"Just about here," he muttered with his hands full of

her bottom and his face buried in the tangle of her hair. "Except…" He straightened up and released her ass. A second later, a finger of night air touched her cleavage as he opened the zipper on the jacket.

"Nice," he muttered as he leaned down and kissed the creamy swell of her right breast. He trailed the tip of his tongue down its side and into the valley of her cleavage.

"Oh Christ!" she gasped. Her skin was ultrasensitive, but what was really driving her insane was the way her clit begged for the same treatment. It was pounding with the same insane tempo as her heart. She flung her head back, offering her cleavage to him.

But the position gave her a view of the rest of the table. Ramsey was settled beside Syon, only a foot away, his dark eyes on her. There was an unmistakable flare of lust in his gaze. It slammed into her, rocking her with a jolt of need before it brought clarity back to her and she scrambled off Syon's lap.

"What?" Syon growled until he looked to his left and realized it was Ramsey. He gave a shrug and reached for her again.

"Not on your life," she warned.

"The idea turned you on," Ramsey accused. "I saw it."

Kate scooted back and crossed her arms over her breasts, eliciting a grunt from Ramsey. "So is your big plan to show me I'm some kind of slut? Does that keep your ego stroked? What's the big deal, Ramsey? Can't you deal with a woman who has more to offer than lip service?"

His jaw tightened, his eyes narrowing. "You're a bitch."

"And you're both being pricks who have one-track minds when it comes to what women are on this planet for."

One corner of Ramsey's mouth twitched. "You've got balls."

It was exactly the sort of compliment that suited him.

"Even if they are pushed halfway to your chin." He looked at her cleavage and smacked his lips before jumping down and wandering over to where Drake was standing near the edge of the overlook.

Syon was wearing a disgruntled look that irritated her. "Relax, Kate," he drawled before tipping his beer back. "Ramsey is just messing with you because you're the new guy."

"Yeah? Well he can get the fuck over it." She suddenly felt like she was missing an obvious fact, something she really should have considered. He and Ramsey were tight—really, really tight. "Are you bisexual?"

Syon watched her from beneath hooded eyes. His lips were pressed into a hard line that made her squirm. She'd put her foot in it now for sure.

"Sorry, I didn't mean that question to come out sounding like that," she said, trying to lessen the blow. But an epic screwup was an epic screwup.

Syon suddenly cracked and started laughing. He ended up leaning all the way back on his elbows and tossing his head back so his hair teased the worn surface of the picnic table. The rest of the guys looked over but didn't budge, turning back to look at the view after a moment.

"What?" she demanded. "It's a fair enough question. You and Ramsey have been double-teaming me."

Syon sat back up and smirked at her. "You should have seen your face…" He chuckled some more.

"You know, it's wise to keep the seamstress happy.

I just might forget to remove a pin or two when you go out on stage," Kate warned him. "It's cool if—"

"No," he cut her off. "I'm not bisexual, and neither is Ramsey. We've both been drunk enough together to know for sure."

"I'm not sure I want to know what you mean by that," Kate said. And she was pretty sure she didn't want to dwell on just why his answer pleased her so much.

Syon smirked at her, showing no mercy for her sensibilities. "It means we've had a few drunken orgies. If either of us had any desire for the other, it would have been satisfied. He wants to put his hands on you, not me."

"And you're cool with that?" she asked.

He moved faster than she'd thought possible. One moment he was stretched out beside her, and the next he was half over her, one hand pressed flat against the top of the picnic table beside her hip.

"I want to explore every type of pleasure we can experience, from the simple to the edge of whatever boundary you decide you can't cross."

He pressed a kiss against her lips, claiming her lower lip between his teeth and gently biting it.

"I want to make you scream for me," he said when he released her lip. His eyes flickered with need so intense, she felt it scorching her skin. "And gasp, and shudder, and—"

"I get it," she said.

"Do you, Kate?" he asked in a hoarse tone that unleashed a desire to let him do whatever he wished with her.

No holds barred.

He curled a hand around her nape, squeezing just

enough to send a shiver down her spine. "Ramsey is the only man in this world I trust unconditionally. If you want a ménage—"

"I haven't even decided if I'm having a relationship with you," she said, feeling like she was trying to hold him off with a slingshot. The person she was kidding was herself.

She was such a liar. Her body was ready to jump right into hard, raw sex with him.

"Then allow me to add my thoughts to the decision-making process."

He pressed his mouth down on top of hers. The kiss was every bit as hard as his body. There was no mercy, no tender playfulness this time. Only hard purpose. She was sure she was melting.

But he let her up, just about the time her thoughts had scattered enough to have her ready to do whatever he wished, wherever he decided he wanted it. She was a breath from surrender, and the glitter in his eyes told her he knew it.

"Come on," he demanded gruffly.

He pulled her along behind him toward his bike. The vibration of the ride back into town, coupled with her struggling feelings, nearly drove her over the edge. She felt poised on a ledge. Her clit was begging for release, but she was battling with her rational side, trying to maintain some shred of self-control around this man.

Syon headed toward a high-rise hotel with mirrored glass siding. They roared up in front of the valet parking, practically causing a riot as all the valet attendants rushed to be the ones getting the keys to the Harleys. The losers looked glum when their gleeful comrades climbed aboard the sleek motorcycles and peeled out of the turnaround, making way for a flood of paparazzi.

Syon claimed Kate's hand as the cameras started snapping pictures around them. She twisted her hand, trying to escape the press, but Syon held it tight. There were squeals as passersby recognized the rest of the band. Eager fans reached for their idols, and the hotel security tried to keep them out of the entryway. Ramsey was surveying the crop of adoring fans near him and selected one, offering his hand.

She shook with excitement and tugged her girlfriend through the throng with her. Ramsey grinned and draped an arm over each of their shoulders.

"It's like when you get two prizes for the price of one at one of those carnival crane games," he called over his shoulder before passing into the lobby of the hotel. Syon shook his head mirthfully and tugged Kate away from the fans who were perplexed—and crushed—to see Syon arrive with a woman already on his arm.

Inside, a man wearing a black polo with the Toxsin logo on it stepped up and handed Syon a key card.

"This is Cid, Toxsin's road manager," Syon introduced the man.

"You need it, I get it for you," Cid said as he handed her a key card. He turned to hand keys to the other band members. "We'll go over the ropes tomorrow."

Syon punched the elevator call button and slid his key into the security slot. The door slid smoothly open, and he swept her inside. She expected the rest of the band to join them but when the elevator doors closed, they were alone. He wrapped his arms all the way around her.

"I can't wait to see if you have ginger curls between your legs too…"

She'd passed the point of being in control enough to form a coherent response, so they rode up to Toxsin's suite in silence. When they reached the top floor, the sound of the rest of the band with their fangirls broke through.

Syon had her out in the hallway before she managed to brace a hand against his chest. "Look, we're working together," Kate said, wondering if it was too late to try playing the professionalism card.

"You're so wet, I can smell you," Syon countered. He forced her back until he had both hands flattened on either side of her head on the wall behind her.

"You're crowding me," she said. "We just met."

"And we hit it off." He countered her argument in a smooth voice that made her nipples tighten. She wanted to be mad about it but honestly, it was a total rush to be turned on so completely. Part of her had to admit to enjoying the intensity. She ended up smiling in spite of every reason she should have been fuming at him. Chemistry was chemistry. And, oh boy, did they combine with a serious sort of reaction.

"You like to dominate," she said with a half laugh.

One side of his mouth twitched up as a look of approval glittered in his eyes. "I'm not into slave play, but yes, I like to control…"

Her lungs were frozen for a moment, leaving her suspended between breaths. The idea of letting him take control captivated her brain. It would be…well, epic.

Mind-blowing.

Yeah, and you'll wake up tomorrow morning knowing you are a pushover.

He reached for her wrist. "Let's find a bed, Kate…"

"No," she uttered, but honestly, she was talking to herself more than him. She tried to pull him to a stop and ended up skidding on the carpet for a few steps before he gave a frustrated grunt and turned back to face her.

There was a squeal and a burst of feminine laughter from around the corner. It hit her like a bucket of ice water—she wasn't his fangirl; she was his costumer, damn it.

She was pretty sure she wouldn't be able to live with herself if she folded. Her dreams of being a serious designer demanded more self-discipline than that.

Kate closed her eyes and found the remnants of her composure. "Good night, Syon. It was a great date."

Frustration needled her, but she opened her eyes and refused to bend.

Syon regarded her from behind narrowed eyes. "I don't go in for games, Kate."

Her temper heated, but she drew in a deep breath because she realized she was sending the guy mixed signals. She owed him an attempt at an explanation. "Look…I've known you for a whole forty-eight hours, Syon. Yes, you turn me on, but I don't know you. It isn't a game; it's called forming a relationship. That's the sort of thing I go for."

"You're just as hot as I am to keep this going," he said, trying to cut through her protest. "So stop being a cock tease."

"Stop being presumptuous." She propped her hand on her hip. "Going on a date does not mean there is going to be sex."

"Sticking your tongue into my mouth while I'm kissing you says there is!" he growled.

"Stop taking this so personally, Syon. There are plenty of other men who have to actually get to know a girl before they get naked with her."

She'd caught him off guard. One of his eyebrows rose in question. "You're trying to get a commitment out of me."

"Even if I were, I wouldn't apologize." Her temper sizzled. "I realize you're used to nailing everything you see—"

"Only the pussy," he drawled.

She rolled her eyes at his tone. "See? That's exactly why you and I need to go to separate beds. I'm here as a crew member."

"We don't have any female crew members," he argued.

"Well, you're the one who ambushed me into this," Kate replied. "So I'm a crew member now. I think there needs to be a clear line between crew members and fangirls."

He crossed his arms over his chest. "What do you want, Kate?"

Confusion clouded her thoughts. "I just told you."

"What, then? You want money? I'll double your contract fee."

Her jaw dropped. Then she took a swing at him. She never landed the slap, at least not on his face. Syon raised his forearm to block, and she ended up hitting nothing but hard muscle, leaving her hand stinging.

"Asshole!" she snarled. "I am *NOT* a whore."

"Everyone"—he stuck a thick finger out toward her—"*everyone* wants something from me. You're no different."

His eyes were lit with a jaded conviction that sickened her. No one should be so certain they were being used by everyone around them. It doused the flames of her temper, leaving her miserable. They really lived in different worlds. His wasn't any more perfect than her own.

"I'm sorry."

He stiffened, drawing back as their gazes connected. A guarded look appeared in his eyes before he shrugged, pulling his flippant sex-god side back up to cover his momentary vulnerability.

"Don't be. My life rocks," he informed her. "I don't need you or your pity. Just your leather skills."

"Well, I'm glad we got that clear between us." Her pride was stinging, but there was no way she was going to let him see it. She turned around and started down the hallway, blurry eyed and pissed. Fortunately, she found the room number written on the little paper envelope her key card was in only a few doors down. She slid the key card into the lock and pushed her way into the room.

The air-conditioning was droning away, soothing her flushed cheeks. Her bags were already on the luggage racks. It was a lavish bedroom, with a separate sitting area. But she didn't have any will to appreciate it.

Syon slammed into the suite his bandmates were partying in. There was already a scattering of clothing on the floor. He unzipped his jacket and shrugged out of it, flinging it aside to join the mess.

"The Marquis!" a feminine voice cooed.

He turned to find a topless brunette greeting him

with a bright smile. Her bare breasts bounced as she approached him, but all he felt snaking through his gut was revulsion.

What the fuck? Since when wasn't he interested in a pair of good tits?

Since he met Kate.

"You're so fucking *hot*!" she squealed. "I bet your cock is gorgeous…"

She reached for his fly, and he stepped back.

Shit!

Ramsey looked up from where a blond was sucking his dick. He was leaning back in a plush armchair with the chick kneeling between his spread thighs, but his attention was completely on Syon. The chick meant nothing to him but a moment of entertainment. That doubled the feeling twisting Syon's insides.

He shook his head and turned to leave.

"Hold on, sweetie," Ramsey said.

Ramsey caught him in the hallway, completely unabashed to be stuffing his erect cock back into his pants. "What's up with you, bro?"

"Nothing," Syon barked. "I'm just not in the mood."

"You're in the mood," Ramsey argued. "So why the hell aren't you between Kate's thighs?"

Syon growled. "She's making sure I know she's a team member."

"Yeah, and she had her hands all over you about an hour ago, so what's the problem?" Ramsey demanded.

"Apparently *I* am!" Syon slammed his fist into the wall, leaving a hole in the drywall. He stared guiltily at the damage. "I'm a dumbass tonight, Rams. Forget I exist."

"No fucking way." Ramsey reached out and grabbed a handful of Syon's shirt to keep him from stomping away. "Let me have Cid pack her ass out of here. We don't need this kind of tension. We've got a ton of our assets tied up in this tour."

"That's why she has to stay. We can't look like shitfaced amateurs." Syon shook off Ramsey's hold. "I checked her out. She does mind-blowing custom work. My pants don't fit right because I couldn't get worked up enough in front of the other guy." He snorted and shot his buddy a hard look. "That won't be a problem with Kate for sure."

Ramsey gave a grudging nod. "Fine, get your ass back in that suite and fuck it out of your system. We've got plenty of pussy to go around. And tomorrow, Kate can be a team member. You can let her measure the boner she's too prissy to ride."

Syon looked at the door but shook his head. He wasn't even sure he'd decided to decline the offer; there was only pure reaction, and it sent him away from the excess going on in the suite.

"I'm going to…write something," he said.

Syon stormed down the hallway to his own room and shut the door behind him. His guitar was set up again in the corner of the suite, the sofa pushed aside to make room for his practice area. His cock was throbbing, and he was pissed as hell. Without a second thought, he turned up the amps and played out his frustrations, making the strings squeal and ping.

But when his anger settled into something deeper, he began to make notes and put them together into something that made his blood pulse.

Relationship?

He didn't have to do relationships.

In fact, it was a whole lot brighter of him to avoid them. Success was a cruel little bitch in that she twisted everyone around him into leeches. No one came to him without a plan to get something out of him. His bandmates were the only exception.

He needed Kate to cover his ass; that was all.

He refused to let it be anything else.

She needed earplugs.

Syon was playing. Kate was sure of it. There was something about his rhythm that she recognized, even though she didn't know the tune. Her memory offered a perfect recollection of what his fingers looked like when he was playing, and her clit throbbed in response.

When he finally stopped, her mouth went dry. Her body felt on edge even though there was no reason to think he'd come looking for her again.

Ha! You screwed that opportunity!

Actually, she wished she had screwed it, literally. Maybe she'd be getting some sleep if she had.

Yeah, but sunrise would have been a bitch to face.

She growled and punched her pillow.

Someone's squeal pierced the hallway. "Come and get me!"

There were pounding footsteps and then a thud against the wall that shook her door. The girl laughed loudly as someone growled, and there was another rattle from her door.

"*Oh yes!* Fuck me!" the girl shouted, and the

door began to shake in a very recognizable rhythm. "Harder… *Harder!*"

Was it Syon?

Would he be that big of a jerk?

You don't have a right to be mad about it.

But she was.

"It's so good! Ramsey!"

Kate buried her head beneath her pillow and screamed. She didn't have the right to feel relieved either.

But she did.

—⁓—

Kate rubbed her eyes and waited for coffee to brew in her little kitchenette. The scent of java helped improve her mood as she marveled at Toxsin's ability to party. The noise hadn't died down until well after four.

She was going to have to do more sleeping on that tour bus.

You need to stop caring. He's a rock star.

It was well after noon when she made her way to where her shop was set up. The Toxsin crew knew what they were doing. Her machines were assembled in an easily accessible fleet, every case opened so she could see into it. Even her cutting table was ready. Racks of costumes stood around the room, each with a band member's name marked on it. The scent of leather was familiar, easing some of the tension from her neck.

At least this part of the deal she knew she could handle.

And do it really fucking well.

Someone rapped on the door, and she turned around to see one of the black-polo-shirted crew members standing there with one of those pigtail earphones stuck in his right ear.

"Do you need anything, Ms. Napier?"

"Well…" She scanned the room again. "Actually, I need to drape out the members of the band. Not all today, but if any of them have time…I'll start there. Mr. Braden is a priority."

He reached down to press the button on the little microphone clipped to his shirt collar and relayed her instructions.

She turned back around and started taking inventory.

"You've got one coming down," polo-shirt guy said. "They have a sound check in an hour."

"That's plenty of time," Kate assured him, biting back a question. She'd know soon enough who was going to come through the door.

She'd thought Syon was the one she couldn't really deal with, but Ramsey stalked into the suite and sent her look that made her blood boil.

He was spoiling for a showdown.

The problem was, so was she.

Professionalism…

"Thank you for coming. I'll try not to take up too much of your time."

No, not too much time at all, because the sooner her task was finished, the sooner she could stop holding her breath. She reached for a bolt of muslin and tore off two pieces to begin draping him so she would have a perfect pattern tailored to his specific measurements.

Ramsey grunted, and she caught the hint of a warning in his eyes. He shrugged out of his leather jacket and tossed it on the cutting table, presenting her with his bare chest. She ignored the urge to scan the perfection and started by pinning the fabric at his waist.

A half hour of total, awkward silence later, and Kate took the patterns off Ramsey.

"All done," she said.

Ramsey gave her one last acerbic glare and turned to leave without another word. Her temper got the better of her as he was shrugging back into his jacket.

"Okay, explain your problem with me." Kate pushed some hair that had worked its way free of her clip out of her face, and glared back at Ramsey.

"Don't have a problem with you," he blew her off and continued toward the door.

"Bullshit." Kate tossed the mock-up over the back of her chair and stepped into his path. "I thought it was just me throwing off the all-boy vibe, but I'm dangerously close to thinking there's more to it than that." She stepped aside. "By all means, take off and prove you're nothing but a prick who's worried I'm going to somehow stand in the way of you scoring tonight."

He jutted out his chin, started to shake his head, but stopped. She could see the indecision in his dark eyes. He ended up crossing his arms over his chest and sitting on the edge of her cutting table.

"Syon means a lot to me. A fucking hell of a lot, and he's got it bad for you, but you…" His eyes flashed. "You don't think he's good enough. That's what's pissing me off. He's going to get his heart shredded by your holier-than-thou 'tude."

Ramsey considered her. "You're not the first bitch who looked down her nose at him or me. So don't expect me to kiss your ass because you don't like my attitude or the way I live my life. It pisses me the fuck off to see you disapproving of the way my best friend spends his free time. He's walked through fire to be what he is today and doesn't owe you shit."

He started to walk away. Kate lunged after him and hooked his arm. He jumped and turned around to snarl at her.

"You've had your say, now it's my turn," she informed him.

"Is that right?"

"It is," Kate snapped. "For the record, I didn't say Syon wasn't good enough for me."

Ramsey snorted.

"What I question is how healthy this environment is for a relationship." She pointed in the direction of the hallway. "Do you even remember the names of the girls passed out in your bed or wherever you left them?"

Ramsey shook his head without a shred of remorse. "Most of them don't want me to. They want a buzz and a mind-blowing experience, and they sure as shit don't want it to follow them back to their nice, respectable lives. You know what I've got down the hall? One's a school teacher. She's getting married next summer."

"She told you that?" Kate asked incredulously.

"No." Ramsey reached for his jacket and pulled three cell phones out of the inside pocket. "I found that little tidbit right…here." He dangled a smartphone from his fingers. "I was trained to disarm complex programs. These little civilian devices are a piece of cake for me."

"You hacked their phones? What's wrong with you?" She paused as his words sank in. "You should tell her fiancé."

Ramsey only shrugged and slid the phone back into the jacket pocket. "It's not my shit-pile life. She might even make a good wife, now that she can enjoy her memory of fucking a rock star when hubby can't go down on her worth crap."

"That is so messed up, Ramsey. She's got no right to use you like that."

"I used her too."

He was trying to blow it off, but Kate wasn't buying it. She could see the pain in his eyes. He changed the subject.

"Syon hasn't touched another woman since he saw you."

She failed to hide just how much she appreciated hearing that. A little bubble of happiness just rose in her chest and sat there, glowing. Even the knowledge that the time frame under discussion was a whole two days didn't dampen her joy. Ramsey bit something back after reading her emotions off her face.

"Just…understand this. We spent years playing together before our parents decided to ship us off to the military so we would grow up and lose our adolescent dreams of playing in a band. It turned out to be the best thing that ever happened to us, but this is what we are." He opened his arms wide. "It's the fire that's been in our bellies since we were eight years old. I'm sick of seeing Syon torn between what he loves and his damned desire to please the rest of the world."

"You're sick of being judged," she said as understanding dawned. It was a painfully clear sunrise too. Success didn't promise happiness, even on the level Toxsin was experiencing it.

Ramsey's eyes narrowed. "This isn't about me."

"Yes it is."

He shook his head, but Kate reached up and cupped his cheek to stop him.

"It's about you because of the connection you share with Syon."

Ramsey lifted his chin to sever the contact. "He's the only family I have, since my blood thinks I'm infecting the youth of America with Satan's plots...or some shit like that."

He turned and started stalking toward the door.

"I've worked my ass off for what I have too, Ramsey."

He froze. She watched him fight the urge to turn around and fail. He faced her with a grudging expression.

"Professionalism is the foundation of my business." She spoke quietly. "Jumping my clients doesn't fit that image. My reputation is all I have. If you guys trash my performance on this tour, everyone who works for me will suffer. I've got a damned good reason to think before acting. Syon made this my workplace. So...I have to hold on to my professionalism."

He studied her for a long moment. She could see his outer shell cracking, granting her a glimpse of the wounded soul behind his public persona. His lips twitched, just a bit, into a genuine grin. "I'm beginning to see why Syon is fascinated with you."

"Huh?" Confusion stole her composure as Ramsey strolled back toward her with that sexy prowl of his. She tipped her head back to maintain eye contact and didn't care for the feeling of exposure that washed through her.

"You have integrity." He reached out and tapped her on the lips with his index finger.

Kate jumped back, feeling like a live wire had touched her.

Ramsey laughed, low and deep. "That's sexy. Really sexy. Sucks that you prefer Syon."

"Yeah, I heard how pitiful your night was as you longed for my company."

He smiled before moving back toward the door and knocking on the drywall. "It's not that thin." His eyes flashed. "What can I say? I do a fantastic job at everything."

Kate groaned and pointed him toward the hallway. "I've got all I need from you, thanks."

He licked his lower lip. "No, you're still hungry."

She raised her voice. "Bye!"

He chuckled knowingly at her before disappearing into the hallway.

She was going to be insane by the end of the tour.

Chapter 3

SYON WAS AVOIDING HER.

It really pissed her off.

Liar... It stings.

Well, that too.

The other members of Toxsin had come by her suite for fittings, but Cid showed up with Syon's missing-crotch pants instead of the singer.

"Pull a pattern off these."

The road manager tossed the garment at her. She caught it but dropped them on the chair next to her. "I don't clone. I do my own work. Always. I need a fitting."

Cid was close to fifty by her guess but hiding it extremely well. His body was toned and fit, and only a hint of gray was visible where his hair had grown out at its roots. He fixed her with a hard look.

"You're here to work on our schedule. Mr. Braden hasn't had time for a fitting. In case you missed it, he's a celebrity."

"My work is custom." Kate pointed at the two pairs of partially completed pants hanging on a rack, waiting for fittings. "If Syon wants a pair of pants that fit, I need him down here."

She needed his ass and his hard-on, but she was avoiding thinking about the particulars.

Cid didn't like her tone. Something slithered through her that left a very unpleasant aftertaste in her mouth.

She realized she was getting a glimpse of what it was like to ruffle the feathers of those who considered Syon their bread and butter. If Syon told Cid to be a dick to her, he would without getting a single hair out of place. Cid knew who was signing the paychecks and didn't give a shit about how many feelings got hurt while he was ensuring his meal ticket. Toxsin was bringing in big money, and that meant there were going to be big sharks swimming in the tank. No one was on tour who didn't know when to abandon fair play.

"I'll see what I can do."

The road manager left with an air of importance and no hint of remorse in his expression.

She should have dived back into the work she had.

Should have, but she walked across the suite and glared out at the San Francisco skyline instead. The sun had gone down hours ago, but the city was far from sleepy. There was a buzz and pulse that she could feel through the double-paned glass windows. Traffic was flowing below her, people thick on the sidewalks. Cafés were open, catering to the night crowd. It seemed too dedicated to spend the night working for someone who couldn't be bothered to make time for a fitting.

Okay, she was miffed that she didn't rate high enough for an hour of his time.

Kate shook off her grumpiness.

Syon had gotten his eight hours out of her. So it was quitting time.

She picked up her phone and trolled through Facebook and a couple of travel sites to see what the city offered for night entertainment. Surely there was a local hot spot somewhere close with a band or signature dinner dish that she could enjoy.

Her phone chirped. It startled her, but she grinned when she recognized the name of one of her Bay Area clients. His name was Clarence O'Malley, but it was a whole lot safer to call him by his preferred nickname.

"Hello, Conan."

"Why didn't you tell me you were coming to the Bay Area?"

Kate smiled, feeling ridiculously rescued. "It was last minute. Um…how'd you know?"

"You're logged into Facebook, with the location app. You're too cute to have that turned on, you know. Someone like me might use it to stalk you," Conan said.

"Um…yeah."

Conan chuckled on the other end of the line. "You doubt my badass-ness?"

Kate laughed and reached back to rub her neck. "Never. Just your level of desperation to resort to stalking. Last time I checked, you had a small harem."

"Maybe. Get down to the lobby."

"You're here?" she asked incredulously.

"Yeah, I drive my ass down to your end of the state because no one can sew leather like you. Just shut up the shop. Let's grab a cold one and get some chow. Got a couple of guys I'd love to introduce you to. Can't wait to tell them you were in my pants while you're sitting close enough for them to see how hot you are."

And that was why he liked to be called Conan. He claimed to be a barbarian at heart. Which made him just interesting enough to be fun.

"You're on," Kate said.

She wasn't going to hang around waiting for Syon. She'd put in a full day. If she was going to be on tour, she might as well enjoy the sights a little. She could catch up on her sleep on the road.

She swung around and took a moment to run a brush through her hair and apply a fresh coat of lipstick. The elevators were express ones, and a few moments later, she was striding through the polished marble floors of the lobby. Conan had pulled up on a chopper. The doormen were eyeing him as security eased closer.

Not that she blamed them. Conan was rather typical as far as her clients went. His shaved head had a tattooed skull on the back, and his forearms sported more ink. He had a huge, square-cut jaw, and his nose bore the evidence of being broken. When he grinned, one full gold crown winked at the suit-clad security men watching him. The only way he wasn't typical was in the fact that he ran a very lucrative business. The bodyguards edging in on him would have been surprised to discover themselves dealing with a man who could afford to rent out one of the exclusive penthouse suites. Ripped jeans and all. The guy owned several Armani suits, but needed to be beaten half to death before putting one on.

He revved the chopper and whistled when he spotted her. Kate swung the shoulder strap of her bag over herself, cross body.

She reached out and steadied herself with a hand on his shoulder before lifting her leg to get on behind him. There was a roar as Toxsin pulled into the half-circle drive, taking control of the space completely. Conan turned his head to admire the chrome work on the Harleys. Kate slid her leg along his back.

"What the fuck?" Syon ripped off his shades. "Get the hell off that chopper, Kate!"

She wasn't completely on the back of the bike yet. Surprise kept her frozen. Syon threw his helmet and launched himself off his Harley.

"Know this dude?" Conan asked her, his attention on Syon. There was a clink as he kicked the stand into place. "His tone says he needs his ass kicked."

"That's the only action you're going to get tonight," Syon growled.

Conan was off the chopper the second Syon got close. Kate stumbled back as they faced off.

"She's not worth it." Ramsey grabbed Syon by the shoulder and tried to pull him back. "If she'd rather be in his pants, let the bitch go."

"Oh, she's been in my pants alright…real deep."

"Conan—" Kate protested.

Syon's growl cut her off as he took a swing at Conan. People screamed, and paparazzi moved in, their cameras rolling. Conan bared his teeth and launched himself into the fight. Syon snarled and went after him with blood lust on his face.

"Stop it!" Kate skirted around the tail of the chopper and tried to lunge between them. Ramsey turned and hooked her around the waist. He dragged her out of the way and scooped her up when she tried to fight him. She got out only half a sound of protest before he dumped her into someone else's arms.

"Get her out of here."

"Wait…"

Taz didn't pay attention to her. He turned and carried her back up onto the curb.

"Forget this shit." She kicked her feet up and succeeded in getting one knee loose. She put her leg down
and pushed out of Taz's hold.

Taz snorted and let her stand up. A second later he
had her over his shoulder. There was still the sound of
flesh hitting flesh behind her. She looked up as Taz
hauled her through the front door of the hotel, to the
delight of the paparazzi snapping pictures.

"Put me the fuck down!" Kate yelled.

Taz dumped her in an elevator but pushed her back
into the corner as he jammed a key card into the slot.
He stuck one finger out at her. "You can walk or I'll
carry you."

"Like hell you will."

The elevator jerked and started pulling them toward
the top floor. "I want out of here. You guys are insane!"

"Yeah, we are." Taz shrugged.

His nonchalant attitude left her frozen for a moment.
It was long enough for them to make it to the penthouse.
She dove out the door the second it started opening.

She refused to work for crazy people.

Percy would have to understand.

She was inside her suite before she realized Taz had
slid smoothly through the door behind her. She spun
around and pointed at the door. "Get out."

He caught her wrist and jerked her arm around. She
popped into position like a rag doll; one moment she
was facing him, and the next he had her arm locked up
in a martial arts move that made sweat pop out on her
forehead. The pain was just enough to keep her from
challenging him, because it was going to hurt like hell
if she did. He pushed her toward the bed. There was the

touch of something smooth against her wrist and a click before he released her.

She looked down and realized he'd handcuffed her to the huge headboard.

"What are you doing?"

He'd retreated a few paces and shoved his hands into his pockets. "Making sure you're here when Syon wants you. You two need to talk."

"Fuck what Syon wants." She snarled and jerked on the handcuffs, but they held. "Unlock these."

Taz shook his head.

"Are you some kind of idiot?" She jerked on the handcuffs again. "This is illegal."

"Did you have to take up with someone else so fast?" Taz looked disgusted. "Is this your idea of some sick game?"

"What?" She shook her head, trying to make sense of what he was saying.

"That dude." Taz pointed out the window. "You cut Syon deep."

"Wrong." The door hit the wall as Syon kicked it in. The handle punched right through the drywall with a dull sound. "I don't give a shit whose pants you're hopping into."

"I made his leather pants," she explained. "Conan's jerking your chain, dumb ass."

And Syon had blood trickling down his chin.

It froze her in place. Horror wrenched her gut and left her stuck between breaths. Nothing else mattered at all.

Syon had gone still, his gaze locked with hers, one hand stopping in midswipe on that trickle of blood.

"That makes sense." Taz sounded surprised. "A lot of

sense. *'She's been in my pants real deep…'"* He started to laugh softly. "That dude totally got you."

"You too," Kate said.

Taz shrugged. "Yeah. Sorry if I hurt your shoulder."

"Get these cuffs off me," she demanded.

Syon reached out and pushed Taz toward the open door. It was still open, the doorknob stuck in the drywall.

"They're making up!" Taz yelled down the hallway. Drake and Ramsey must have come up. "She made that dude's pants, that's why she was in them."

"Like hell we're making up," she yelled after Taz. "Get your ass back in here with the key, Taz!"

Taz stopped and tossed a key back; Syon caught it and yanked the door loose. Chunks of drywall dropped to the floor as he shoved it closed with a slam.

"Are you done with him?"

"Done with who?" She jerked on her hand again; this time the cuff bit into her wrist. "I swear, if you don't unlock me…"

"Yeah, yeah."

He flipped the key over and fit it into the lock. He was too damned close again. The scent of his skin filled her senses. Just the brush of his fingers against her hand sent a little thrill through her.

"You're making me crazy."

She rubbed her wrist and glared at him. "That's my line. Where the hell does Taz get off handcuffing me to the bed?"

Syon's eyes narrowed. "He won't be getting off. Not with you."

"Like that's any of your concern. Is Conan alright?"

"Yeah. The dude can hold his own. Had to stop when

the cops showed up." He wiped the blood away, but a fresh trickle appeared. For some reason, the sight of it deflated her anger, which pissed her off again. Couldn't she even be mad at the guy when he deserved it?

"Shit. You have a show tomorrow night."

She rolled over the bed and came up on the other side. "So what?"

Kate rolled her eyes and went into the kitchen. She yanked a plastic bag out of the cabinet and filled it with ice. "Put this on your jaw before you get a bruise."

She settled the bag against his jaw.

"That's what makeup is for."

He wrapped his arms around her, and the bag dropped. Syon buried his face in her hair instead. "All day I've been thinking about how you smell."

His words were muffled, but she still heard the low, raspy sound of need in his tone. It was like being shocked with a set of jumper cables. She flattened her hands on his chest and tried to push him back. "Really? Then why didn't you show up for a fitting?"

She hated how hurt she sounded, but the words were out of her mouth.

He cupped her nape, pressing a kiss against her neck. It sent a tingle straight down to her toes. She squealed, struggling against his hold, feeling the tidal wave of arousal beginning to crash down on her.

He let her go, and she bounced onto the bed.

"That's why."

She jumped up, her face flaming.

"I tried to stay away because every time I get near you, all I want to do is lick you." He threw his arms into the air. "You want me to do it too."

She had her mouth open to fire off a retort, but it died when he locked gazes with her. The world shifted again the second her eyes connected with his caramel ones. She did want him. Bad. She shifted, her clit feeling crushed inside her pants.

"So I gave you some space and came back to find you on another dude's bike." He shook his head. "You're fucking making me…jealous!"

It was a strange compliment. Really strange, because he was pissed off. At least she thought he was, until she looked closer.

Apparently, Syon was just as overwhelmed as she was. The need burning between them was so tangible, it interfered with everything else.

There was a hint of uncertainty in his eyes, and it hit her straight in the heart.

"What are you doing?"

Kate rolled her eyes at him. "Taking my clothes off."

She popped the lace holding her corset top closed and untied the knot.

"Why?" He wasn't waiting for her answer but shrugged out of his leather jacket with a violence that strained the seams.

A rush of cool air hit her overheated skin as she yanked the lace free, and the front of her top sagged open. Her thin top was transparent, allowing him to clearly see her nipples.

"Because we're too old to hold hands and smooch on the back of your bike while we work up the nerve to justify our actions and give in."

He groaned, his eyes narrowing and his jaw tightening. "I want to do that…later."

He tore off his shirt, and it ripped as he yanked it over his head. The sound hit her heightened senses, driving the heat up another few degrees. Getting out of her clothing was a necessity. She felt trapped by her pants, the leather too thick, too hot to tolerate.

He was chiseled.

And bulky with muscle.

A fatal combination.

She tore at her pants, knotting the lace with her clumsy fingers.

"I want to do it," he growled; then he scooped her off her feet and dropped her back onto the bed, savage enjoyment glittering in his eyes as she bounced in a jumble of limbs.

"I haven't stopped thinking about dragging these off you…"

He captured her ankle and pressed a kiss against the inside of it. She gasped, arching her back as sensation took complete control of her. There was no thought, just writhing as he pulled her ankle boot off and dropped it.

He chucked her other boot across the room. "I want to tear this leather off you like a Christmas present."

"Don't"—the word got stuck in her mouth—"tear it."

She was panting, desperation twisting up her insides as he attacked the lace keeping her fly closed.

He fought with the knot. "You need to start wearing skirts."

His lips split with a wide grin when the lace broke. He thrust his fingers into the fly, stroking across the sensitive skin of her lower belly.

She freakin' purred.

The sound rising up from the contact between their skin swamped her, dragging her down and rolling her in pure enjoyment.

"Yeah…I like that sound."

He plunged his hand in deep, reaching all the way to her mons. He teased his way through her curls before stroking her belly again.

"Like it a whole hell of a lot." He gripped the waistband of her pants and tugged it over her hips. She was so eager, she lifted her butt for him. She landed back on the bed as he pulled the garment down her thighs and past her ankles with a grunt of male satisfaction.

"Perfect."

His gaze targeted her mons. The tip of his tongue slid over his lower lip as he reached out to finger the bikini briefs she had on. Expectation showed brightly in his eyes as he hooked the elastic waistband with his index finger and pulled it down to expose her.

"Hot damn…*ginger curls*…"

His tone made her shiver, anticipation punching her in the gut as he dragged her underwear down her legs and threw her panties across the room.

"I fucking dreamed about seeing these…"

He dropped to his knees, spreading her thighs.

"Wait…"

He looked up her body, searing her with the glint in his eyes. Her insides liquefied. The promise glowing those orbs set her clit throbbing at an insane rate.

He moved his hand along her inner thigh, stroking her, petting her with a touch that sent a little moan past her lips.

"How long?"

He had made his way to her hip, her clit begging for its turn to be under his fingers.

But he pulled his hand down her leg, to her knee, and then back down in a slow caress to her hip again.

"How long should I wait?"

She jerked, her hips lifting, but he held her down with both hands on her thighs.

"You smell so *hot*…"

He was hovering over her spread body, his breath teasing her open slit.

"So…sweet…" He leaned down and pressed a kiss against her belly, right above her mons.

"Don't…" Her voice was nothing but a rasp, speech darn near beyond her grasp. She just needed…needed to be touched. "Don't…wait…"

She curled up, reaching for his shoulders. She wasn't close enough. He wasn't close enough. She caught his shoulders and let out a little sound of victory. She used the grip to pull herself to the edge of the bed and flatten herself against his bare chest.

The contact was catastrophic.

Every bit of thought she had was laid to waste. There was nothing but a flood of sensation sweeping through her. She lifted her hips, certain she could climax by just grinding against the bulge still covered by his leather pants.

"We're not fucking rushing this."

He pushed her back down and held her there with his body. He was hard and heavy, and he hovered just an inch above her lips.

"I'm going to eat you out."

"I can't—"

He shoved her protest back into her mouth with his, kissing her with a hard passion that broke something loose inside her. She arched and dug her nails into his shoulders, sucking his tongue and thrusting hers up to tangle with it.

"Ah…yeah…claw me…"

He surged up, arching his head back so she was staring at the corded muscles running up his neck. She pulled her hands down his arms, hesitant at first, but his chest vibrated with a growl of enjoyment.

"Again," he ordered her, pressing forward and making contact with her clit.

"Oh…damn…"

She was on the edge, a breath away from climax. Desperation made her crazy. She wrapped her legs around his body, pulling him against her as she reached up and raked her claws down him again.

Sweat was popping out all over her skin. Her nipples contracted into tight little pebbles. She was straining toward him.

"Not yet, baby."

He sounded like he was a thread away from losing control. She slapped his shoulder.

"Yes…*now*," she insisted.

He rose up off of her, enraging her with the separation. "Don't tease me, Syon."

He flattened his hand on her belly, easily putting her back on the bed. "You're not ready yet."

"I've never been so ready." She was pretty sure she was baring her teeth at him, but she didn't give a rat's ass. "Get your cock out."

He reached down and opened his pants. She froze, mesmerized by the idea of getting a look at what she'd thought about so vividly. Time was moving like molasses, flowing in a thick, sweet ooze that tantalized her senses.

"Like this?" He'd opened his fly and reached inside. She'd never realized what a turn-on it could be to see a man handling his own cock. Syon pulled his length into view, his fingers just as hard as his penis. It was huge with thick veins running from head to base.

"Yeah…like that…" She wanted to taste it, stroke it, lick it, but most of all, she wanted it deep inside her. She was spread wide-open and didn't care a bit what she looked like. Just so long as she got what she wanted.

"I want to fuck you, Kate."

He clasped his cock, the huge, swollen head making her insides ache. Her mouth was dry, and she had to lick her lips before forcing a word past them. "Yes."

It was more of a moan.

A needy, hungry little plea.

He leaned closer, guiding his cock toward her spread body. His forearm muscles were corded, the veins standing out as he touched his cockhead to her labia. She hooked her heels around his thighs, pulling him toward her, lifting her butt off the bed to get in position to take him.

He thrust two thick fingers inside her instead.

"What the fuck are you doing?" she demanded, her eyes popping open.

He used his body to pin her down again, hovering over her lips as he worked his fingers in and out in a slow motion that was driving her mad.

"Getting you ready, baby…and you aren't ready… just yet."

"I sure as hell am!" she snarled, rolling her eyes at him.

He bared his teeth at her in response. "Not until I find your G-spot."

He was stroking her insides, slowly teasing all sides of her passage and pausing when she gasped.

"There it is…"

She had no idea what he was saying. She was only aware of what his fingers were doing to her. He'd found some spot that pushed her into a completely new realm of sensation. It was so intense, she wasn't sure if it was pleasure or pain. But the motions of his fingers made it impossible to clear enough of her mind to think about it.

All she could was moan.

And moan louder.

She was being twisted and pulled and jerked from the inside out. Her clit was an insane throbbing point, wanting attention just as much as the spot Syon's fingers were on. It was building, like the roar of a train coming down the track straight for her. She was lying across the tracks, waiting for impact, knowing that she was going to scream when it happened.

"*Now,*" he snarled.

She opened her eyes, trembling with excitement. She lifted her arms in welcome, but he didn't press down on her. He lifted one of her legs and slid onto the edge of the bed. He pushed up against her, his legs scissored with hers, and drove his cock straight up to the spot he'd been massaging. Every thrust rubbed against her clit and finished with a hard connection to her G-spot.

She strained toward him, desperate for the next thrust. Her heart felt like it was going to burst, and she didn't give a damn if it did, so long as he kept moving, kept hammering into her, kept bringing her closer to the edge of oblivion.

Sex had never felt so good.

So absolutely necessary.

There wasn't a single force on the planet that would have gotten her to stop.

It was obsession. Complete. Total. No holds barred.

"Yes..." she yelled. "Oh...fuck...yes!"

"Right there?" He ground himself into her so deep, his balls slapped against her thigh.

"Yes!" There wasn't any other word left in her vocabulary.

She was twisting, straining against him, the bed rocking insanely as everything inside her ripped apart. Pleasure slammed into her harder than she'd ever experienced. She clamped him against her, her thighs burning with the effort.

"Oh yeah!" he growled, pumping hard and deep into her. "Scream for me, baby..."

She didn't have any choice. Pleasure was searing through her. It was so intense, she cried out, feeling like her spine might just snap.

He growled low and deep, his cock hard enough to break. He was stretching her, plunging deeper than anyone ever had, pumping into her harder and harder until he yelled. His come spurted inside her, sending another wave of pleasure through her. She started gasping for breath when it hit, and she flailed as it gripped her. Syon held her in place, pumping through his climax until he ground out a soft word of profanity.

———∿∿∿———

"He was jerking my chain?"

Kate winced. The question was a reminder of how reckless she'd just been.

It was reality tsunami time.

The impact was going to sting.

"Does reality really have to return?" she asked.

Syon stroked her back, moving his hand along her spine in a slow, sensual motion. It felt so tender, she buried her face in a pillow and just willed the night to swallow them.

"Does it bug you that I didn't use a condom?"

She groaned. Feeling like her stupid level was at an all-time high.

Syon snorted. "Yeah, color me a dumb ass."

"I'm on the pill but—"

"I'm clean," he offered. "Get tested every month, and you're the first time I've ridden bareback."

She lifted her head and locked gazes with him. "Really?"

He nodded, looking away for a moment. Syon was lying on a stack of oversize pillows, his bare chest a portrait of perfection.

"Me too."

He looked back at her. "Then why the pill?"

She smiled at him. "Most girls go on it to regulate their cycles, not so they can have unprotected sex. But I can see how you probably only meet the type who do it for the sex factor."

"Don't discriminate against me because I'm a rock star. I know what a quality girl looks like. Why else would I ambush you into coming on tour with us?"

She bit her lower lip, trying to decide if she wanted to go anywhere near that topic. He reached out and used his thumb to pull her lip from between her teeth.

"It would have been within my contract rights to make the original artist produce more pieces."

Danger...

Oh hell, she was in dangerous waters now. The kind that could get her a massive heartache.

"I wanted the chance to get to know you. Couldn't cancel the tour." He shrugged, looking unrepentant.

"So you...kidnapped me?" she asked.

"Persuaded."

"Ambushed," she corrected.

His gaze lowered to her bare breasts. "You don't look too unhappy for a captive."

"I was pretty pissed off a little bit ago," she reminded him. "And great sex doesn't trump that issue."

His expression became guarded. There was a hint of stubble on his face, giving him a less-than-civilized look. It made him seem more male, if such a thing were possible. One thing it definitely did was blur the line between what she thought she wanted from relationships and what was making her blood boil. He was pushing her out of her comfort zones, and she'd be a liar if she didn't admit she liked it.

"It did," he said in a low whisper.

The intensity in his tone touched something deep inside her.

"Did...what?"

"Hurt. Seeing you on the back of that dude's bike… the sight…tore something," he offered at last, his jaw tight with the admission.

At least she wasn't alone.

That thought sent a tingle of guilt through her. "Conan was just taking advantage of the opening you gave him to dick with you. He's the sort who thrives on that kind of buzz."

"Where were you going with him?"

His gaze had slipped down to her breasts. Hunger softened his features as he reached out and cupped one. She still had on her thin chemise top, and she really loathed it just then, because it left her wide-open. His fingers sent a thrill through her, her skin ultra-aware of the connection. Her heart was accelerating.

"Where?"

"Ummm…" She tried to keep her brain from disengaging. "Just dinner. He's a client and noticed I was in the area. He called and asked me to share supper with him."

His expression tightened again. "And you just agreed to take off with him?"

She sat up, removing his hand from her breast so she could think.

"I wasn't going to wait around here when Cid said you weren't coming for a fitting. It felt like…moping. And I didn't like knowing you were avoiding me just because I didn't have sex with you on the first date. You shouldn't have been pissed because I wanted to stick to my standards."

"I wasn't pissed." He sat up. She felt a charge in the air between them; her belly tightened.

"Yes you were."

"Only at myself." He folded his legs back, leaning toward her.

Her mouth went dry. He looked like he was getting ready to lunge at her. But he gripped the bedding, his knuckles turning white.

"Because I shouldn't have ripped into you about my own insecurities regarding people seeing me as a meal ticket." His eyes narrowed. "As for ditching the fitting, guilty as charged. But I was a little afraid I wouldn't be able to keep my mouth off yours and you'd jab me with a pin."

She snorted at the image. "Might have used my scissors."

His gaze settled on her mouth. "I love the way you taste. It's annoying how much I think about it."

"Gee. Thanks." Her words might have been flippant, but her tone was husky.

Damn.

She just couldn't help it. There was something about the way he was looking at her—his jaw tight with frustration over the way she affected him—that set her blood on fire. It was the sort of thing warm, fuzzy words could never convey.

It was raw.

Savage.

And it curled her toes.

She rolled over and stood up with some notion of escaping the potent storm of stimulation she was stuck in, but her damned knees wobbled. The bed moved, and a second later Syon closed his arms around her and pulled her back onto the foot of the mattress.

"Syon—"

"Shhhh… I didn't mean to freak you out," he said.

"I didn't say—"

He covered her lips with his hand, sealing her retort inside her mouth.

"It knocks me for a loop too, the intensity between us. So do me a favor and don't deny it. I don't need to feel like a wimp," he said, trying to placate her.

She sighed. "Like that could ever happen."

He nuzzled against her neck for a moment, his breath warm and setting off a swarm of tremors that raced down her skin. "I'm getting the feeling neither of us has any idea how to deal with the way we react to each other."

She swallowed but couldn't quite get the lump out of her throat. He was dead on the nail head, and it made her feel like she was standing on the edge of a cliff.

For a moment, he held her. She wiggled, because there was something about his embrace that was just so damned…tender.

She was pretty sure she couldn't deal with tender from him. He'd already melted his way through her common sense, her reservations, and she didn't need him blowing a hole straight into her heart.

"Conan's okay. He told the cops we were rehearsing for a video."

He nuzzled against her neck, licking her skin and setting off a ripple of sensation.

"Taz is an asshole for handcuffing me to the bed."

Syon shifted and pulled her top off. He chucked it across the room, but the moment he released it, the thin fabric fluttered like a butterfly on its way to the floor.

"Taz is just calling what he sees." He was wrapped around her again, cupping her breasts and teasing her nipples with his thumbs. "Not his fault we're both uncomfortable with the charge between us."

Her body was starting to pulse again, her clit aching.

"I can't do that again. At least, not right now."

He smoothed his hands down her arms. "Got to work up to it this time…"

His voice was a dark whisper. He placed her hands on the foot rail of the bed and grasped her hips, raising them so he could get behind her.

"Seriously, Syon. I can't take that intensity again… not just yet."

"Trust me, baby…you can, with the right coaxing." He held her hips and teased the opening of her body with the tip of his cock. "I'm a lot better at sex than not being a dick."

She scoffed at him.

He chuckled, flattening one hand on her belly. "You're so damned wet."

She was.

And hungry for more.

"Ready for me," he rasped against her ear. The head of his cock slid through her folds, slipping easily through the wet flesh.

A moan got past her lips before she even realized it was coming.

"Very ready," he told her in a tone that was edged with dominance. He thrust into her from behind. "I've done my homework, baby…"

He settled deeply inside her, letting her adjust to having him there.

"All the little facts about sex…"

He pulled loose and thrust forward again, his pace

smooth and slow. He massaged her belly, working his fingers closer and closer to her throbbing clit. Driving her wild with anticipation.

"Read all the studies on what women say they want…"

He teased her slit, slipping into the wet folds on his way to her clitoris.

"You make me sound like a test subject."

He caught her earlobe between his lips. She shuddered, lifting her bottom for his next thrust, astounded by just how good it felt. He was stroking all around her clit with his fingers, without actually touching it. Need was building up inside her again, the pinching ache leaving her as he slowly rode her from behind.

"I don't want to just fuck you."

His fingertip was maddeningly close to her clit. She curled forward, trying to get it on top of the throbbing mass of nerve endings. He kept her in place by cupping her mons.

"It worked for me," she said, breathless again.

"I want more than that." His tone had hardened. "So do you."

Her brain tried to reengage. "Syon—"

He fingered her clit, and she was jerked away from reality with a jolt.

"Just…shut up…and feel, baby." His voice was strained, his pace increasing. "I want to make you feel…as insane as you make me feel," he rasped against her ear.

She sank back down into the waves of need and sensation. She didn't think she'd ever been so wet. He was gliding in and out of her, his cock harder than she'd believed possible.

It made her shudder.

And gasp.

The bed was rocking again, squeaking as he gripped her hips and started hammering her. He was adjusting her position, slowly changing the angle until she gasped.

"There it is…" he groaned, tightening his hold when she would have squirmed away from the sheer intensity. He held her steady and thrust straight back into her G-spot.

"I don't think…" She was panting, sweat trickling down her sides.

"That's the idea."

He was using short thrusts against that spot inside her, making sure he didn't withdraw too much and lose connection with it.

She lost the ability to form thoughts again, tossed back into the vortex of churning need. Her heart was hammering again, making her pant as she shoved herself back into every thrust. She had never realized how sensitive her body was. She felt every last millimeter of his cock. Her body made wet sounds as he moved.

"Oh…yeah…" he ground out, his grip tightening on her hips.

The hold sent a thrill through her that made her shudder. She felt captured, controlled, and yet unleashed. He was dominating her but freeing her too. The contrast was extreme, and she ended up yelling as climax tore through her once more. This time, she actually felt her body tightening around his length, gripping his cock as pleasure reduced her to a moaning pile of quivering flesh.

"That's it…yeah…that's it!"

He was pumping a second load into her. His come hot against her insides. He held her with a hard grip on her hips as the last shot of his seed spurted into her, keeping her in place for that last moment while he was suspended between breaths.

He cussed when he drew breath again. The bed bounced as he flopped over onto his back and pulled her with him until they were laying sideways, most of the pillows on the floor. Their breathing was as rough as the air-conditioning that hummed in the background.

Epic.

Just…epic.

Chapter 4

HER BELLY GROWLED LONG AND LOW.

Kate stretched out her leg and pushed her face into the pillow, still feeling like movement was beyond her.

The bed moved, and she jerked up, her eyes widening when she caught sight of the naked man in bed with her.

More like naked god…

Syon was bare-assed and completely lickable. From his rumpled hair to his tight backside.

He reached over and grabbed the phone on the night-stand. "Send up some chow. Just a bunch of breakfast plates. Little of everything."

Someone said something on the other end of the line. He frowned. "Check the room number, buddy. This is the penthouse floor. I don't care what time of day it is. Make it happen if you want your tips."

He dropped the phone and wiped his eyes before grinning at her. He pushed his hair out of his face, looking like a gigantic golden bear.

"Let's catch a shower before the food arrives."

He rolled over and pulled her with him. The suite had a huge walk-in shower with three showerheads, and he made full use of it. He walked right into the spray and let it soak him as he shook his head to make sure his hair was completely wet. It was incredibly personal to be able to see him in that moment, a secret intimacy she'd never realized could touch her as deeply as it did.

It set off another little warning bell in the back of her head. He was becoming an essential part of her world too easily.

Get a grip, girl...

She hadn't expected him to spend the night. Kate bit her lip to keep the thought from spilling out of her lips while he adjusted the water temperature. She was leaning against the vanity, trying to decide what to make of his presence and her reaction to it.

He turned and caught her in his caramel gaze. "You okay?"

"Yes."

She was.

Yup.

Sure was.

Liar...

He was studying her with those amazing eyes, his expression becoming guarded as she hesitated to join him.

"Didn't expect me to be here?" he asked.

She lifted one shoulder, but the motion felt forced. She let out a long breath. "To be fair, I don't think I thought that far ahead. You sort of have a way of disarming my entire thought process."

As in, her brain completely fried every time he kissed her.

His lips twitched, his expression softening into something she was pretty sure qualified for the term "cheeky."

"You took your clothes off first." He extended his hand in invitation.

"I did." She pushed away from the vanity. "You loved it."

"I did."

The shower was an enormous, stone-tiled thing. Done in a warm honey tone, it had a bench seat and a collection of bathing items. She put her hand into his and felt herself losing her grip on her brain again.

Obviously the Syon reaction of choice.

The water was splashing all over him, running down his body in torrents.

And she wanted to lick it off him.

"I think I should have left my clothes on last night."

His jaw jutted out, his expression hardening defensively.

"Because I missed the opportunity to appreciate all of you." She grabbed a washcloth. "A real shame."

He relaxed, something flickering in his eyes that looked like relief. She popped open a bottle of bodywash and drizzled it onto the cloth. "You've got to be putting in hours of resistance training."

"Yeah. Need to have the whole package." He swept her from head to toe.

"You know what a cardio workout is too."

"Well, there is no fitness fairy."

She stroked the cloth across his back, turning him away so his cock was out of sight. Her self-control was slipping again. The hard flesh might have been out of sight, but it certainly wasn't out of mind. The idea was there, teasing her with the memory of just how good sex with him had been. Seriously, she needed to have at least one more bout, just to make sure she hadn't been hallucinating the night before.

Maybe it had just been sensory overload. Doomed to fade after the intimate explosion.

He made a low sound of appreciation as she

washed his back, leaning forward to brace his hands flat on the tile wall of the shower. She swished the cloth back and forth across his tight shoulders and onto his lower back.

"I couldn't have waited last night for you to do anything to me." He arched up as she touched the top of his ass. "Which is a disgusting lack of control. I'm not seventeen."

"Seems pretty fair to me." It probably wasn't the brightest idea to be making confessions. It was one thing to be overwhelmed by him, another to let him know it. "I couldn't wait either."

He looked at her over his shoulder. "I never play fair."

She bent her knees and drew the cloth along one thigh and down his calf.

He didn't play fair? No shit.

He turned around when she straightened, and she got stuck in mid-motion, the cloth hanging from her hand as she was reaching for the bottle of bodywash.

Her brain just fried.

In the buff, Syon was perfection. Her breasts felt heavy; her nipples drew tight. It was an uncanny effect, like someone turned her senses up to high.

"Mmmm…my turn…"

She jumped back when he tried to claim the washcloth. "I'm not finished."

His eyes narrowed. "You'll be screaming when I finish you off, baby."

It was a hard promise, one backed up by the glint in his eyes. The stubble on his chin added to the uncivilized picture he presented.

The combination made her insides churn.

He scooped up the bodywash and clasped a hard arm around her in one of those whip-flash motions of his.

"I think it's time to multitask."

He crushed the bottle in his hand, drizzling it all over her body like icing. He dropped it and pulled her tightly against him.

"Now let's dance, Kate…" She hadn't noticed the sound system, but the shower had a control pad set right into the stone wall. He punched a couple of buttons, and the first bars of "Insatiable Craving" filled the bathroom.

"I sang this to you the night we met…"

He rubbed his body against hers, rotating, grating, holding her hips and twisting her in the opposite direction so he was sliding across her, the bodywash lathering gently with their motions.

She shuddered, pleasure shooting through her from the full-body contact.

"That's it."

He turned her around and ran his hands down her front. Standing up behind her so closely, his cock nestled between her buns. The water was pouring down, but she felt overheated. He started rubbing her at her collarbone, slowly stroking his way to her breasts.

She lifted her head and tipped up her chin, making sure he had a clear path to her breasts.

"I love these."

He cupped them, his fingers moving through the lather of the bodywash, slipping and sliding around the soft globes as well as teasing her hard nipples.

"Perfect…handfuls…"

She let out a soft snort. "They're that."

He positioned her so the water washed the soap off her breasts.

"Don't hate your curves…" He worked his hands down her body. "You're sexy as hell…*buxom*."

From anyone else, she was pretty sure the word would have sounded idiotic, but there was something in his tone that made her feel ultra-sexy. Like "buxom" wasn't just a nice way of saying "well fed."

He slipped his hands down to her hips and clasped them. "Perfect for wrapping my fingers around…"

The bodywash was almost gone now, and her heart was accelerating, the idea of what they could do now that there wasn't soap on their skin driving her wild. She reached behind her, found his thighs, and purred.

"I normally last so much longer"—he bit her neck—"but not with you."

She stiffened and opened her eyes. The idea of him with other women bugged her. He stopped moving and turned her around so he could see her expression.

"Sorry. That was me being an insensitive dick."

"I get it."

He clasped her against him, still swaying with the beat. "But I don't like it."

She pulled her fingernails down his chest and pushed him back. He went, not because she was stronger, but because he was watching to see what she had planned. He ended up sitting on the stone seat with a gleam of anticipation in his eyes.

"Are you jealous, Kate?"

His big cock was jutting up, the head ruby red, his skin shiny with water, making her pulse with need. Today, she enjoyed it, letting it rip through her and savoring the burn.

"Pretty sure." She reached out and boldly clasped him, wrapping her fingers around him at the base and pulling her hand up to the head. His flesh was silky smooth but iron hard.

And thick.

Crap. She never expected to see such a thick cock.

Much less ride it.

He reached around her and cupped her butt, lifting her up to straddle him.

"*Good,*" he rasped out, clasping her hips and guiding her over his cock. "I'd better not be alone in this."

She tried to take control by seating herself, but he held her in place and lifted off the seat, sending only the tip of his cock inside her. It set off a shudder that went up her spine and down her legs, curling her toes.

"How do you do that?" she asked, fighting his hold and trying to plunge down on him.

He chuckled ominously and lifted her up and turned around. A second later, she was sitting on the bench, breathless from the abrupt power shift. One moment she was in the saddle and the next she was on her back.

He pressed her thighs wide, exposing her and leaving her fighting a surge of vulnerability. The seat was wide enough for her to lay all the way back. The placement of several rolled-up towels suddenly struck her as very purposeful because her head ended up on them.

"You want to be fucked," he said slowly, just slow enough that she was hanging on his words.

Her mouth went dry, and she had to swallow before responding. "No, I want to fuck you. On top."

His eyes flickered with hunger, but his jaw tightened. "I like you just like this…all mine to play with."

She felt that way.

Excitement speared through her, but it collided with her pride. He was already overwhelming her so completely, she wasn't ready to let it go any deeper.

But all the brawn she'd been admiring allowed him to keep her there, at his mercy. It wouldn't have been so bad if it hadn't made her so breathless. Somehow, he'd uncovered a deep, dark secret she hadn't realized she had.

"I'm very demanding when it comes to my toys…" He pressed her knees wide, shifting his gaze to her pussy as it spread open. "I need to explore every function."

"Oh…yeah." Her voice was sultry and breathless.

He shot her one quick glance that made her shiver before focusing on her spread body again. She was riveted by the sight of him standing over her. He sank down to his knees as the song ended and another one began. The shower was still going full blast, steam rolling around the ceiling in a soft cloud.

But none of it mattered as he hovered over her spread sex, his breath teasing her clit before he opened his mouth and laid his tongue on her.

She moaned. A hard sound that was wrung from her.

"I love the sounds you make."

She forced her eyelids up and found him looking up at her. He teased her with a fingertip, dipping into her slit and rimming the opening to her pussy. "Love knowing I make you make them."

He thrust up inside her, and she whimpered, needing so much more. She tightened around him, trying to grip his finger.

He let out a groan. "You gotta do that to my dick."

"Sit your ass back down, and I will," she promised.

His lips curled. "You're not asking very nicely."

"You don't want me to be nice," she responded in a sugary-sweet tone.

His face tightened savagely and he gave in and sat next to her. She rolled over to get to his cock. Cupping his balls, she captured the entire head inside her mouth before he got a grip on her shoulders. She swirled her tongue around the thick crest on his head before pulling free. She kept her grip on his balls and squeezed as she made eye contact with him.

"You make a nice toy, Syon Braden," she cooed.

He cupped her butt and settled her over his cock. "Play with this part of me."

He pushed her down onto his length. She gasped, the penetration setting loose a slight twinge of discomfort.

He held her still, his cock buried to the hilt inside her. "Sore?"

She shrugged.

He studied her for a moment before his lips rose into a very satisfied grin. She slapped his shoulder.

"Don't be so pleased with yourself, savage."

He lifted her and let her slide down his cock as his lips parted. "Can't help it. You loved every second of getting that way."

She was seated completely on his length again and tightened her internal muscles around him. He sucked in a breath, his grin fading.

"So did you."

"Yeah, a whole lot," he agreed.

He shifted beneath her, lifting her and thrusting into her again before she clamped her thighs around him and held herself down long enough to tighten her muscles around his cock again.

He jerked, his breathing becoming harsh. "I'm still going to eat you out."

She wasn't sure if it was a promise or a threat, but it set off a tremor inside her.

"I might beat you to that one." She tightened again and again before he lifted her and hammered several hard thrusts into her. She was sinking into that vortex again, her insides melting into an inferno of need. But she wasn't finished. She looked him straight in the eye. "Be…the one…to hear you…groaning."

"We'll see."

"We sure will," she promised.

But thoughts were drifting away again. She fought to maintain control, tightening around him and wringing hard sounds of enjoyment out of him. All the while he held her in place and lifted up to penetrate her, hitting her G-spot with just enough force to push her closer and closer to climax. She needed it now, instead of just craving it.

"That is…fucking…intense," he groaned out.

She was going to need another shower, because the effort was making her sweat. She tightened and released; he lifted and thrust; she twisted her legs around him tighter and fought to stay seated on his cock. Her clit was throbbing madly, so close to release, but his cock was iron hard now, ready to burst. She struggled to hold back the orgasm, just long enough for her to grip him one final time.

His jaw was tight, his head tilted back, and his lips curled away from his teeth. His fingers were digging into her buns as she felt him giving in. He was thrusting into her, little pistoning motions of his cock that rubbed the hard length against her clit. His come started to burn against her insides as she was ripped away from everything and tossed into a wave of pleasure. It rolled her and sucked her down. She clung to him, the only solid thing in her world as the orgasm tore through her and left her gasping.

―⁓―

Ramsey was in the suite when they stepped out of the bathroom.

Kate shrieked, recoiling and falling back into Syon.

"What the fuck?"

He lifted her off her feet and went right through the bathroom doorway without a second's hesitation, setting her on her feet in the hallway.

"Ramsey is *here*," she groused at him, trying to wiggle free and get back into the bathroom.

"He's like a cat, always shows up when the food does. That's why I ordered so much," Syon explained like it was no big deal his band buddy was sitting there while she was naked. He wouldn't get out of the way, but kept moving down the hallway, pushing her closer to Ramsey with every step.

Accepting defeat, Kate pushed away from Syon and hightailed it around the corner and back into the bedroom.

"I'll purr if you pet me," Ramsey called after her.

She slammed the door in reply. Her face was flaming, but the food smelled so good. Her belly grumbled loudly, and she cursed before dressing and opening the door.

He'd already seen everything she had. But her cheeks remained on fire as she approached the table. Ramsey made a low sound under his breath. One that sounded like a purr. She shot him a deadly look.

"There is way too much blood in my caffeine system at the moment," she warned him. "I might just pack you off to the vet to be spayed."

He smirked at her. "Naw. You like cock too much for that."

Syon reached over and thumped him on the head. "Not yours."

Ramsey gave him a "get real" look. "She hasn't had a sample yet, so how do you know?"

"Well, second place is first loser," Syon informed him smugly.

"I'm in an alternate dimension," Kate said.

They both flashed her grins, unconcerned with her sanity dilemma. She decided to look at what was offered for breakfast.

At one in the afternoon.

Room service had outdone themselves. Or at least the waiter had made sure his tip was going to be big by bringing up a huge amount of food. The table was covered in dishes. Ramsey and Syon had flipped off the stainless steel covers on some of them and were sitting back, chowing down. There were carafes of juice and insulated pitchers of hot beverages.

Ramsey offered her a lazy grin and picked up one of the pitchers. "Coffee?"

Kate grabbed a mug and used a second pitcher to fill it. She took a long sip before shooting Ramsey a hard look. "Let's discuss some ground rules."

He sat the pitcher down and picked up his fork. "Think I might have pissed off your girly."

Syon pushed a chair out for her with his foot. "Eat, Kate. Ramsey is…how did you put it last night? Jerking your chain."

"Very funny." But she choked on a giggle. "It is funny. In a payback-is-a-bitch sort of way." She pulled a cover off a plate and investigated the contents.

Ramsey snorted and smirked at her when she cut him a glare. Syon had his mouth full of scrambled eggs, but his eyes were glittering with amusement. They were like a pair of eight-year-olds, friends to the end. It made them both adorable in a crazy way that tugged on her heartstrings. Syon had his guard down—completely down—and she realized it was a privilege to get to see him this way. She suddenly understood Ramsey's attitude during his fitting a lot better. They really were tight, and that was something she knew the value of. Friendships like that didn't come along every day.

So she wasn't going to be the party pooper.

Or the bitch who needed to bolster her own confidence by trying to change the man she was hooked up with.

"Is this the part where I deal with privacy becoming a casualty?" she asked as she twisted the top off a small jar of strawberry preserves and started spreading it on a slice of toast.

"At least I left the shade down."

She'd bitten into the toast before Ramsey commented. With her mouth full, all she could do was shoot him a questioning look. He hopped out of his chair with a smirk and pushed a button on the wall. There was a low, motorized sound as what looked like the wall between the bathroom and outer room rose up. What she'd thought was a wall was in fact a window, covered by a colored shade.

That rose all the way up to offer a full view into the bathroom and shower.

"Oh shit." She almost choked on the toast. "Who in the hell thinks to put a transparent wall into a bathroom?"

Who would want a view of the toilet?

"Guys with too much money who have had so much sex they need to get creative to get off." Ramsey was rummaging through the other offerings on the table. "Slave play. Fetish stuff. Toilet humiliation."

"I'm eating," she said, cutting him off.

"You're cute when you're pissed," Syon said.

"Taz says to clean the cuffs before you give 'em back."

"They didn't get dirty," Kate said as she pointed her knife at Ramsey. "Ground rules. You don't get to see me naked."

Ramsey pouted. Syon reached over and shoved him half out of his chair. "You heard her."

"Alright." Ramsey righted himself. "Touchy. I thought you two would be a little more mellow now that you've—"

"None of your beeswax," Kate interrupted him.

Ramsey bit into a piece of bacon in reply. Syon was watching her, a guarded look creeping back into his eyes. He shifted his attention between her and Ramsey, taking in the scene. She lifted her mug and extended it toward Ramsey.

"And I like my coffee with cream."

"Do you normally sweat during fittings?" Syon drawled softly. "Seems a bit…unprofessional. Like you're nervous."

Kate pulled a pin from the cushion she had strapped to her wrist and waved it over the fabric she had draped along his groin. "Sure you want to rattle me?"

He chuckled ominously. "Yes." The tip of his tongue appeared on his lower lip, sending her heart into a gallop. "You're fun when you're pushed past your limits. And I'm betting you like my cock…uninjured."

She sent him a withering look. "I need this draping."

He made a low, throaty sound of male satisfaction. "I love feeding your needs. But remember, I need there to be room for a major hard-on."

She drew in a fresh breath and concentrated. It was getting close, but she needed it perfect. Reaching out, she worked the fabric with her fingers along his hip line. Then from his inner thigh up…up…and over the bulge of his erection.

She looked up at him but settled her hand over his cock. "It was harder when you came off stage in Los Angeles."

Syon had his arms crossed over his chest. "Guess you'd better find a way to make it work. I hired the best and expect it."

"You ambushed me," she corrected. "It would serve you right if these pants crawled up your ass."

He snorted.

"Umm-hmm." She stepped back and considered the draping. "Well, I guess if I have to make it work…"

She popped the first latch closure on her corset top. The weight of her breasts separated the front, drawing his attention instantly.

"I love how you troubleshoot," Syon drawled.

She opened the second one, giving him a view of the sides of her breasts.

"It's really having an effect," Syon continued. "A very desirable one. But I should warn you…my resolve to keep you is…hardening."

She heard the truth of it in his voice. A deepening in the timbre. It stroked her senses, making her nipples tighten into hard little points.

She opened the last one, and her corset split open. This one had straps, so the garment stayed on her body, only open to give him a full view of her chest. She didn't have a chemise on, so her breasts were in full view.

"Stay right there, or you'll ruin my work," she ordered him.

He snorted but settled back into his stance. She stroked the sides of her breasts, slowly trailing her finger down one until she got to her nipple. His eyes narrowed.

"Let me see if we've found the solution."

She reached out and stroked the bulge of his cock. It was iron hard now, and she had to adjust the fabric.

"That's it."

She straightened up again to take one last look. "Got it."

"You're going to get it as soon as you take this fabric off me," he warned her wickedly.

She stood still, fingering one of her puckered nipples, enjoying the moment of having control in her hands.

The door to the suite pushed in.

"In here, we have a full leather studio for outfitting the performers."

Cid walked in, a guy with a huge camera right behind him. Kate gasped, whirling around, but not before the cameraman hooted.

"Right on!" he commented as Cid led him forward. "Perfect shot of those tits!"

Kate succeeded in getting her top closed and turned around to see Cid flashing a smug smile at Syon.

"This is the team from *Roadkill*. Local fan-based blogosphere," the road manager said as he introduced them to Syon. Kate was as insignificant as a used coffee cup.

An ultrathin girl was with the cameraman, impeccably dressed in a hot dress with a plunging neckline and short enough that it showed off her tiny butt. She smiled at Syon, batting her eyes and boldly licking her lower lip before she pushed a microphone up to his mouth and started asking questions.

Syon didn't miss a beat. His voice was liquid sex. The girl's eyes took on a sultry mode as she flashed him an inviting look. Kate unpinned her draping, trying not to look at the camera.

When they were finished, Cid guided them off to find the rest of the band.

"I got to get ready for the show." Syon sounded disappointed. "Didn't expect the interview." His eyes narrowed. "We'll have to wait."

"Does Cid know how to knock?"

Syon shrugged. "I'll talk to him about it. Don't worry. Those shots won't get out. I've got to get over to the arena for sound checks and warm-ups."

Kate looked up from her worktable. She felt the real world jerking them apart. Like they'd been hiding, and now their cover was being ripped away. It was a little strange to discover something as normal as work obligations getting between them. But that added only another layer to their interaction, that touch of normalcy that made it seem much more real.

She was definitely scaring herself now.

She pointed at the draping she had laid out on the table. "Got work to get to myself."

His expression was guarded. He gave her a single nod and turned around.

It was stupid to get emotional. He was a rock star.

So…she should get busy making him look like one.

At least working with leather restored her balance. It had always been her comfort zone, since she'd first discovered what she could do with a sewing machine. She stroked and worked with the pattern. Time melted away while she was focused on getting it perfect. It wasn't going to be some universal size. It was going to fit Syon perfectly, with just the right amount of give.

In the right places, of course.

She spent a lot of time going through her stock of hides, searching for the right color and then for one that had a great finish. She settled for a magenta-colored one, deciding it would go stunningly well with Syon's eyes. Adjusting it on the tabletop, she circled it several times, making sure the pattern was in the best spot before going in with her shears.

She loved the scent, the sensation of cutting through it. But most of all, she loved being mentally mesmerized by the project. Time wasn't a factor. Perfection was.

Syon provided an amazing image for her to try and fit, the over-the-top persona of the man merging with her insatiable love of working with hides.

She turned up the music and let herself be absorbed by her project. Syon thought she was the best. She intended to show him exactly how right he'd been.

———

"I thought you'd be flying high after getting into Kate's pants." Ramsey grunted as they came off stage.

"My game wasn't off," Syon defended himself. They were both covered in sweat, their hair tangled after the wild performance they'd just given.

They went down the backstage steps as the crowd roared behind them. The noise bounced off the ceiling designed for sound retention and rained down on them. The overhead lights still flashed, making sure the fans left on a high.

"You were pushing hard." Ramsey reached the performers' backstage room and ripped a towel off a rack to mop his face.

Syon jerked his hand toward the screaming behind them. "No one sounds upset."

"I know the difference." Ramsey grabbed a bottle of water and drank down a third of it. "Just sounded like you and Kate worked it out."

"We did." Syon reached for some makeup-remover wipes. Tonight the crap was driving him batty. He needed it off. Fast.

That wasn't the real problem, but he took out his aggression on his face, working at it until every last trace of eyeliner was gone.

"I need some air," he said when he was finished.

Ramsey was still nursing the water bottle. He studied Syon for a moment, his eyes narrowing when he came to a conclusion. "She wasn't here."

Ramsey hit the nail on the head.

"So what?" Syon shrugged.

Ramsey knew him too well. Syon lifted his hand to wave it off and started out the door. Cid was coming through it, blocking his path.

"Brilliant, mates! Fucking brilliant."

Cid's beaming expression faded a tad as he looked at Syon. "Why the clean mug so early in the night? I've got plans for you." He dug his tablet out of his suit pocket and stroked the screen. "Two clubs to visit, and I hear there's this topless joint near the waterfront that has a reputation for wild parties." Cid looked up with a smirk. "That should be great for some publicity."

"I'm out tonight," Syon said.

Cid caught his arm. "Whoa there, partner. You can't buy this kind of publicity. The fans want to see you party. It's all about image. We need those birdies tweeting."

"I'm not in the mood."

"Get in the mood," Cid said. "We're not sold out in Seattle yet. A few pictures in the tabloids will take care of that. You can sleep on the road tomorrow. That's what drivers are for."

Ramsey hooked him around the neck. "Some guys actually have to work for a living. We have to party. It's rough, but we signed up for it."

"Yeah."

And he felt just as trapped as someone reporting

to a cubicle. He didn't crave the insanity of a club. What he wanted was Kate and the opportunity to take her for a ride on the back of his bike. She was right; they didn't know each other, and he wanted to change that.

Actually felt like he needed to change it. Fast. Before she slipped away.

She hadn't shown up at the show.

That stung.

It shouldn't have.

He should have been thinking about her sleeping because he'd worn her out, and how much energy she'd have when he crawled back into her bed.

But all he had on his mind was the fact that her face hadn't been in the crowd, and he'd wanted it to be.

Wanted it really fucking bad.

"Text me the address. I'll meet you there."

"Whoa…" Cid hooked his arm and turned him around. "You're not thinking about going back to the hotel for the costume chick?"

Syon stepped back. "So what if I am?"

"I'll tell you what." Cid slid the tablet into his pocket. "The fans want to see hot guys living it up. Not you necking with your seamstress. You pay me to manage, so let me do my job. These clubs are pushing your music right now. They expect a visit for that play time."

"Yeah."

It was the professional thing to do. Ramsey and Taz were watching him, waiting to see what he'd do. He shrugged and grabbed his leather jacket.

"Let's party."

—◦◦◦—

"You're drunk." Taz plopped down in the booth beside him.

"Nope."

Taz gave him a long look. "You are, and a promise to a bandmate is a promise."

Syon turned to point at Taz. The girl trying to give him a lap dance giggled as she was dumped across Taz.

"Oh my God!" she squealed. "I so can't believe it! You guys are so hot!"

Her skirt was about the length of a packing strap, and her top looked more like a slingshot band. She was a bundle of bare flesh and hair and excitement.

Drake appeared and scooped her up. She kicked her feet up with another giggle as he turned around and set her down.

Syon started to get up, but Taz caught his arm and twisted it, so he sat back down with a twinge in his elbow. The little pain cut through the haze of alcohol.

"Maybe I'm a little drunk," Syon admitted.

Taz nodded, smiling at the horde of girls gyrating on the floor in front of them. Tops were going up, nipples flashing at them as the dancers worked themselves into a frenzy that had the men in the club howling with approval. The bartenders were sweating as they tried to keep up with demand while Toxsin's music blared.

"Don't worry," Taz said softly, handing over a beer bottle. "Your wingman is here."

The bottle was filled with water, but no one in the place would know. Taz was sipping off a similar one and grinning at the dance floor. He nodded his head in time to the beat, doing a good job of making everyone think he was buzzed on suds. In the dim light, no one was able to see how focused his eyes were.

He was stone sober. Taz rarely got drunk, and when he did, they had a blood oath between them to be there and keep each other from doing something stupid.

Syon tipped the bottle back, trying to hydrate. He was only a little buzzed. Just enough to make him stupid. Like letting someone onto his lap in a public place. At least Cid would be pleased with that.

"Did I let her kiss me?"

Kate wouldn't like that.

"Almost," Taz confirmed. "Another few seconds, and she would have had you in a lip-lock."

His brain hurt, but he tried to focus. "Uh…" The thought escaped him, dropping off into the haze clouding his head.

"You're welcome." Taz motioned to some of the security guys to keep the horde of partying fans back. "Got a car coming."

"I love you." He couldn't ride.

Ramsey was on the dance floor, the girls pushing in around him. Cid's security detail was keeping watch, but Ramsey was living it up.

When the car arrived, they followed the security guys out past the pole dancers. The guys in the club instantly filled the void, coming out of the shadows to hook up with the disappointed girls on the dance floor. The owner of the club shook Cid's hand before he piled into a second car with his personal assistants.

Yeah, the business side. Cid was working out great.

Ramsey hooted and ripped off his shirt. He tossed it

out the window as they pulled away from the curb, to the delight of the screaming fans.

—⁓—

The door burst in, and Kate sat up with a start. Sound asleep, she ended on her feet and wobbled as she tried to make sense of her surroundings.

"Right here, Ramsey!"

A topless girl was laughing as she danced through the suite. "It smells like leather in here. So hot. I'm going to suck you off right here."

Ramsey was grinning at her, his erect cock already jutting out through the open fly of his pants.

"I'm going to rip those pants off you," the girl declared.

"No ripping," Kate instructed, her wits clearing enough to talk. She realized she was watching Ramsey slip on a condom and turned her head.

"Stay out of my business, bitch. He's mine."

There was a wet sound and a groan from Ramsey. Kate stumbled through the door and made it down the hallway to her personal suite. The clock read four thirty in the morning. She didn't bother turning on the lights, but yanked off her clothes before crawling into the bed.

It was lonely without Syon.

Don't be a wimp…

Exhaustion took her back down into sleep, but it wasn't a complete escape. She still felt Syon, longed for him, and knew he wasn't there with her.

And that she had no logical reason to expect him to be.

—⁓—

Someone pounded on her door. Kate rubbed her eyes as she heard a key card being used.

"Rise and shine. Check-out time in forty-five."

It was one of Cid's guys, one of the black-polo-shirt-wearing dudes that seemed to always be dodging the road manager's heels. There were girls too. Marketing personnel, publicists, or so they claimed. From what she could tell, they were Cid's personal entourage. Catering to his whims, always on his coattails.

Among other things, she was sure.

Ramsey's escapades from the early-morning hours rolled through her memory.

Yeah, catering was the word alright.

You knew what you were getting into.

True.

And yet, she was still struggling to get into the flow.

She heard more pounding on doors up and down the hallway.

Kate rolled over and stretched. She was still tired, but the clock read eleven fifteen. Guess it was a good thing someone was in charge of making sure they were all on schedule. She showered and dumped her clothes back into her suitcase.

She needed to get into the rhythm of life on the road. Staying up until two wasn't going to work.

But it had been worth it.

She made it down the hallway to where her studio had been set up. She hesitated only a moment before knocking on the door. She gave Ramsey exactly ten seconds before she used her key and entered the suite.

The rocker was nowhere to be seen.

Neither were the pants she'd spent the night making.

Horror flashed through her, raising her hackles. She forced herself to take a breath and take a second look.

Nope. No pants hanging on the rolling rack where she'd put them.

Instead, there was a scattering of women's clothing, empty beer bottles, and torn-up pieces of leather. The pants Ramsey had been wearing were on the floor, torn beyond repair.

"I'm going to kill him."

Ramsey's voice sounded off in the hallway. Kate turned and caught sight of the rocker by the elevators. He was French-kissing a blond woman who was in the elevator. The doors started to close, and he pulled his head back. Kate gained just a glimpse of the girl as she waved good-bye, but it was long enough to see that she was wearing the pants she'd made for Syon.

"Stop!"

Ramsey flipped around, but the doors shut.

"What the hell are you doing?"

Kate dove toward the control panel, slapping the button, but the car was gone.

"You got a hard-on for my date?" Ramsey asked.

"No, I want the pants I spent last night making back," Kate snarled at him. "What the hell do you think you're doing letting her take my work?"

Ramsey flattened a hand over her mouth. "My head is splitting."

Her eyes bulged, and she started to lift her knee. Ramsey jumped back, allowing her to see how many people had come out to watch.

Well, she wasn't backing down. "You and your date tore through all of my work."

"Easy now…"

Cid hooked her and crowded her through the doorway of some suite.

"See…here's the thing," the road manager said.

Kate shoved away from the guy, but he pushed her farther into the room.

The road manager pointed at her. "Image is key." He stressed each word like she was some high school student sitting in the principal's office.

"No kidding. That's what I'm pissed off about. I spent all night making those pants," she snapped.

"That's why you weren't at the show?" Syon's voice was like a live current, stroking her senses.

Awakening her.

She looked past Cid, losing interest in the road manager. Syon had walked into the room, Ramsey and Taz on his heels. His hair was tousled, and his shirt hung open.

And he made her mouth water.

"You're out of pants," she answered. "Of course I was working. I needed that draping to start…"

A horrible thought occurred to her.

"Ramsey better not have screwed with my patterns."

Cid waved her off. "Make some more. The publicity will be worth it."

"And what kind of publicity will you get when your performers go on stage in their jock straps?" she demanded.

Cid's expression tightened. "That's your problem, and I'll pack your ass out of here if you let it happen."

He started to poke her in the chest with his finger. He went stumbling as Syon pushed him out of the way. "Keep your hands off her, Cid."

"Then tell her to mind her mouth."

"What the hell?" Kate demanded. "You've got security set up around the room where the instruments are, but not around my studio?"

Cid looked at her like she'd lost her mind. "Your work doesn't rate on that scale."

"I don't what?" She propped her hands on her hips. "You can find yourselves another leather artist if that's where I rate."

"Like hell," Syon cut her off. He hooked her around her waist and pulled her away from Cid.

"Get the fuck out. Everyone."

"I am not staying in here with you."

She wasn't sure why she was pissed, just that it hurt to see him. Uncertainty was eating her alive.

Ramsey made sure everyone else went out the door and closed it without a backward glance. It left her alone with Syon. Which hurt.

And that pissed her off.

She tossed her hair back and faced off with him. But that allowed her to lock gazes with him, and the moment she did, it felt like a spear went through her. He was so close. So within reach. She suddenly questioned why she was mad or if it was worth it.

That hurt her pride. She was folding, crumpling under the weight of her attraction for him.

"I worked all night on those pants."

For him.

Syon had crossed his arms over his chest and stood watching her from behind a guarded expression.

"Cid's attitude is…counterproductive," she added.

She was struggling to dredge up professional

language. Really struggling because all she wanted to
do was cuss.

"He's an asshole. It's his job," Syon said offhand-
edly, obviously not interested in the topic. His gaze cut
into hers, something else on his mind.

She blinked at him, surprised by how easily he'd
agreed with her. "Well doesn't his job include not letting
your wardrobe walk away on Ramsey's party partners?
I put my heart into my work."

His expression cracked at last, his lips twitching into
a genuine grin.

It confused her and frustrated her. She tossed her
hands into the air. "Why are you grinning?"

He moved toward her, opening his arms. She recognized the intent in his eyes and instantly recoiled.

Ha! You mean you're retreating.

Yeah, whatever worked. If he touched her, she'd
lose track of the conversation. Her pride wasn't willing
to bend.

"We're not done talking, Syon."

He captured her, gathering her against his chest so her
face was buried in the open front of his shirt. One breath,
and she was struggling against a rush of pheromones.

"I heard what I needed," he muttered against her hair.

She flattened her hands against his chest and failed
to push, because she was too delighted to be in contact
with his flesh again.

Had it been less than twenty-four hours?

It sure felt longer.

"I missed you."

She froze.

"At the show. Thought you didn't think it was

important." He threaded his fingers through her hair and pulled her head back so their gazes met. "It was sold out, and I missed you."

"I wanted to…get the pants finished. The pair you have pinch."

He scooped her off her feet and carried her backward. She had no idea where he was taking her and didn't really care.

She was in his arms.

He sat her on a table, kicking a chair out of the way. He cupped her cheeks, gently rubbing them. "I wanted to sing to you."

She gasped, something tearing inside her. His voice was thick with emotion, and her eyes grew glassy.

"I got caught up in my work."

He chuckled. "Yeah, you're passionate."

"That's the pot calling the kettle black."

He made a low sound of agreement and slid his hands down to her cleavage. "A trait you love about me."

"Maybe." The word "love" was a little heavy. But everything about Syon was over the top. He was a study in extremes.

He lifted one eyebrow. "The lady requires proof."

"I thought we were checking out." It was a half-hearted attempt to maintain her sanity.

He popped the first latch on her corset top as one side of his mouth curved up roguishly. "The crew is still tearing down the stage. We can handle a late check-out charge."

"But…" She suddenly noticed how many footsteps were moving around in the hallway outside the closed door. Other doors opening and closing. Conversations

as the rest of the band and entourage made their way out
of the hotel. "Everyone will know what we're doing."

"I hope so." There was a blaze of determination in
his eyes.

"Syon," she admonished him, her cheeks feeling like
they had caught fire. "I am not that kind of girl."

She was working her way away from him, wiggling
across the tabletop. He cupped her hips and slid her
back, spreading her legs around his.

"I know."

He caught the sides of her dress and pulled it up.
"That's part of it, though. I love knowing I push your
buttons so hard you can't resist me." He stroked the
outside of her thighs, sending ripples of sensation up
her spine. "I love knowing it isn't in your nature to
give it up so easily. I want everyone to know I drive
you that insane."

"You sound so arrogant. So full of yourself."

Territorial.

He caught her underwear and twisted it until it
snapped. His eyes glittered with intent.

"Tell me you don't like hearing me say that." His tone
was challenging.

He leaned down and drew in a deep breath. "Tell me
you don't like hearing me say that my cock is so hard I
don't fucking care who is waiting on us."

She shivered, her insides clenching with need.

"I…I…*oh shit.*"

She leaned back as he tugged the ruined scrap of her
underwear off her and tossed it aside.

"Brace your hands behind you."

"Why?"

His lips twitched menacingly. "Because I want to see you waiting for me."

Her belly did a flip as excitement tore through her. She braced her hands behind her, intensely aware of how easily he'd reduced her to a quivering mass of need. He hovered over her, his breath hitting her lips and making her tremble.

"And I love smelling how wet I make you."

Her lips parted as she gasped. A soft, desperate, betraying sound. "I hate how easily you undermine me."

Her heart was on display now. Wide open for the wounding.

"I hate how bad it hurt not to see you there last night."

"I—"

He cut her off with a kiss that stole her breath. It was softly seeking at first. Slipping and sliding across her mouth as he licked and teased her lips with his. He cupped her cheeks, holding her head softly as the kiss continued.

Tender.

But so hot, it felt like her core was melting. She sat up and pushed the open shirt over his shoulders, needing more contact with his bare flesh.

He shrugged out of it and opened his fly, earning a soft sound of appreciation from her as he pulled his length into view.

"Back," he ordered.

She hesitated.

One of his eyebrows rose. "Lean back and wait for me to touch you, baby."

"I've never been one for dominance games."

"I'm not playing games," he said. "I'm going to tease you."

He pumped his hand along his cock. He was so hard the veins stood out along its length. Anticipation pulsed through her. She leaned back, curious about what he had planned.

"Now open your legs." His tone was sin incarnate, beckoning her closer to whatever he wanted to do with her. "Show me your pussy, Kate. I want to see if it's glistening."

It took more effort than she'd anticipated to do as he commanded.

Shit. He is commanding me.

Her pride reared its head but her logic shot down the protest. She liked his demand. It made her feel more desired, more attractive than she had ever felt before.

"Beautiful," he offered as she opened her legs.

He stepped forward between her legs. He grasped each of her heels and set her feet on the table. The position bent her knees up, and he cupped them, pulling them even farther apart.

But what she was focused on was how close his cock was to her slit. It was an unbearable bit of information, tormenting her with just how much she wanted him inside her.

"Fuck me." She was done waiting.

"With this?" He gripped his cock again. "Or these?"

He released his cock and stroked her open sex with two fingers. She yelped when he glided across her clit. He chuckled.

"With your cock." She was breathing hard, making speech a challenge. "Deep…and hard."

"An interesting proposal."

He teased her clit with the head of his cock, slipping

it through the fluid coating her folds. She arched back, surrendering to the storm of need. It was even more intense when she just let go. Let every thought slip out of her mind in favor of enjoying the sensation the connection of their flesh produced.

It was off the scale, mind-blowing. Pride, sense of self didn't come into it. She folded into the sensation, becoming part of it.

He cupped her hips, bringing her closer as he slid into her. She wrapped her legs around him, pulling him toward her as he sank farther.

"Hard and fast?" he questioned, burying himself so deep she felt his balls against her butt cheeks.

She opened her eyes and shot him a challenging look. "Try to impress me, if you can."

A savage light brightened his eyes. His cock twitched inside her, making her eyes close as she hummed with pleasure.

"Uggh…" he growled, pumping two hard, fast thrusts into her.

She moaned, matching him, straining toward each thrust, groaning when he penetrated all the way.

"Too hard?"

He'd caught her nape, lifting her head back up so he could see her expression. His was savage. She was mesmerized by it, by the sheer lack of boundaries. He was sweating, his jaw tight as he struggled to hold back his desire.

"Kate?"

"Harder," she demanded, tightening her legs and lifting herself off the table to take his next thrust.

His fingers tightened on her neck. "I don't want to…"

"Let go?" she finished for him. "Completely?" She reached out and drew her fingernails down his chest. "I want you to. I don't want to be alone either."

Her voice was sultry and demanding. "Harder," she insisted, straining toward him. Her thighs ached from the way she was lifting her body off the table, but the burn mixed well with the hard motion of his hips.

He jerked and grabbed her hips, holding her in place as he hammered off another round of thrusts.

"Is that all you've got?" She had no idea why she was saying what she was, only that it fed the tension coiling inside her gut. All of the frustration and uncertainty was combining to make her bitchy, and the bitch inside her craved satisfaction. "More!"

His lips split and curled back. It was savage and hard, just like the rest of him.

She purred with approval.

The table was rocking, groaning, but she didn't give a shit if it collapsed. Syon ground into her, working his body. They were both gasping, straining toward each other, demanding satisfaction.

When it came, it burst inside her like a grenade, blowing everything to bits in an instant of white-hot insanity. She never knew what hit her, could only ride the shock wave as it rolled her into oblivion.

Syon cussed as he came. "Shit! Goddamnit...*fuck. Fuck, fuck.*"

He ended up catching his weight on his hands, his head resting on her chest. They were both panting, the silence in the room deafening as they let their heart rates slow down.

"Fuck," he said again, this time with a touch of guilt.

He lifted his head and slid his hand along her cheek. "Did I hurt you?"

She shook her head, suddenly shy. Had she really just done that? Had dirty, hard sex? She tried to look away, but he kept her head in place, his gaze boring into hers.

"I'm not sure I'm comfortable with the way you get under my skin either, Kate."

It was the same thing she'd been thinking. He pulled free with another groan and arched to stretch his back.

"I need a shower after that," Kate said.

He grinned at her and wiped his hand through the sweat on his forehead, pushing it up into his hair. "You're a demanding one."

She hopped off the table. "Well, if you can't keep up…"

He swatted her on her butt. Her dress had fallen back down, but she jumped and ran toward the bathroom.

The best part was Syon was hot on her tail.

⚬⚬⚬

Ramsey caught her arm when she made it back into the hallway. All traces of his hangover were gone. She stared at him for a moment, impressed.

"I was drunk," he offered, "and being stupid last night."

"Could only wingman one of you," Taz said as he passed by. "Couldn't risk Syon's cords. You can play with a cold."

"Wingman?" Kate asked.

Taz stopped and offered her a shrug. "Yeah. One of us always stays sober. In case we need to keep one of us from doing something stupid."

"Taz was covering my butt last night," Syon explained. "Rams slipped the leash."

"Like I said, I was being stupid," Ramsey said. "I wasn't that drunk."

Drake spoke up. "I didn't think you were, or I would have stuck on your tail."

"Won't happen again," Ramsey finished. "The messing with your studio part, anyway." He sent her a wink and a satisfied smirk that had his band buddies rolling their eyes.

"Thanks."

Kate caught herself looking at the members of Toxsin in a completely new light. They were serious musicians and devoted to one another. But they'd made it a priority to talk to her together.

That rocked.

Cid whistled from the end of the hallway. "Let's load and roll!"

She bristled at the sound of the road manager's voice. Syon hooked an arm around her back and massaged the tight muscles of her nape. He leaned in and kissed her temple. "Someone has to be the detail stickler, 'cause I don't want the job. It might take up all my free time."

She cut him a side glance. "Well, I suppose I could see benefits to you having free time."

———

Her phone rang somewhere between Oregon and Washington. Kate sat up and missed the ceiling of the bunk by about an inch. The bus was rolling smoothly along, the sun setting outside the window.

"Hello?"

"Sweetie!" Percy drawled on the other end of the line.

Kate crawled out of the bunk, grinning. "Hey, sorry

I haven't called." She had to brace herself against the vibration of the bus.

Percy brushed her apology aside. "Don't worry about it. I know I would have kept my mind on my clients, if I were there. And my eyes and hands if they'd let me."

She blushed beet red. "I bet you would."

Percy laughed. "I'm terribly jealous. That Korean drummer looks positively decadent. Steve drooled over the pictures of you two."

"Huh?"

Percy scoffed. "You're all over the tabloids, my dear, and all over him, I might add. Being carried off in style." His voice became a purr. "Caveman style."

"What?" Horror cut through the fog sleep deprivation had left her in. "What pictures?"

Percy laughed at her.

"Percy."

"Just google Toxsin, sweetie."

She sat down at the desk and turned on the computer.

"I hear you tapping away, so I'll go. You've got a package waiting for you in Seattle. Steve helped me pick out some luscious skins for those man animals."

"Yeah…thanks."

She ended the call as the mobile hotspot engaged on the computer. She clicked on one of the links, and a picture of her slung over Taz's shoulder filled the screen.

"Oh, shit."

Cussing didn't change the full-color image of her, butt up, on the guy's shoulder. But there wasn't any mention of the fight. She trolled through the other links, but came up dry when it came to the fight Syon had had with Conan.

Shit.

And double shit.

She was in over her head. Cid had done his job alright. Bought off the right people and left the juicy bits out to fan the flames of Toxsin's reputation. She felt nauseated but not because of the motion of the bus. It was the sheer size of the road manager's reach. His cronies suddenly seemed a lot more threatening than they'd been before. Not a single one of them was a fool; that was for sure.

She'd better watch her back, because her reputation wouldn't survive if they turned on her.

———

"This is frustrating," Kate groused.

Syon kept her head where he wanted it with one large hand threaded into her hair.

"Yeah. Glad we fucked first."

Perched on his bike, with the Space Needle behind them and the light from a half-moon, he was kissing her senseless. Long, deep, hungry kisses that were melting her insides.

"Smooching is fun…until I realize how much I want to get inside you."

He angled his head and kissed her throat. A wet, full-contact kiss that ended with a soft bite. She shivered, her toes curling as her clit throbbed. Cars buzzed past them on the road, and a soft giggle came from another couple who were a dozen yards away in the roadside pull out.

"But you wore the skirt," Syon cooed appreciatively as he slid his hand along her thigh.

"Kinda stupid on a bike."

He raised his head. "I'll keep you off the pavement."

The picture of her over Taz's shoulder came to mind and she froze. Syon's hand stilled against her.

"What's on your mind?" he asked.

She shook her head, not wanting to kill the moment. She tried to kiss him, but he held her back.

"Spill it, Kate. Something's bugging you."

She shrugged and rolled her neck, but he didn't release her. "Cid managed to keep all the pictures of your fight with Conan out of the media; couldn't he have stopped that shot of me on Taz too?"

The road manager could have. She knew it. The real issue was why he hadn't and what Syon thought about it.

"Cid is an asshole," Syon said, pulling back a few inches.

It felt like ten feet.

"But a useful one. He knows how to pack the seats."

"*You* know how to pack the seats," she said. "I get the whole argument, but honestly, it's starting to piss me off a little bit to hear your music sold short. Those fans don't scream because of some pictures in the tabloids. It's something your music touches inside them. Sets loose, really."

His expression became very sensual. "I like setting loose your inner desires."

She pointed a finger at him. "That's a two-way street."

His expression tightened, becoming guarded again.

"Not even." She reached out and stabbed him in the chest with her finger. "Don't think for one second I am going to surf this insanity current alone. Your ass is coming along."

Syon's lips twitched. But his expression stayed hard. "Being around me means you're going to end up in the tabloids."

"I'm not griping about that."

"Yes, you are." He started to pull his gloves on. "You're used to having control. You won't have it completely with me."

"No shit."

She hadn't meant to let that slip out. Something flashed in his eyes that set off a tingle of warning in her.

"I don't like part of it either," he said, "but not enough to live in a cage. I pay Cid and a couple of good lawyers a lot to deal with the worst of it."

"Cid must be good, or you would have been in jail over that fight. Even with Conan vouching for you. The cops could have slapped you both with disturbing the peace violations."

"I'm not sorry. He was asking for it." Syon offered her a looked that said "bring it."

She ended up laughing at him. "That's part of Conan's charm."

"Mine too."

He was dead serious. She eyed him for a long moment. "Maybe."

Something flickered in his eyes. It set her on edge, because she got the feeling he was planning something. He leaned in, flattening his hands on the seat of the bike on either side of her hips. Her heart reacted instantly, beating faster.

"I want to take you somewhere I can fuck you."

Her lips went dry.

His eyes narrowed. "Do you want me to do that, Kate?"

She rolled her lips in, a surge of lust igniting her insides. "How do you do that?"

One of his eyebrows rose. "Turn you on?"

She nodded, fixated on him, on his mouth, and the fact that she desperately wanted to kiss him again.

"It's only fair, since you make me crazy." He pressed forward, connecting with her mouth. He teased her lower lip with two slow licks before pulling away.

"You've only known me a week."

He pressed another kiss against her mouth, this one harder, more demanding.

"And you took your clothes off first."

She stiffened, but he kissed her again and kept kissing her until she stopped trying to wiggle away.

"It keeps me sane"—he was kissing his way across her cheek and onto her throat—"knowing I'm not alone. I'd be on my knees if you refused me."

She scoffed at him. "You wouldn't have to go far for solace."

He lifted his head and locked gazes with her. "Don't sell me short. I'm more than the tabloid persona. I want to be liked for more than Toxsin."

"I know. Sorry, that was hitting below the belt."

His eyes were lit with need. "I like that game too, but we need the right venue for it."

He offered her a hand and pulled her off the bike when she took it. He swung his leg over the Harley and waited for her to mount behind him. He was more complex than she'd ever expected, more real. Guilt chewed on her because she'd judged him before getting to know him.

But she was glad to have been proven wrong.

When they were riding, he was in control completely. Maybe it was one of those things she shouldn't dwell on too much, but at the same time, she got the feeling that he enjoyed being in command of her. They wove through the streets, making their way to the hotel near the center of town.

The horde of fans was there, wearing Toxsin T-shirts and plenty of leather. A few hopefuls were playing guitar on the sidewalk, trying their best to be noticed. Not to be outdone, the paparazzi were there too, their cameras ready.

Syon drove up the main driveway, ignoring the entrance to the parking garage. The crowd roared with approval. He lifted his helmet off. A group of Cid's polo-shirt crew started pushing the fans back from the walkway to the entrance doors. Fans screamed louder as they good a good look at Syon.

Cell phones were lifted up, a hundred little flashes going off like fireflies. Syon offered Kate a hand as one of the crew members took their helmets. She put her hand in his, conscious of the people watching. He pulled her along toward the doors but stopped halfway from the curb to the revolving entrance.

Syon pulled her against him and kissed her.

It was a hard kiss of ownership. A declaration of intent. He pressed her lips apart, capturing her squeal as he turned her in a small backward circle to hide the fact that she was recoiling.

The crowd went crazy.

"Great ass!"

"Sexy redhead!"

"Give her some tongue!"

Syon didn't disappoint his fans. He kissed her thoroughly. She wanted to resist, wanted to hold on to some small part of her dignity, but all that went through her mind was the fact that she hadn't found another picture of him kissing anyone.

It was an admission. A very public one, but a very personal one too.

"Lucky!"

"Bitch!"

Syon finally lifted his head from hers, sending her a very satisfied smirk before he turned her around and pushed through the huge rotating door that led to the hotel lobby. One of Cid's guys was there with a key card, but when Kate extended her hand for one, Syon shook his head.

"You're bunking with me," Syon said as he turned and headed toward the elevators.

Two girls standing there moaned with disappointment. One spoke up anyway. "Can we join the party?"

"Sorry." Syon pulled Kate into an elevator. "It's private."

The girl pulled her top down, giving him a view of her tits before the door slid shut.

"It's very private," Syon informed her.

The penthouse suite was set up for him. Syon pulled her through the outer sitting room to the master bedroom, which was massive. His guitar was sitting in the corner, the spot had a bird's-eye view of the city. It was a full three-room suite, candles lit to welcome them. Her suitcase was in the corner, her clothing hung up in the closet.

"Why did you kiss me like that?"

Syon was stripping off his gloves, pulling each fingertip free before removing the protective gear.

"To prove a point."

She recognized this side of his persona. But she'd only seen it before when he was conducting business.

Cold, hard, completely dominating business.

Her belly did a little flip, and she shifted, feeling very much on edge.

Syon tossed the second glove aside.

"That you're mine. I don't want there to be any question."

Satisfaction glittered in his eyes, but it was the hunger drawing his lips tight that made her nipples bead.

"Says who?"

It just slipped out, but she wasn't sorry. She propped one hand on her hip and faced off with him. "I'm not yours because you stage some stunt for the paparazzi."

His lips curved. "You're mine because I make you wet."

She shifted, far too aware of how correct he was. "B.O.B. could help me with that."

His grin broadened. "I like your ginger mode."

She rolled her eyes, but it was a mistake to look away from him. Syon scooped her up and carried her to the bed. It rocked as he followed her down, kissing her breathless once again. He thrust his tongue deep into her mouth, sparking a firestorm of need in her pussy. She'd never been so bluntly aware of how much she wanted to have intercourse. With Syon, she was in heat. He held her down, smoothing his hands along her arms and pulling them up above her head.

She grasped the rails of the headboard, the iron cold from the air-conditioning.

The candlelight was perfect, granting them some sort of permission to just dive into the waves of sensory overload.

"I want to unwrap you."

He worked on her top, popping the lace and pulling it free of the grommets. When he had it open, he spread it wide, exposing her chest. She started to move, intending to help him strip her.

"Stay," he barked. "Don't move. Wait on my whim."

He sat back on his haunches, his gaze sweeping her from head to toe. She shivered, so aware of him looking at her. Her confidence wavered, but at the same time swelled because he was in no hurry to stop.

"Do you like being on display for me?"

She nodded, not sure she could form words.

He cupped her knees and raised them up to her belly before straightening them, her feet pointing at the ceiling.

"Stay."

He slid his hands down the outside of her legs, over her calves, past her knees, to the bottom of her skirt. He kept going to where the zipper was hidden along her left hip. She was so aware of him and of the sound of the zipper separating. He pulled the tab all the way down before hooking his hands into the waistband and pulling it up her legs. He had to stand up to remove it, because her legs were still pointed at the ceiling.

She gasped, the sight of him yanking her skirt away twisting her insides.

"Open your legs for me."

She'd crossed her ankles, but unlocked them and watched his face as she spread herself for him, the yellow flicker from the candles turning him golden. He stood there, above her, making her breath catch, and opened his fly. His cock was swollen, jutting out the moment he allowed it freedom.

"Oh yeah…" She curled up and rose onto her knees,

reaching for his cock, cupping his balls before licking her way up the shaft.

Her leaned forward, bracing his hands on the wall above the headboard as she circled the head of his cock with her tongue.

"Shit…" he growled. "Suck it…"

"Not yet." She licked him again, making a slow pass along the ridge of flesh that crowned his cock. "You're going to wait for it."

She toyed with his balls, recalling just how he'd driven her crazy with foreplay.

It was time for payback.

"I'm going to make you lose it this time."

She cut him a look and purred when she got a glimpse of his face. It was savage, hard with primal enjoyment, and she'd put that look there.

She stroked his cock, closing her fingers around his girth and working her hand along its impressive length. She ached for another round with it, but she was going to make him groan first.

"Oh shit!" he hissed when she took him inside her mouth. "Yeah, baby…suck it down…"

She'd never wanted to give a blow job as much as she did at that moment. This wasn't a payback, tit-for-tat thing. She wanted to drive him wild.

He was jerking toward her, fucking her mouth as she played with his balls and worked her fingers along the portion of his cock that she couldn't take inside her mouth. She lifted up and came down, rubbing her tongue along the underside of his cockhead to tease the cluster of nerve endings there.

"Yeah…suck me…suck me hard…"

His voice was guttural, the moment hard and blunt. She tightened her lips and hand, working her mouth up and down as she listened to the sound of his breathing.

He gasped, groaning as he sucked his next breath through his clenched teeth. He was driving toward her, holding her head as his cock hardened to the breaking point.

"Argh…"

He started to spurt, giving up his come in a thick eruption that she sucked him through. It was more erotic than anything she'd ever done, the shift of power intoxicating in a whole new way. She sat back, pleased beyond measure by her victory.

And it was a victory. When Syon opened his eyes, there was the promise of payback.

He dropped to his knees and stripped her chemise top from her, but he didn't remove it completely. He twisted it around her wrist and knotted it.

"Does that hurt?"

She was still stunned to discover herself bound. He lifted her chin so he could see her expression.

"No. It doesn't hurt."

Pleasure lit his face, and a moment later he pushed her onto her back, using his chest to flatten her on the bed. He pulled her arms above her head, and she felt him tying the ends of the top to the headboard.

"It's my turn, baby."

She trembled, both from the timbre of his voice and the look in his eyes. He pulled up and off her, sliding his hands down her body to her breasts.

"Perfect tits."

He teased them with just his fingertips, sending a

thousand ripples of pleasure across her skin. She twisted, unable to stay still. Her nipples had contracted into tight beads that he leaned over and licked.

"Oh, Christ." She jerked as his tongue rasped over one nipple, lapping, licking, before he moved over to the other one.

"I like them wet like this…" He came back to the first nipple and treated it to another round. "From my tongue."

The air-conditioning was cool against her nipples when he left them and ventured lower. He grasped her panties and pulled them free.

"And I like seeing this part of you glistening too."

He pushed her knees open, but honestly, she was shameless at that point. She was ready to have him, in any position he demanded.

"So wet."

He trailed his index finger through her folds, stopping at the opening to her passage.

"So inviting."

He rimmed her, circling her opening with that fingertip, the look on his face making her breath catch.

He thrust inside, drawing a moan from her as she lifted up to take him.

"So tight."

He added a second finger on the next thrust and worked them in and out of her.

"Were you sore?" He pushed deep and scissored his fingers inside her, setting off a whole new round of hunger. "From my cock?"

"Yeah…" Her voice was thready and desperate.

He moved his thumb up until it was resting on top of her clit.

"I love the sounds you make when you come."

She jerked, the need simmering inside her reaching a critical heat level. She'd never been one for talk during sex. But once again, Syon was taking her to places she'd never realized she wanted to go.

"Suck me." It should have sounded cheesy, but instead she discovered it so erotic, she writhed.

His lips split into a grin. "Yes, ma'am."

A moment later she lost all concept of the world around her. Syon hovered over her spread slit for just a moment, long enough for her to feel his breath against her tender parts. Just one moment before he licked her.

She cried out, gripped in sensory overload. She was a hairbreadth from climax, but he didn't linger over her clit long enough to let it burst.

"Not just yet…" He teased her slit, thrusting his tongue into her pussy and licking his way up to her clit. He closed his mouth over the throbbing point and worried it with his tongue.

She jerked.

And cried out.

And wound her legs around his shoulders as she lifted off the bed in a frantic attempt to ride him. She was twisting up and off the comforter, certain that every muscle she had was going to snap because she was drawn so tight.

Syon didn't give her the release she was desperate for. He teased and licked, always pulling back right at the moment she was sure she was going to fly apart.

"Syon!" she screamed. "You…asshole!"

He chuckled against her clit, the vibration tormenting

her even more. She whimpered, mentally surrendering all attempts at control.

"Like that, do you?"

He looked up her body, his lips curved into a huge grin. "Like I said, baby. I want to sing to you."

He lowered his mouth and captured her clit again. This time, he mumbled against her, the sound intensifying the motion.

She arched up, her body tightening around his fingers as she climaxed. It wrung her like a dishcloth. She jerked against her bonds, twisting and tumbling through the waves of pleasure. Syon sucked her through it, finally rising up when she collapsed onto the bed in a pile of quivering muscles.

She was dimly aware of him unknotting her wrist and gathering her against his body. The air-conditioning was a welcome relief from the heat burning across her skin.

"I love singing for you, Kate."

"You must have pulled some strings to get the candles in here." Hotels had a ton of fire regulations. But Cid often had a cigarette in his hand too. Obviously the fine for smoking in the rooms didn't worry him.

Kate trailed her fingers through Syon's chest hair. He was toying with her breast.

"One of Cid's more useful job components."

She tried not to stiffen at the mention of the road manager, but he chuckled and sat up.

"When I write music, I like stuff turned off. It gets me in the zone. The candles set the mood."

His expression had softened.

"Neat."

He pressed a kiss against her lips. A slow, seductive kiss that made her sigh. "Stay right here."

He rolled off the bed, and she rolled onto her side to watch him. He moved across the room and sat down in the corner. He picked up the guitar and slung the shoulder strap over his head, taking a moment to type something on the laptop that was nearby.

He looked up, his lips curving when he caught sight of her.

"Stay just like that."

He started working the strings. His face became a tapestry of concentration, his fingers forcing his thoughts into notes. The tempo increased, and her heart accelerated. She was tapping the surface of the bed with the rhythm, feeling like she was part of the creation happening right in front of her.

When he pulled out the last note, he opened his eyes and grinned at her.

"Show me how you'd move to it."

She rolled out of the bed and landed lightly on her feet. "Hold on." Kate pulled a dress from the closet and shrugged into it. Her shoes were also unpacked, and she pushed her feet into a pair of black heels. One of her corset tops was there, with the latches, and she closed it right over the dress.

"Now I'm ready."

The dress only fell to midthigh. Her lack of underwear didn't bother her. Syon started again, this time turning up the volume. He made the guitar squeal, working the strings until she was gyrating with the rhythm.

"Yeah…fuck yeah…"

He was off the stool, bowed back as he worked the

instrument and made it perform. There was a glint in his eyes and a sensuous set to his jaw. She was pulsing, moving with the music, letting it inspire her.

"That fucking rocks." Ramsey was suddenly there, pushing his way toward Syon, his own guitar in hand. "Cue it up again."

Ramsey peered at the laptop screen before setting his fingers on the strings. He looked up at her and licked his lower lip.

But a moment later, he joined in, switching his attention to the screen to read the music. Syon took the lead, but Ramsey kept pace with him like they were part of the same being.

They reached the end of the song, and there was suddenly a round of squealing from behind her.

"This is so hot!"

"I want to party!"

Ramsey actually scowled at the two girls chugging beer near the doorway. "We're working. You both gotta go."

Taz and Drake were suddenly there, pushing the girls toward the door, their expressions serious.

"Hey, how come we can't stay?"

"Why is she staying?"

Taz put them through the door and closed it firmly. He flipped the lock and walked over to look at the laptop. He started nodding his head as Drake unrolled a thick mat that was an electronic set of drums.

"Cue it up."

She felt like a third wheel, suddenly unsure if she belonged. Syon looked up. "Dance again, baby."

"Yeah," Ramsey agreed.

The music started again, and she let her doubts dissipate with the beat. It was time to live in the moment.

And it was a fucking epic moment.

———

"You're a goddess, Kate."

The ache in her neck was suddenly worth it. Her fingers were swollen, and she had pricked several of them, but Syon was standing in front of the mirror in new pants. He turned and looked at his backside as Ramsey came out of the back bedroom.

"A fucking leather goddess!" Syon added.

"I would have bet on the sausage hound doing a better fit, but you smoked his ass," Ramsey said as he joined Syon. "Must be all her personal knowledge of your person."

"Which I don't have of you," Kate said.

"Not my fault." Ramsey sent her wink.

There was a rap on the door, and Cid strode in. He swept them both up and down quickly. "About time those got done."

Kate bristled. The road manager missed it because he had eyes only for Syon and Ramsey.

"Got a reporter down the hall who wants an interview."

Syon nodded and started toward the door, but Cid put out a hand to stop him.

"Let's talk about image."

Ramsey turned to eye the road manager.

"No steady girlfriends. It cost me a fortune to get those pictures of you kissing her pulled."

"Wait…you paid to have them pulled?" Kate asked.

Cid didn't even glance her way. But Syon did.

Kate turned away, feeling like a knife was buried in her chest.

Google it? What the fuck was that worth if Cid was going around paying the paparazzi off?

"Let's give the fans the dream life. It doesn't include playing house. Okay? Great."

Cid carried on as though she wasn't in the room and pulled open the door. There was a frenzy of people out in the hallway. The air of excitement was tangible as concert time drew closer. Crew members and entourage folk were waiting to fawn over Syon and Ramsey. They had their tablets out and security headphones on. A makeup artist even had a mobile box hanging off her hip from a cross-body shoulder strap. She eyed Syon and reached into her box to pull out a blending square.

"Go blow her skirt up," Cid added as the crowd seemed to pull Syon and Ramsey into it. He followed them out, never giving her a second look.

Kate busied herself with putting away her tools.

But she was pissed.

Liar.

Well, there was no way she was going to admit she was hurt.

Nope.

It still stung. She rolled up her tape measure and put it away, sweeping up some ends of thread from the surface of her worktable. Two more hides were set out, ones she'd decided would suit Drake and Taz well. But they didn't call to her. She fiddled with her box of tools instead, trying to ignore what was chewing on her.

It was show night. The top floor of the hotel was

teeming with an excitement that was tangible. The brigade of polo-shirt-wearing crew was in high gear as they set about making sure the next performance of Toxsin was spot-on.

She'd done her part, and it seemed that no one had any interest in her doing anything else. The hallways quieted down as more and more people left for the arena.

She twisted off the cap of a single-serve whiskey bottle from the minibar and realized she had never felt quite so lonely.

Or like Syon was so completely out of her reach.

She snorted at herself and tossed the contents of the bottle down the drain. New rule time, she decided. Rule number six. No pity parties. She nodded with satisfaction.

Now all she had to do was figure out how to stop breaking her own rules when it came to Syon.

—~~~—

"Brilliant again, mates!" Cid rolled into the backstage performers' room, framed by two of his female employees. "All the chicks are tweeting about you. Ticket sales are popping as we speak."

He extended his hand, and one of the girls laid his tablet into it. "Cid has more magic in store for the evening. First up is a club with an ice bar. I bet the manager you guys could raise the temperature."

"I'm out," Syon said, wiping away his makeup.

"We've been over this ground."

Syon turned away from the dressing-room mirror. "No, we haven't, but we will, just as soon as I straighten things out with Kate."

"What are you talking about?"

Syon brushed by Cid. His passion was riding high. Not that it was unusual, but tonight he needed to take it to Kate. He was being drawn to her and didn't give a rat's ass what anyone thought about it. He wasn't going to think too deeply on the subject.

Just act.

———∾∾∾———

"You missed the show."

Syon didn't knock, but it was his suite too. His shirt was open, giving her a glimpse of his six-pack.

"You're not working this time."

Kate jumped, dropping her phone. Her cheeks heated as Syon picked it up and spied the game of Angry Birds she'd been using to distract herself.

"Not sure how it's your business."

He was still wearing the pants she'd made him, and she couldn't help but admire them. But that set off another little jolt of pain. She'd put her heart into those pants, and he was…well…a dick.

"We've already established that Cid is an asshole, Kate. Don't let him get between us."

She propped her hand on her hip. "Your words are the ones coming between us. You told me to google you to see if you've been kissing other girls, but what is that worth if Cid is just buying off the paparazzi?"

"Not everyone has a price."

Kate scoffed at him, feeling hollow. "You knew I wouldn't find any pictures when I went looking, so what you used to establish trust with me is bull."

"I knew you wouldn't, because I haven't kissed anyone else, baby."

"Don't call me baby," she said. "You don't get to call me that."

A hard glint entered his eyes. "Yes I do."

She shook her head. "I don't think so. Not when your road manager is buying up pictures you challenge me to find. I thought you were being sincere."

"You know what I am."

He was moving closer, cornering her. She wanted to stand her ground, but her belly was twisting, making her tremble, and she moved away from him.

"What do you mean by that?" She tried to hold on to her pride. That potent sexuality of his was hitting her with gale-force winds. But she hated herself for being affected now. Hated herself for not having more self-worth.

"You have to decide to trust me." He was almost in arm's reach, his jaw tight as he held her gaze. "I told you I haven't kissed another woman in two years. Either my word is good enough, or the problem we have has nothing to do with Cid. It's a trust issue. You told me Conan was jerking my chain."

She shuddered. The look in his eyes cut straight through her. "Yeah. I did."

He captured her wrist, closing his fingers around it and pulling her against him. "Are you asking me to blow off appearances because you don't trust me?"

"No." She hated the way it made her feel just to hear him say that.

He tilted his head to the side and fitted his mouth against hers. For a moment, he thrust every thought out of her mind, licking and kissing her until she opened her mouth, desperate for a deeper connection. His scent was filling her senses, his chest hard beneath her fingertips,

and all she wanted was to sink down into the vortex of
sensation he created.

"Not yet."

He'd pulled away, holding her back when she would
have followed him.

He spun her loose and pointed her toward the closet.
"Get dressed."

"For what?"

"I've got to work, and you have a point to make." He
nodded. "Something hot. To defend your turf."

Understanding dawned on her. "You must have
pissed Cid off by coming back here."

"Happy?" There was a trace of bitterness in his tone
that grated.

She shook her head. "I'm happy you're here, not that
you left before dealing with business."

He didn't believe her. He crossed his arms over his
chest, retreating behind a hard expression.

She wasn't taking it.

"Trust is a two-way street, Syon," she said. "Either
you get that I'm not jumping you for your status, or don't
get on my case about taking your word on the pictures."

He pushed out his jaw, but she refused to move. It
was far more serious than she'd ever imagined she might
be with him. Part of her was stuck in a moment of disbelief to find herself actually there.

Was she having a relationship?

Because it sure felt like it.

And that scared her.

"I'm here because I couldn't blow you off, Kate."

Oh shit. She was getting into a relationship.

"It scares me too."

He was reading the emotions on her face.

"Sorry. I don't mean to be…well…" She had no clue what she really wanted to say. Syon opened his arms and came toward her. He slid his hand along her cheek, sending little ripples of delight through her. Only these ripples touched her heart. It was more than sexual pleasure; this was heart deep.

"I didn't mean to get involved either."

"Yeah."

It was a simple reply, but one that fit. His eyes were full of need, the need to be understood. She slowly smiled.

"I'll get dressed."

His expression became sensual. She backed up, her hips swaying. "Sit right over there"—she pointed at a chair—"and wait for me. Or we won't be going anywhere."

Ordering him around gave her a heady sensation, but the wolfish smile he flashed her made her shiver.

Oh yeah.

The guy made her shiver.

And she'd so gotten in over her head.

———

"Kate!"

Ramsey called out to her over the mass of bodies on the dance floor. He was wearing only a leather vest with his pants, the front of it open to show off his pierced nipple with its stud bar.

"I love what you do when you get in my pants!"

The girls rubbing against him reacted instantly. Some of them laughed; others shot her dagger looks as they made it clear the singer was theirs. He pulled one closer by her hips, leaning down to whisper something in her

ear. It was a sensual picture. One that sent a zip of heat
through her, if she were honest enough to admit it.

"Like I said, Rams is a cat. He likes to prowl."

Syon turned her around and caught her up against
him. People were crowding close, the loud music sinking
into them until the only thing to do was move to the beat.

"Let him. It's fun to watch," she said.

Syon's expression turned sensual. He cupped her
cheeks, moving her backward into the mass of dancing
bodies; the situation had a vibe that was slightly savage.
There was a glint in his eyes that told her he wanted to
put her on display. A bolt of awareness shot through her,
unleashing a wildness she'd never found the right place
to let loose before.

"He's watching you now."

Sensation prickled on her nape. They were surrounded by a crowd of sweating people, more skin on
display than anything else.

But she could have sworn she felt Ramsey watching
her exclusively.

"Do you like it when he watches me?"

It was a horrible thing to say. A nasty thing.
Something polite people didn't say.

But so true, so freeing to say.

And she wasn't interested in hiding behind the facade
of correctness.

Syon leaned over, his breath hitting her ear as he used
his bigger body to dance her back another few steps.
Her insides were tightening with anticipation, waiting
for that first contact with Ramsey.

"Yeah. I like it when he watches you," Syon
rasped against her neck before he raised his head and

captured her gaze. "I like watching you getting turned on by the idea."

The music was pounding around them, the dance floor crowded. It was Syon's beat too. She lifted her head, raising her arms up to dance, working her hips in a rhythm that was deeply intimate. He pushed the mass back, keeping a spot open for her. Somehow, he had a drink in his hand, and he took a long sip and leaned down to transfer some of it into her mouth. There was the tangy taste of dirty martini and the bite of the alcohol. It stung just the right amount as Syon kissed his way across her jaw before delivering a bite to her neck.

She purred, the sound more of a warning than a response. Prowling felt just about perfect. She caught his earlobe between her teeth, biting into it just enough to make sure he felt her strength.

"Yeah, baby…don't play nice with me."

His tone was deep and raspy. He slid his hands down her corseted sides to her hips, cupping them and moving in time with her. She drew her claws down him, enjoying the sight of him baring his teeth at her.

"Ramsey isn't the only animal on the prowl tonight." She lifted the drink out of his hand and tossed back another swallow. Her blood was pumping, burning off the chill that had settled on the bare skin of her shoulders from the night air. "You want everyone to see what an animal you are." He finished off the drink and leaned in until their lips were only a fraction of an inch apart. "I want you to see me choose you."

He gave her neck a squeeze. Just a sample of his darker side. She shuddered and eased back, swaying as she tried to catch the beat.

Other people joined in. Women and men slid right
up to them both, joining them in a sort of ménage à trios
dance. She was turned away from Syon by a woman
who had dark, sensuous eyes. Kate moved with her for
a moment before Syon reached out to reclaim her.

Heat speared through her.

There was a possessive look in his eyes, one that sent
need clawing up her insides. She let it climb, allowing herself to be split off again, this time by a man,
because she knew Syon was watching. He butted his
way between her and her impromptu partner, bumping
chests with the guy before cupping her jaw and sealing
her mouth with his.

"Oh yeah."

"So hot…"

"Kiss me too."

The voices were background noise. An erotic addi-
tion to the pulsing beat of Toxsin music. Someone new
slid up behind her, a harder presence; she felt awareness
rippling across her skin.

"You're hot, Kate."

Ramsey's voice was dangerous. It slithered through
her like dark temptation, luring her away from the light.
Syon was still dancing with her, moving his hips in time
with hers, brushing her with his erection as Ramsey
cupped her hips from behind. Syon kept her chin in his
hand, watching her intently.

She was pretty sure she was going to melt into a puddle.

Her core felt like it was molten, and Syon's eyes were
glittering with enough passion to reduce her to a pile of
cinders. Ramsey leaned over, his hair brushing her nape
and setting off another round of sensation.

She was teetering on the edge. But it didn't bug her. Part of her was enjoying the sensation of falling, like a form of freedom she'd never been bold enough to reach out and touch.

She was hungry for it.

Strangely fascinated by it.

She turned, facing Ramsey, and reached out to grab his nipple bar. He backed up a step, baring his teeth at her.

She stuck out her chin at him, dancing up to him and tossing her hair before Syon was pulling her back around to face him.

She went to him, sliding her hands up his chest, skin to skin through the opening of his shirt. The connection was jolting, making her smile as Ramsey caught a handful of her hair and pulled it tight. He leaned over her shoulder, making full contact with her back.

She shuddered violently.

It shattered everything inside her. Every boundary she'd thought unbreakable was crumbling into particles too fine to recognize.

"Kiss him," Syon demanded.

She hesitated, licking her lower lip as she teetered on the top of the ledge. Syon tilted his head and fitted his mouth against hers. There was a roar of approval from the crowd as he kissed her hard, thrusting his tongue deeply into her mouth before pulling away.

"Kiss him, Kate."

She turned, not sure if it was her idea or Ramsey's and Syon's hands doing it for her. She caught the scent of Ramsey's skin, drawing in a deep breath to make sure it intoxicated her.

Different.

Yet part of Syon.

It defied thought. The only thing that mattered was the pulsing need moving between them. Syon pressed up behind her, his cock hard against her lower back. Ramsey's was hard against her stomach as she rose up on her toes to connect with his lips.

His kiss was a slow exploration of her mouth. He teased her lower lip, slipping along it before licking it. She tried to kiss him harder, but he held her back, gripping her nape to control her, and made sure she felt him doing it. He pulled away, just an inch, and shot her a look full of dominance.

She twisted his nipple bar in response. For a moment, they were caught in a tangle of defiance and the need for control. He demanded; she hissed in his face. Syon chuckled behind her.

"She's ginger, Rams."

"That's the best part," Ramsey said before claiming her mouth in a soul-shattering kiss.

There was nothing nice about it. He pressed her mouth open, storming her senses with a kiss that awakened a need to shove back at him. She grabbed his hair and kissed him back, to the delight of those watching. They roared with approval, trying to touch her.

Syon and Ramsey weren't sharing. They moved her between them, blocking those groping hands and keeping her for themselves. She lost track of who was touching her where, twisting around to kiss Syon as she trailed her fingers down Ramsey's open vest.

Her senses were reeling, her blood pulsing with the beat, her body on the edge, but she didn't want to give in. She wanted to resist release, because it would end the moment.

Syon didn't give her a choice. He cupped her mons, rubbing it hard as Ramsey thrust against her back. She shuddered, sensation tearing through her. Syon captured her cry with his mouth, Ramsey holding her up as her knees went weak. They held her through it, rocking her, supporting her, delighting her…

Completely.

Chapter 5

The air-conditioning was on.

Kate felt the slight vibration of it as cool air brushed her chest.

"Waking up hungover is a lot better when it happens next to you, Kate."

Her eyes flew open wide. She was staring at Ramsey, and he was looking at her chest. Her corset was missing, only her thin, transparent chemise top still on.

"You've got mouthwatering tits, girl."

He reached out and traced one of her nipples, his eyes closing against the light.

She looked down, her breath coming out in a little rush when she realized he was still wearing his pants.

"Yeah." Ramsey opened his eyes and caught her blushing. "Would have been a shame to be too drunk to remember having you."

"The three of you were wasted," Taz said from somewhere across the room, taking her level of horror to the top of the scale.

The bed rocked as Syon sat up behind her. He dropped a pillow over her chest as she turned to look across the suite. Taz was busy pounding the keys on his laptop, his short black hair in its normal spikes.

"You owe me sushi tonight for hauling your butts back and separating you from the posse that tried to join you in an orgy. Pretty sure one of them bit me. I might need a rabies shot."

Kate groaned, suddenly recalling the dance-floor climax she'd had. "I only had one drink…"

"More like three…maybe four," Syon said as he rolled over and landed on his feet. "For a Scot, you're sort of a lightweight."

She flipped him the bird but yelped when Ramsey swatted her butt.

"You need some discipline, Kate."

"Well, you need—" She'd rolled over and sat up but stopped when she caught sight of Ramsey. His eyeliner had run and smudged around his eyes, making him look like a badger. "A date with a shower."

She finished up with a snicker.

He sat up, settling his feet on the floor and smirked at her. "You're one to talk."

Syon chuckled, stretching and arching back until his spine popped.

Kate sat hugging the pillow. Her head was hurting, her mouth dry like she'd chewed on a cotton ball some-time during the hours she couldn't remember. All she could do was blink and try to absorb the scene.

Had she broken something?

Put the nail in her own coffin?

That thought terrified her completely. It opened a door she'd been avoiding looking at. The one that opened into a relationship she would regret losing.

Syon was ordering room service, and Ramsey wandered off into the suite, a door shutting in one of the other bed-rooms. Taz had slipped on a pair of headphones that covered his ears entirely and was cussing at the game he was playing.

"Hey…"

Syon crawled back across the bed and cupped her chin. Time started crawling by as she turned to look him in the eye.

She was scared.

Plain and simple.

What she didn't expect to see was uncertainty in Syon's eyes.

"You okay?" His expression tightened as silence sat between them. He was steeling himself for her reply.

She nodded, but he wasn't accepting it from her. It was a halfhearted response, one designed to protect her feelings.

"Come on." His tone was tight. He grasped her hand and pulled her off the bed. He maintained his grip as he tugged her into the massive master suite. He turned on the water in the shower and stripped.

She was still hugging the pillow when he turned around to look at her.

"You've seen me now, Kate. Everything about me." His eyes narrowed. "I need the excess…"

Steam was billowing up from the shower. He walked backward into it, letting it engulf him. The water hit him and ran down his hard body.

"You are excess."

That was why he sent her into a vortex. The screaming fans were all just addicted to the vapors coming off him. Fascinated by the raw energy radiating from him.

"And Ramsey keeps me grounded. Keeps me from thinking I'm the only one who craves it. I'd have lost my mind without him around to make me feel grounded."

She dropped the pillow, reaching for him. She

wanted to keep him from disappearing into a place where he felt alone. She could see it in his eyes. The desolation. The loneliness.

He waited for her, watching her strip off her top and skirt before walking into the water. It hit her skin, awakening all the sexual needs she'd never gotten satisfied the night before.

"Next time, I'm not drinking."

His face became a tapestry of hunger. There was lust, hard desire, but also something deeper. Something intimate.

"I want to have my wits when you take me back to that place you share with Ramsey."

Obviously, she was crazy.

"Sure about that?" he asked, cupping her hips and squeezing them until a zip of pleasure speared through her insides.

"When you jump out of an airplane, there's only one direction to go." She reached out and handled his cock, closing her fingers around the thick phallus and pulling her hand up to the head. "I'll have to hope my parachute works."

Or it was going to be a deadly crash.

"Me too."

He lifted her up, bearing her backward and pushing her against the tile. Her knees spread to allow his body close, his cock burrowing between the folds of her sex as she lifted her hands and clasped his shoulders.

He thrust forward, her body eager for the penetration. It was more than the water from the shower; it was the state of semiarousal left from the night before. Her brain was clearing, bits and pieces of the night rising above the alcohol's grip. She'd climaxed but gone to sleep hungry for deep satisfaction.

Her position against the wall didn't give her much room to move and get what she wanted.

He knew it too. He was pressing her body to the tile with his chest against hers, holding her in place and keeping her from seeing his expression. She tried to arch, to take his thrusts, but he kept her still.

"Take it." He twisted his hand in her hair, holding her in place. "Take it, just the way I want to give it to you."

He was being savage, and there was something about it that pleased her. Something brutally honest about the moment.

"Then you'd better give it all to me," she hissed. "No bullshit excuses about me not being able to take it."

He rammed himself deep, both of their hearts hammering.

"I can take anything you can dish out. Maybe you get away with that crap with the rest of the world, but there is nothing about you I can't understand. Don't be too chicken to share yourself."

He snorted at her. A second later, her feet were on the floor. He turned her around, and she ended up with her hands braced on the seat as he thrust back into her from behind. He could get more force behind his thrusts now, each one feeling like it was driving the breath from her.

He was holding her hips, keeping her prisoner and not even allowing her to move back into his thrusts. She grasped the edge of the seat and used her hands to push herself back, drawing a snarl from him when she succeeded.

Their skin was wet, making slapping noises when they connected. She fought to push back, delighting in every grunt she wrung from him. "I'm not going to let you hold back."

He wrapped his arm around her body, still pumping her from behind, but now reaching down and fingering her clit.

"Same goes for you, Kate."

Everything shifted. What had been a struggle between them, morphed into a fight to hold back climax. She reached back and grabbed his thighs, trying to work him faster, but he rubbed her clit, pushing her closer to the edge of mindless pleasure. When it came, she screamed, the sound bouncing crazily around the title walls. She dug her nails into her thighs and heard a strangled sound. He ground himself into her, roaring as his cock burst inside her. His come was hot, stinging as it hit her insides. She tightened, like a second orgasm, an aftershock that rolled through her with only slightly less force.

"I love that thing your pussy does when I get you off."

He was slowly pumping her, his cock feeling like it hadn't lost any of its stiffness.

"Are you a female ejaculator?"

"Hmm?" She was suddenly tongue-tied. Which was stupid, considering she'd woken up in bed with not one but two rock stars. But the topic shocked her to her core.

So much for being a sophisticated, modern woman. Syon had busted her back to fourteen with one frank question.

"Female ejaculator," he repeated without a hitch.

He withdrew and sat down. Reaching out, he pulled her onto his lap and settled her on his length. "It's rare, but your G-spot is sensitive, so maybe—"

"I don't know."

She was embarrassed, feeling awkward. He held her down when she would have lifted off him.

"You make me want to impress you, Kate." He was still shaking, his release shocking his system. "But I can't do that by being a good guy."

She smiled, shaking her head. "You gotta be you. It's what makes you irresistible."

He lifted her chin, locking gazes with her. "Did I break something between us? Today or last night?"

Her eyes widened. "I was wondering the same thing...when I woke up with Ramsey...there..."

"With me there." He smoothed his hands down her back. "Us..." He shook his head. "Anyone else, and I'd..." His face tightened. "I want you to come to the next show. You need to see. You'll understand if you see."

"I'll be there," she promised.

She kissed him. Softly, slowly. He framed her face, cradling it as she started to ride him. This time, there was a gentle build up, but one that culminated in an explosion that left them clinging to each other.

"Thank you, Denver!" Syon raised the microphone over his head as the Pepsi Center filled with screaming fans. It was sold out, every seat filled, and the pit was a crush of bodies all straining to get closer to the performers. The surge of bodies was like watching a tribe, all of them melding into a single entity, united by one driving force.

The music.

It was the force that promised them liberation. In the moment, they could immerse themselves in it. Everyone in the arena was there with a sole purpose in mind.

To jump into the current and ride it over the falls.

Drake started up on the drums, setting a beat that made Kate squirm in her seat. Dead center at the end of the catwalk, she had a seat that normally went for over ten thousand dollars. She could touch the edge of the catwalk and possibly Syon when he made one of his runs down it.

You've touched him...

She grinned.

Yeah, and licked, as well as a few other things.

Pressing in around her were women willing to pay for that privilege. They were decked out in Prada and other designer labels, most of them looking like they'd invested in their personal enhancements as well. No one was sitting down. Drake was tearing up the mood with a drum solo that made it impossible to sit. Taz was laying down a bass rhythm that tickled her insides. It was a deep, dark feeling of impending madness.

That insanity was delivered when Ramsey and Syon joined in on either side of the stage, their fingers coaxing sounds out of their guitars that shot through the building and left Kate panting. It was more than their fingers. It was a whole-body experience.

Back in Los Angeles, she'd wondered if she'd just been overwhelmed, if the intensity would fade, but it hadn't. If anything, she was caught up even more this time, the music hitting her deeper, more intimately as Syon took to the mic to add lyrics.

His voice was rough velvet—smooth when it needed to be, but cutting as he sang out.

His soul was on display.

No one else knew it, but she did. What he was pulling

on that stage was his inner demon. The one the rest of the world was too chicken to let be seen.

It was an awesome sight.

Kate realized why the crowd was roaring, why she was on her feet shaking her fist in the air. It was because he was a leader, setting them all free, saying exactly what was on his mind, singing it out without remorse for who was offended.

Everyone wanted sex, but Syon was bold enough to say it out loud. Ramsey backed him up, completing the moment as the lights flashed around them and the song came to an end.

Syon was halfway down the catwalk when he finished, bowing back, pushing the last notes out of him. He forced it into the world, and everyone experienced the intensity of life, that thing everyone thought about, wanted to be, but were too practical to act upon.

Too scared to release.

He opened his eyes, drawing a gasp from her because she recognized the hunger in them. It turned her on, tightening her nipples. He locked gazes with her, caressing the strings of his guitar as he played the first, fleeting notes of "Insatiable Craving."

He was singing to her, applying the words to her as he prowled toward her. People stretched up, straining to touch him. They ended up stroking his ankles as he passed them, but he was completely intent on her.

The intensity was mind-blowing. She strained toward him, reaching for just a fleeting moment of contact. The people around her were crowding her, pushing their way closer to their idol. She didn't care. She threw her head back and laughed.

—⁂—

"Now that was fucking brilliant!"

Cid was in top form. Two of his personal assistants were at his elbows, each of them looking like they'd spent the day doing nothing but getting ready. From head to toe, they were buffed, primped, and dressed to kill. She'd never seen makeup so perfect or detailed.

The performers' room was hot because of all the bodies in it. The roaring crowd could still be heard behind them.

"Denver PD just called for backup to deal with the party in the parking lot," Cid crowed. "Perfect!"

"Kate is good for the show," Taz spoke up.

Cid stiffened, cutting her a quick look. No one else really caught it, but she did.

Ignore him. He's just pissing on his turf.

The guy saw her as a threat. She was sure of it now. She'd have to keep her eye on him.

"They've got more churches than bars in this city, so I want you guys to do a little riding. Got a few private invitations, but what we really need is connection with the masses. I've got the guys bringing your bikes around. Kerry and her team are going to fix you guys up with light makeup."

Cid was good at what he did. Kate had to give him some credit. There were at least ten team members in the room, all of them organized and working together to keep Syon and his band looking top-notch. The makeup crew wore blue polo shirts. They didn't hesitate to move right in and start using their sponges and brushes. Cid was going down his performance notes with the help of his tablets while the heavier stage makeup was removed and lighter coats applied.

"Costume production is going well, so don't be afraid to play hard out there."

Ramsey cut Kate a glance, one eyebrow raised.

"Is there a problem with my note?"

Ramsey snapped his head around to look at Cid. "I like looking at her more than you, Cid."

The other members of the band laughed, a couple of the crew joining in. Cid's cronies didn't though. They cast her long, calculating looks.

The power shifts were like everything else Toxsin did—extreme.

Syon hopped out of his chair and captured her in a hug. "Me too," he said as he nuzzled her neck.

"If you're going to fuck, take her to the dressing rooms," Cid tossed over his shoulder.

"What the hell?" Kate demanded.

Syon stiffened. "Kill your attitude, Cid. Kate's not a groupie."

"Yeah," Taz chimed in, surprising her. "She's taking me out for sushi tonight. I don't hang out with groupies."

"You should," Cid shot back at Taz. "Your image needs a shot of heat. About ten of them. Time for you to get over that high school sweetheart thing."

"I told you before: don't even make a reference to Joi." Taz was suddenly dead serious.

Cid opened his arms. "Come on. It's been what? Three years? At least Kate isn't a prude."

"Warned you."

Taz grinned evilly at the road manager, looking a

whole lot like a martial arts fighter who was getting ready to whup some ass.

And love every second of doing it.

Cid actually stepped back. "Okay. Got it. I've forgotten her name."

Taz looked disappointed for a moment.

Syon chuckled. "Yeah. Sushi." He kissed Kate again, trying to smooth out the hard set of her lips. "We owe Taz sushi. He takes sushi very seriously."

They did owe him, and the reason made her blush. But it restored her good humor too. Ramsey was suddenly there, falling into step.

"Wait up," Drake called as his makeup person refused to let him out of the chair.

They walked between rows of security men who had their arms out wide to hold back the fans. Barricades had been set up, but they were being pushed out of alignment by the surging crowd. Syon draped his arm across her back as the cameras snapped around them like fireflies.

Toxsin crew members pulled up on the Harleys, gaining a roar of approval from the fans. They slid off the bikes, and Syon and his buddies took their places.

"Take a ride with me," Syon cooed to her. She shivered, enjoying the tremor.

She climbed on behind him and pressed up close. "I do enjoy rides…with you…"

Syon pulled away, in command of the bike. The engine roared with a vibration in the seat that teased her clit. The wind was crisp on her face, but it was the hard body she was holding on to that captivated her the most.

Cars slowed down as they passed, windows sliding open to reveal fans. Long-haired guys with tattoos

and piercings screamed out. Girls in the bare mini-
mum of clothing sent saucy looks, and more than a
few flashed them.

They made several passes through the area around
the arena before Taz took off, and the rest followed
him. They made their way down to where the streets
narrowed and more signs were written in Korean. It had
to be close to midnight, but the sidewalks were still full.
Groups of teens looked up, some of them gasping with
surprise and raising their fists into the air. Taz called
back to them in Korean.

For once, he was the wild one, tipping his head back
and howling. He pulled up in front of a huge restaurant,
built to look like a vintage Asian house. Two Korean
girls in native dress smiled at them from the door before
they bowed in perfect unison and greeted them.

Taz stopped and bowed. Syon pulled Kate behind
him, and they stopped to bow to the girls as well. It
seemed to be their duty to greet every person entering the
establishment. Inside, there was a huge counter with bar
seating and sushi chefs working behind it. Taz called out
to them, and they raised their hands in acknowledgment.

Waiters were carrying huge trays of food around,
some of it steaming hot. There was a cloud of moisture
hanging out near the ceiling. There was the clink of
dishes and conversation in an Asian language. Two
more women in native dress hurried over and bowed
to Taz.

"We're going upstairs, guys," Taz said. "Got a private dining room."

He reached out and shook the manager's hand. Kate
watched a folded bill transfer between their hands before

the girls led them up a staircase. The manager secured a thick red rope across the opening once they'd passed.

Upstairs, the noise level was considerably less. The soft sounds of Korean music floated around as they were taken down a hallway with walls that looked like they were made of bamboo and rice paper. One of the girls slid a door open and welcomed them in.

"Nice, Taz," Drake said as he walked in and landed on a pillow that was meant to be sat on.

"Take your shoes off." Taz was slipping off his boots at the door, still on the other side of it. One of their escorts was looking at Drake like he was a parasite.

"Oh…sorry. My bad." He rolled over and got to his feet before making his way back to the door. An older woman had appeared from somewhere and was actually dry mopping the floor behind him. Taz reached out and smacked him on the ear.

"Where were you raised, in a barn?" Taz asked.

"Hey," Drake complained, but the girls laughed happily with their chins down and their lips pressed tightly closed.

Once she was in the room, Kate realized there was an open place beneath the table for their legs if they didn't want to sit crossed-legged on the pillows.

"So, where's the geisha?" Ramsey asked as he pulled up the edge of the tablecloth and looked beneath. "The one who gives us blow jobs while we eat, and we all try to figure out whose cock she's got in her mouth."

"Geisha are Japanese," Taz said as he settled in. "And I came here to eat."

The food started coming and didn't stop.

Neither did the sake.

"Come on, Kate…try the octopi," Taz insisted.

"Yeah, Kate, you don't want to miss the octopi," Ramsey said.

"She won't," Syon confirmed. "I make sure she gets plenty of tentacle."

She stuck out her tongue at him.

Syon growled suggestively and stuck his foot out under the table. Kate ended up putting the octopus in her mouth to cover her shock as he pushed his way past her knees and right up to her pubic mound.

Taz had moved on to challenging Ramsey to a drinking bout. Drake happily made sure their sake cups were filled with the same amount.

Kate had to swallow the food quickly as Syon used his toes against her clit. His sock and her panties were the only things between them as he rubbed his big toe back and forth across her clit, stirring up the hunger the concert had left her with.

Taz and Ramsey slammed their cups down and started arguing over who had won.

"We need to go buy the chefs a drink," Taz suddenly announced. "Let's go downstairs."

He was up and moving toward the door, Drake and Ramsey falling in behind him.

Kate didn't make it out of her seat fast enough, because Syon was still playing with her. Before she knew it, Taz and the others disappeared, leaving her alone with Syon.

"Perfect," Syon said with a dark promise in his tone.

Syon removed his foot, giving her enough time to clear her wits. He slid beneath the table before she realized what he was going to do.

"Syon…"

Her voice became a squeak as he hooked his fingers around her underwear and pulled it down her legs.

"I want ginger," he said, his voice rasping as he pushed her knees apart.

She felt his breath on her cleft. "Syon…not here…"

"Oh yeah, baby." He ran his thumb down the center of her slit. "I came here to eat…"

Words failed her. She was suddenly intensely conscious of her slit. Syon teased it with his thumb, moving from her clit to her pussy with a slow motion.

"First time I saw you…I wanted to know if you had ginger curls." He pushed his fingers through her pubic hair. "I love them."

"Someone is going to walk in on us." She tried to push away from him with the help of the table, but he had his hands on her hips and held her still.

"Guess you'd better bite your lips." He used his thumbs to pull the folds of her pussy open. "'Cause I am going to eat you out."

The first touch made her shudder. She ended up grasping the tablecloth as her fingers curled into claws. She raised the edge of it just enough for her to see the back of Syon's head where it was buried in her lap.

"Mmmm…" he muttered as he licked through the center of her slit. *"Good."*

He was rimming her pussy with his tongue, sending her heart pounding. Her clit was pulsing, begging for attention.

Syon didn't disappoint her. He lapped his way back to the little bundle of nerve endings and teased it.

"Oh…damn," she gasped.

He chuckled and closed his mouth around her clit. Pleasure ripped through her, raising goose bumps all over her body. She forgot about being walked in on. Forgot about where they were.

Forgot everything except the way Syon was eating her out. He might have started slow, but there was nothing timid about his actions now. He was lapping her and sucking her, working his tongue against her clit in hard motions that were driving her to the edge of madness.

"*Yeah...*" she muttered, on the edge of climax. She pushed her hips toward him, twisting her hands in his hair. "Like that..."

She strained toward him as he worked his tongue. He pressed hard, pushing her toward the explosion and sucking her through it. She ended up sprawled out on the floor, the oversize pillow beneath her as Syon pulled a napkin from the tabletop and cleaned her.

It was strange to have him attend to such a personal chore. Stranger still to realize he understood her body so well. He rubbed the top of her thighs with his hands, massaging the quivering muscles before crawling out from beneath the table.

"You're a maniac," she said at last, sitting up and reaching for her wineglass.

"That's what you love about me."

The word "love" was a little sharp.

Only because you're chicken...

With good reason. Syon had women throwing themselves at him. What sort of incentive did she have to offer for him to be monogamous?

But then again, he hadn't insisted she be monogamous. Taz and the others came back, hooting with laughter over their adventure. They settled in as another round of food arrived. They laughed and ribbed each other. The unity was there, like a close-knit family. In a way, it was rarer than family, because what drew them together was the passion inside them. People might enjoy the idea of being rebels, but they went back to their respectable lives when the concert was over. Very few were willing to face the condemning nature of society at large.

She was lucky enough to be having dinner with four of them.

———∾∾∾———

Percy caught up with her again in Milwaukee. "So how is it going, sweetie?"

"I'm not a very good gypsy," Kate confessed. Cid's crew was setting up her shop as she sipped coffee in an attempt to wake up. Her body was protesting, her internal clock thrown so far off, she didn't have any hope of recovering.

But she had to work on the day they were building the concert stage, so it was up with the sun.

"You're going to do just fine." Percy offered her a long-distance pat on the shoulder. "Being on the road is hard, but the work I've seen is fabulous."

"Thanks to your shopping."

Percy made a happy sound on the other end of the line. "Wouldn't miss it. Steve keeps asking when we need to go again. I think he's fantasizing about those studs a little too much."

"Well, I'm sure you can put his passion to good use."

Percy laughed. "You know I will."

The last of her shop was unloaded. The crew was unboxing her machines and setting up the cutting table. It took less than an hour, because she and Percy knew how to design a set kit.

She laid out a new hide, smoothing the winkles and studying the surface intently before laying out a pattern. Drake wanted a small pocket running down the right leg for his drumsticks. Kate considered the pattern, making a couple of new pieces to form the pocket.

"You're intense when you work."

Kate looked up to find Taz halfway into the suite. She lowered the shears she'd been about to start cutting with.

"Yes."

"It shows in your work. You love what you do."

Coming from Taz, it felt like a double compliment. He was more private than the other members of the band.

"I was wondering"—he pulled a tablet from his jacket, looking like he was working up the courage to ask her something—"if you can do something like this. If you have time."

He laid the device on the table. She came around and looked at the picture of Loki from *The Avengers*.

"I like to cosplay when we're not on tour," he confessed.

Kate nodded. "And you want to be the bad boy."

"I am the bad boy."

Kate shook her head. "No, you're not."

Something passed through his eyes. It darkened his expression momentarily before he shook it off. "I've messed up pretty bad when it counted."

"We all do."

He offered her a shrug before leaving. For a moment she felt like going after him. There was something dark inside him, a pain that ran deep. But it was the type of demon only he could defeat.

Maybe he'd tell her more about it when she finished his Loki coat.

"Thank you, Milwaukee!"

The fans roared, and Syon left them screaming for more. Kate fought her way to the backstage entrance. She squeezed through the opening—two of Cid's guys were blocking it and unwilling to move aside more than two inches, it seemed.

But the swarm of bodies behind her made it understandable. They tried to follow her, the men holding them back with pure bulk.

Syon looped an arm around her, pulling her close for a sweaty kiss. She followed him into the performance room, where Cid was ready to run the show.

"I'm out tonight."

Cid turned around, looking at Ramsey like he'd lost his mind.

"Don't think I heard you, mate," Cid said incredulously.

"You did." Ramsey wiped his makeup off. "I've got something I've got to take care of."

"Yeah," Syon joined in. "We've got stuff to deal with."

"Someone's got to meet the press," Cid insisted.

"Fine," Syon said. "I got that."

Cid wasn't pleased. Not by a long shot. A tide of red darkened his complexion, but Syon didn't give him a chance to argue. He turned and jerked his head toward the doors. Ramsey was moving instantly, heading for the door with a hard expression on his face. Kate lost sight of him as they piled into a black SUV and made their way to the hotel.

The normal buzz was missing. Kate felt like the only one not in on the secret. But she didn't get long to ponder it. Their driver pulled around the huge semicircle in front of the hotel and opened the doors to the delight of the fans.

"Got to talk to the press." Syon dropped a kiss on her temple before letting Cid's crew pull him away. The paparazzi were out in good number, snapping pictures of Drake and Taz as they made their way through the huge entrance doors of the hotel. Fans squealed and stretched out to touch them, some of the girls lifting their tops.

Drake stopped and smiled at one. Taz considered him for a minute, judging him sober enough to look out for himself. The girl smiled knowingly, boldly licking her lower lip. Drake offered her his hand, and the security guys let her slide through the barricade.

Kate followed behind them, but not too quickly. The high from the concert was still buzzing her. She didn't want to be separated from Syon.

But a glance over her shoulder showed him facing several cameras. Their overly bright lights were blinding, the soundmen holding up their huge fur-covered microphones.

She needed a shower.

It was a flimsy excuse, but enough to get her through the doors. The roar was dimmer inside. The hotel security was doing a good job of making sure the fans stayed outside. She flashed her key card at one suited man and started toward the elevators.

"You'll listen to me, and listen well."

There was a middle-aged woman tearing into Ramsey. Next to her stood an older man and several other people, two of them actually holding Bibles.

The woman had her finger out and was shaking it at him. "I brought you into this world. It's a disgrace and a shame the way you act. You are coming home with us tonight. You are going to get right with the Lord. Is that clear?"

Kate should have kept out of it. Kept her mouth shut. It wasn't like Ramsey couldn't take care of himself or summon some of Cid's goons with a flick of his wrist.

But he stood there, letting the group converge on him. They were all talking at once, actually shaking their Bibles at him as they closed in like a pack of wolves.

Only Ramsey was like a panther, more than able to take them out.

And he stood there. Taking it.

Damned if Kate didn't feel her respect for him rising. Ramsey was quick to cut down anyone who got in his face, but he was holding his tongue with his family. That made him a decent fellow. Someone with a sense of honor.

The connection between him and Syon was making more and more sense. They only had each other. And not only did they only have each other, but also the rest of the world could be as vicious as it was welcoming to them. The crowd around Ramsey was working itself into a fever.

"Ramsey, don't forget I need your wardrobe checked in."

He snapped his head around. Her heart twisted when she caught sight of his face.

He was in hell. That unique sort of torment that could only come from seeing people you cared about turn on you.

For a moment, she thought she was going to get the brunt of his temper, or at the least, a middle-finger salute.

"And who is she?" the people standing in front of him demanded.

"Costume coordinator," he informed them. "I do follow some rules. Been nice. Bye. Hold the elevator, Kate."

He started toward her at a run. But his expression was one step short of devastated. He slammed into the car as Kate hit the button to close the door. He braced his hands on the hand bar, facing the back wall as the car started to pull them upward.

"Sorry if I overstepped."

He drew in a deep breath and shook his head. "Better that you did. I was about to say something…disrespectful."

"But true?"

He choked a little and turned around to lean against the handrail. He offered her a half grin that really lifted only one corner of his mouth. "True to my way of thinking. Which isn't what my parents want."

"How'd they get past Cid's guys?"

Ramsey shrugged. "They're my parents. I'd be a real asshole if I left instructions for them to be kept out."

His quick exit after the concert suddenly made sense. As did his brush by Cid outside the entrance.

His lack of company did too.

"You're okay, you know that?" she said.

He tossed his head as the doors opened. "No, I'm not." He stopped next to her, leaning down so his breath teased her lips. "I'm the guy your mother warned you about."

He was crowding her, trying to intimidate her, building a wall around himself.

But she saw it for what it was.

He was trying to burn off his frustration by taking refuge in his badass persona. She smiled back at him and tapped the center of his chest with the tip of her index finger.

"Don't take it personally. My mom is a lesbian. She warned me about all guys, just on the basis of gender."

Shock registered on his face as Kate slipped out of the elevator.

"What?"

She was on her way down the hallway and felt him watching her. He lost the battle to let it go, and she felt the vibration of his steps as he ran to keep up.

"Kate? What do you mean by that?" She slid her key card into the door, and he pushed it in. "I really gotta know. Is your mom a lesbian? How are you here?"

His eyes were bright with the promise of a distraction. She smiled in invitation. He walked in, and she pulled one of the beers from the minibar, offering it to him before taking one for herself. She took a sip before shooting him a grin. Ramsey was sitting cross-legged on the floor, nursing his beer. He made a "get going" motion with his hand.

Kate sat her beer down.

"Okay, story time. Once upon a time, at a college far from here, my mom had one too many beers and was talking to a young graduate student who challenged her to question whether or not she really didn't like dick, seeing as she had admitted to having never tried it. Being a lesbian, my mom wasn't on the pill or any

other form of birth control and didn't have a condom
on hand…"

———∿∿∿———

Ramsey could be a kitten sometimes. He snorted at her
from where he was sitting on the floor of Syon's suite.

"Your mom seriously discussed the merits of clitoral
orgasm verses G-spot climax with you?"

"Honest truth," Kate said. "Look, mister, I've been
dealing with my mom's attempts to set me up with her
girlfriends' daughters for years. She's devastated by my
strictly dick sexuality. Blames my dad."

Ramsey rolled back, ending up on his back, and
snickered. He was staring at the ceiling as he chortled.

Syon opened the door, his face shiny from the hot
lights of the press cameras. He looked at Ramsey and
raised an eyebrow.

"Did you skin him and make a throw rug out of him?"

Ramsey rolled over and flipped him the bird. But he
had a smile on his lips. "Have you worked out the bridge
on the new song yet?"

Syon grabbed a beer from the minibar and nodded as
he twisted the cap free. Ramsey swung his leg up and
over his torso so he rolled all the way over and onto his
feet. It was the sort of thing she expected of him—powerful, over the top.

He moved over to the laptop and tapped the screen.
Syon flashed her a smile before he joined him. They both
peered at the screen, lost in the notes, taking solace in
what they were, musicians. Kate watched for a moment,
struck by how much they needed each other because the
people who should have had their backs didn't.

There was a beauty in the way they hadn't let it stop them.

A beauty that touched her heart.

She showered to the sound of them working sections of the song, and fell asleep to Taz and Drake joining in. Sometime in the early hours, Syon crawled into bed with her, stroking her and bringing her body to life. She stretched, caught between sleep and the need churning inside her. Too far gone in slumber, there was no way to resist. She welcomed him, urging him between her thighs as she arched to take his thrusts.

He drove into her in the same rhythm she'd fallen asleep to, building up to the crescendo and hammering her through the climax. He ended up flopped onto the bed next to her, both of them gasping for breath. Kate hadn't quite caught hers when he scooped her up and settled her on his chest.

"Thanks."

Kate lifted her head off Syon's chest and looked at him questioningly.

"For rescuing Rams." Gratitude filled his voice. "I couldn't get away, and honestly, I don't think he would have accepted help from anyone else. His family puts him through hell."

"And he takes it."

"Yeah." Syon reached out and cupped one of her breasts. A soft shiver went through her, and he grinned. "Still hungry, baby?"

He rolled her onto her back and kissed her. Slowly, leisurely, teasing her with his tongue as he drew out the kiss. She threaded her fingers through his hair, which

was still slightly wet from their last round, arching up
and kissing him in return.

"Good." He pushed up off the bed and moved around
to where his guitar was set up. "I want to write something. Light the candles."

The computer screen was the only light in the room.
She got up and struck a match and lit some. Syon
opened the balcony door before tossing a towel over
the laptop to bury the light. He ended up in the shadows, the city lights buffeted by a thin drape that was
ruffling gently.

"Lay back down."

He was fingering the strings, toying with a melody.

"On your side…face me…"

The candle on the bedside table illuminated her. She
felt exposed, in a way she never had. The yellow glow
was more sensual than modern light. She stretched out,
experimenting with the moment. Time suddenly had
little meaning. They might have been in any century.
The current between them was universal.

"That's hot, Kate… I love it. You're amazing, baby."

He was fingering the strings, refining the notes as he
watched her. The soft silver light coming in from outside gave him a sinister look. All of the hard-cut muscles
gained more intensity in the shadows.

"Touch yourself for me…"

She shivered, a little twist of anticipation going
through her. Excitement built along with the tempo he
was playing.

"Show me how you like to be stroked."

The evening air blew in, making the candle flicker.
One died, reducing the light, but it seemed to be like

temptation beckoning her toward it, cloaking her with darkness to bring her deeper into the moment.

She rubbed her hand along her hip, up to where her waist was and then back down.

"Yeah…"

His eyes were narrowed, his lips thin, his jaw tight as he watched her.

"More."

She trailed her fingers along her hip again, but this time, she stroked across her ribs to one breast. Little ripples of delight ran out from the touch, the look in Syon's eyes pushing her forward.

Erotic was a tangible thing with him. It was in the way he watched her as much as touched her.

Like now. He was playing a melody, one that was building. She let the increasing tension in the music drive her motions. She stroked her breast and teased her nipple. It drew tight as he shot off a series of sharp notes.

"Pinch it," he ordered.

She clamped her nipple between thumb and forefinger.

"Yeah…"

He was repeating the chorus, concentrating on the notes.

"Lower. Touch yourself… Show me how you like it…"

She licked her lower lip because it had gone dry. Excitement was brewing inside her, her clit pulsing with anticipation. She lifted her leg and placed her foot against the bed so her thighs were open.

The guitar squealed again.

Her heart accelerated again.

Her breath caught when she touched her own curls. She felt unbearably on display with him watching, but the devotion in his eyes made her keep going.

Syon was still playing, the song rising to a fevered pitch.

"I know you like that little clit touched. Touch it, Kate…*rub it*…"

She felt linked into the rising crescendo, her heart keeping time with the music. She plunged her fingers into her cleft, crying out when she made contact with her clit.

"Rub it… Ride your fingers, baby!"

She really didn't have a choice.

Did she ever when it came to Syon?

Not really. With him, there was only need and the moments between feedings.

"Ride them!"

She was working her fingers in and out of her wet slit, pumping her hips toward them. Her skin turned hot, the blood roaring in her ears, but all she was conscious of was the tempo of the music. She was fixated on his fingers, imagining them against her clit.

"Yeah, baby. I'm the one touching you. That's right… It's me…"

She felt the climax coming. Her mouth opened as she was pulled tight by it. The music was hitting its crescendo; he was forcing it out of the strings, willing it into creation as she cried out. Pleasure slammed into her, flowing through her like a flash flood. Nothing remained standing; it ripped everything up and carried it along until it dumped her, completely spent of mental and physical strength.

Syon threw his head back, breathing deep, rasping breaths as he finished the last few notes.

"So fucking good."

He was suddenly there, in bed with her, his cock

slipping easily into her wet sheath. He'd come up behind her, rolling her and pulling her onto her knees as he thrust into her from behind. He was rock hard, his cock nearly bursting, the hard hammering satisfying that last thing inside her that hadn't yet been fed.

But he was holding back. She knew the difference now. Knew when he was clinging to the remains of decency. Politeness. Neither of which had anything to do with what she craved from him.

"Harder," she demanded. "Fuck me like you want to."

His grip on her hips tightened, his body driving harder, deeper into her. She pushed back against him, but he refused to allow her any motion. She was being claimed in that moment. The savage side of him delighted in knowing she was captured.

His breath was harsh, his cock hardened even more. She tightened her internal muscles and let out a cry. It was savage and full of need. He started coming, his seed flooding her as he pumped her through the climax.

"I hurt you…"

His tone was hoarse.

"No you didn't."

He had collapsed on top of her and straightened up, even though his breathing was still rapid. "I was fucking…rutting on you, Kate."

She rolled over, reaching up to stroke the side of his jaw. "I know. Ramsey's parents obviously got to you too."

He lay there, holding her for a long moment. "You read me too well."

"Good." She stood up and fought to keep her knees straight. "Because you've been a destructive force in my life since the moment I set eyes on you. Fair is fair."

"We're having lunch with my parents tomorrow."

He turned over and rolled off the side of the bed, but she caught his hand. "Say that again."

There was a twinge of uncertainty in his eyes. A hint of vulnerability she recognized and felt privileged to see.

"Is that why there's no partying tonight?"

Syon nodded. "This is our hometown. I made a date with my parents for lunch. Come with me."

She was shocked into silence and touched so deeply, her eyes stung with tears. "Okay."

For a moment, she felt awkward. Syon captured her hand and started tugging her toward the open balcony. He pulled her through the thin drape that was fluttering in the night air. The balcony opened onto the roof and a pool area.

They were both buck naked, but that didn't bother him. He pulled her over to one of the hot tubs and down into the bubbling water. They had a view of the city, the lights twinkling all around them. Syon settled back, sinking down until the water was half-way up his chest.

"Relax. Only Rams is up here."

She sank down to her chin and scanned the area. Syon laughed at her and pointed across the expanse of the pool to a gazebo area.

Ramsey was still wearing his pants, but the fly was open, his cock jutting out. A girl was on her knees sucking on it, but what drew Kate's attention was the way her arms were tied behind her back. Ramsey had a leash wrapped around his hand. The leash was attached to a collar around her neck.

Kate realized she was staring and looked away. Syon

pulled her close, fitting her in front of him so he could hold her close.

"Rams likes to dominate just a little bit more bluntly than I do." He cupped her breast, the bubbles in the water teasing her skin. "I'm a little more hands-on."

There was a snap from the gazebo and a gasp.

Syon smoothed her onto his chest, stroking her arms as she fought off the urge to make an excuse and run back into the suite.

"Why is it important for me to stay here?"

There were more sounds from the gazebo.

"I want you to know every part of me. The seedy too."

She rubbed his thighs. "You don't want to put on a face."

"Not when we're naked."

Ramsey was the counterpart of his soul. It was an odd link, but one that made a strange kind of sense.

"Ramsey keeps you from feeling abandoned by the rest of the human race. I saw that tonight."

His hands froze on her. She rubbed his thighs as there was a harsh sound and another slap from the gazebo.

"Yeah." Syon voice was strained. The admission coming from his soul.

Ramsey was working his date into a frenzy, her cries filling the dark. When he pushed her over the edge, she screamed, but all that came out of him was a harsh grunt.

So one-sided.

There was no tenderness, no companionship.

Instead, he sent her toward the elevators and forgot her before the last of her footsteps had faded. It should have bothered Kate. Should have been a reason to label him a prick. But the sound of the girl squealing with glee in the hallway put an end to that.

"Oh my God! Tina, you'll never guess who I just fucked! Ramsey from Toxsin! He is a god!"

A bitter taste rose in Kate's mouth. There was no baseline in their world, only extremes.

She turned around and seated herself on Syon's lap. "I don't care who you are."

He narrowed his eyes.

"You told me once that everyone wanted something from you." She cupped some water and dribbled it on his shoulder. "I need things from you."

He drew in a stiff breath, emotion brightening his eyes. He clamped her against him, his arms shaking.

"I need too, baby…"

For a moment, they were sealed together by those needs, even undefined as they were. It was just a feeling. A deep, churning knowledge that he soothed something inside her. A thing she'd never named, because it conflicted with everything the rest of the world expected her to be.

What a good girl was.

A decent girl.

She'd always ignored the darker side of her nature. At least until Syon had ripped into her world and set it loose. What did that make her? She wasn't sure. Only that she felt closer to him than to any other person on the globe.

"I should have said dinner," Syon groaned when the alarm went off at noon.

"That or we shouldn't have watched the sun come up." Kate kicked at the bedding and stumbled toward the kitchen. "Coffee."

She wasn't sure if it was a demand or a plea, only that it was an absolute necessity. She held a mug under the machine for the first half cup before putting the pot in place and taking the mug into the bathroom with her. She headed for the second bathroom in the suite, because Syon was in the shower, and she needed to get herself together.

Just the idea of meeting his parents woke her up.

It was a bolt of fear that also left her giddy.

She fussed over her clothing, looking for something just right.

"Perfect."

She turned to find Syon in the doorway. His hair was still slightly wet but styled back from his face instead of spiked out. In place of his normal leather was a pair of jeans and a cotton shirt.

Kate turned to show him the front of the dress she was wearing. Several others were lying on the bed where she'd tossed them after vetoing them. This one had a scoop neck that didn't show off too much, tapered in at the waist, and fell in a loose skirt to just above her knee. She'd slipped into some ankle boots with a low heel.

"Are you sure you want me to come?" She could have bitten off her tongue for voicing her insecurity. But as usual, with Syon, she lacked all sense of control.

"Yeah." He held out his hand for her. "Double sure when I see that you're taking it so seriously." He looked at the discarded dresses. "My dad's going to mess with

you though, and my mom is going to try to decide if
you're knocked up."

"I'm not going," Kate groused at him, turning to look
at her reflection again, specifically at her waistline.

He came into the room and put his arms around her
from behind. She was wrapped in his power again so
easily. "Yes, you are," he whispered against her neck.
"I need you to."

She drew in a deep breath, feeling like something had
hit her in the chest. Syon was watching her in the mirror,
a soft sense of vulnerability in his eyes.

She melted.

"So what's for lunch?"

He kissed her neck again before capturing her hand
and pulling her toward the door. The elevator ride down
was quick and quiet.

But Cid stepped up as they entered the lobby. "Word
with you, mate?"

The implication was clear. Cid wanted her to shove off.

"I've got a lunch date with my parents, Cid."

"Yeah, about that." Cid tried to crowd her.

"Kate's coming," Syon said as he stepped to the side
to make sure there was room for both of them.

"Got the car waiting for you," Cid offered smoothly.
"But this thing with Kate…it's rather new, isn't it?"

"I pay you to manage the tour, not my personal life."

Syon tried to take off, but Cid cut him off, stepping
up close so their words didn't drift. "It's all the same
thing. I explained that to you before I agreed to take
Toxsin on. You take the girl, the tabloids get wind of it,
and suddenly, you aren't the stud any longer."

Syon's fingers tightened around hers.

For a moment, she thought she imagined it.

But she didn't.

"Deal with it, Cid."

Syon's voice was low, but that didn't keep her from hearing how menacing his tone was. A clear warning from the hard, business side of his nature. Cid's eyes widened, but he covered his shock with a smile and a pat on Syon's shoulder.

"Have a blast," the road manager said as he stepped aside.

Syon pulled her along beside him, but she felt Cid watching them. Several of the polo-shirted guys lined the walkway from the hotel doors to where a tinted-window SUV was waiting. Even at noon, there were still a scattering of fans hanging out in the hope of gaining a glimpse of their idols. Paparazzi came out of the foliage, snapping away with their cameras as they worked the telephoto lenses with expert fingers.

The car door shut behind Kate, giving her a barrier to take refuge behind. She let out a sigh before she realized Syon was watching her.

"Does it wig you out?" he asked, retreating behind a stony expression.

"Ah…what part?"

His eyes narrowed. "Cid again."

"He is pissing on his turf a little aggressively."

Syon snorted. "Not sure I care for the visual, considering I'm the 'turf' in question."

Kate shrugged. "Better than me saying he's humping your leg. Because he is."

His expression turned hungry.

"Stay." She had a single finger pointed at him, and it

felt like she was trying to hold a grizzly bear back with a cheese knife. "I am not meeting your parents with my wits dulled by your kisses."

He made a low growling sound.

Kate reached for a can of soda sitting in the center console and shook it up, fingering the tab and pointing the opening toward him. He laughed, but the sound was dark and dangerous.

"Until later," he promised.

―∾∾―

"I'm a bit confused," Syon's mother drawled out in a sweet voice that was nothing more than a different sort of aggression. She fixed Kate with her blue eyes and fluttered her eyelashes innocently.

"I thought I saw pictures of her over one of the other band member's shoulders. But now you're telling me this is your girlfriend?"

"You can't believe everything you see in the tabloids, Mom."

"Hmmm…I suppose," his mother said as she tore off the top of a sugar packet and dumped the tiny grains into her iced tea.

Syon reached beneath the table and squeezed Kate's hand. His mother didn't miss it.

"Oh, for Christ's sake." She put down her iced tea a little too hard, and some of the dark liquid sloshed over the rim of the glass. "What am I doing wrong now? I can't ask a legitimate question when I know for a fact that I saw a picture of this woman over your drummer's shoulder? I'm being too difficult, is that it, Kevin? Too demanding in expecting the woman you bring home to meet your mother be more than one you pass around your band?"

"Now, now," Syon's father interceded. "You know what the psychologist said. Kevin has sensitive boundaries."

Syon's mother nodded at her husband. "I think *sensitive* is too mild a word." She took another sip of her tea and fixed Kate with a look. "So what do you do, young lady?"

Kate had no idea what she ate for lunch. Syon looked like he didn't taste his meal either. When the check came, his dad tried to pay it. By the time they were back in the car, Kate found herself looking at her cell phone.

"That was the longest two hours of my life."

Syon had leaned his head back and closed his eyes. He stiffened as her comment sunk in.

"That was an attempt at levity," she said.

Syon opened his eyes and looked at her. "I guess it was a lot to ask you to sit through that."

Kate moved closer. Syon caught her head and put it on his chest. For a long moment, they just sat together, the sound of the car engine the only noise.

"I liked it," she said at last.

"Bullshit." Syon released her head and looked out the window.

She climbed onto his lap and cupped the sides of his face with her hands to bring his attention back to her.

"I did," she said firmly. "I see where you get your passion from. Your mom has a definite streak of eccentric in her."

Syon snorted. "She's that, alright." He closed his arms around her, holding her for another long moment. "But you couldn't have enjoyed that."

"I enjoyed knowing you wanted me to see it…Kevin."
In a way, it was cool to see him being treated like everyone else, his parents calling him by his birth name.

Understanding flashed in his eyes, and something
else, something very vulnerable. They were standing on
that uncertain ground again. That place where what they
felt didn't make a whole lot of sense.

It was a damned scary place to be. Uncertain to say
the least.

"And I'm relieved," Kate added.

Syon lifted an eyebrow. "How so?"

"If you ever meet my mom, you'll understand."

His lips curled. He leaned forward and kissed her.
She melted into his embrace, enjoying the way her
senses took over.

Because it was a lot less scary than thinking.

Chapter 6

"You rock, Kate."

Taz was excited. His speech took on a slight Asian accent as he turned and looked at himself in the full-length, three-sided mirror she had set up in her makeshift shop.

"I love it."

He did. Kate watched the way he stroked the lapels of the Loki jacket. She'd even made the under jerkin and pants for him.

"You got all the details."

"You guys aren't putting up with me for my good looks. My partner deserves some credit. He got all the leather and trim. Percy is a detail queen." Kate gave credit where credit was due.

Taz shot her a grin. "You're pretty cute, for not being Asian."

"Thanks."

"Got to go show Drake," Taz said. "He's a comic book hound too. He'll be smoked that he didn't think to ask you for something. Should warn you, he likes to be a pirate."

"I'm here if he wants something."

Taz took off, his pace brisk.

Kate took a moment to look at her design book. The Loki jacket was there, drawn out with notes. She'd changed it just a little and then knocked out some limited-edition jackets to be sold at designer cost. The contracted rights would be put to good use. Drake liked to be a pirate? She smiled as she started to sketch out a jacket.

But her neck was killing her. Stiff from too many hours bent over her machines and cutting table. She rolled her shoulders as she stood up and tried to work some of the stiffness loose.

Kate closed up her design book and went back to sorting through the hides, to decide what project to start next. The costume rack was filling up. She enjoyed looking at the growing number of pants on it. Now that the immediate concern was covered, she could turn to doing detail work. She toyed with slashing, making up samples to show to the band members for consideration. The day wore on, the hotel becoming quiet as everyone made their way over to the arena where the concert was going to be held. She checked the time, making sure she wasn't running late.

"We need to talk."

Kate looked up, the note in Cid's voice warning her that the road manager was in the mood for a fight. One look at his face, and she was certain of it. He wasn't afraid to assert his authority.

Piss on his turf, you mean.

But that didn't necessarily make him a turd. Life was a competitive sport. Everyone had to scratch out their spot and defend it.

She laid down her scissors. "Yes?"

"Are the terms of your contract unclear?" he began.

Kate didn't even blink. "Not a bit."

Cid made a wide gesture with his hands. "Oh, I think

there is a huge discrepancy. You don't seem to understand what you're here to do."

She pointed toward the rolling rack of finished pants. It was sectioned off by performer, and she'd even added one of the vests Ramsey was so fond of.

"If there is a problem with my production rate—"

"There's a problem with the fact that you're in here making costumes when I've hired you to make stage clothing," Cid fired out. "Taz doesn't need to be wasting his time playing adolescent dress up. We don't have room on this tour for someone who doesn't have their attention focused on what brings in the money."

"Oh, I'm focused."

Cid was every inch the asshole she'd decided he was. The need to pound her down was glittering in his eyes.

But she wasn't going to take it.

"If you want an accounting of my time, I'll give it to you. Including overtime, which"—she lifted her hand when he tried to interrupt—"is clearly outlined by the terms of my contract. I have produced more than sufficient product, and what I do in my off time is a private matter between me and my client."

"You work for me," Cid insisted.

"During the allotted hours only. Because travel time is part of my hours," she said. "I'll get you that time sheet."

She picked up her shears and looked back at her cutting table. It was a bold move, but slightly more professional than telling the jerk off. He stood there a moment.

"Better be in my inbox by the end of the day." Cid stormed out of the suite.

Asshole...

She'd never met a more fitting subject for the word. What worried her was how crafty the road manager was. He'd planned his little shakedown for when Syon and the rest of the band were doing sound checks. There was also the fact that not a single member of his entourage was in attendance. Which was a real rarity. Cid liked to have someone ready to fetch his cappuccino; that was for sure.

No witnesses.

His word against hers.

Something tingled on her nape, a feeling of foreboding that she had trouble shaking free.

Well, she wasn't going to worry about it.

Nope.

After all, she was a warrior princess.

———

"Kate, my dear."

Kate was suddenly wide-awake. Percy only called her "my dear" when he was going to unleash a life lesson on her.

"What's wrong, Percy?" More importantly, what details did Percy know?

"There is rather more of you on the pages of *Roadkill*'s newest issue than I've ever seen," her partner delivered in a dry tone.

"*Roadkill*?" she asked, trying to place the name. A memory stirred. "I am going to kill Cid!"

Syon lifted his head and sat up, giving her a hard look. She spun around and stood up as Ramsey appeared in the doorway.

"I'm going to pull his balls off," she said into the phone but directing it toward Syon.

Percy attempted a mediation. "Now, Kate, do I have to remind you of how many cameras are on you when you travel with Toxsin?"

"I was in a closed room. With a locked door."

"Oh." Percy made a low sound on the other end of the line. "In that case, his nuts have it coming."

Syon suddenly plucked the cell phone from her hand. "Percy, Kate will get back to you."

He hung up as Kate turned on him. "You don't end my calls."

"When you're contemplating castrating my road manager, I do."

Syon tossed her dress at her, and she realized she'd been standing there in nothing. She was too mad to care. "That film crew has plastered nude pictures of me in their monthly issue."

Understanding flashed through Syon's eyes.

"Wait, how'd they get a shot of your tits?" Ramsey asked.

Syon's lips twitched, a smug look entering his eyes. Kate's temper sizzled.

"We were in a closed room. The door was locked," she hissed. "The terms of the contract concerning the use of my image sure as hell don't extend through locked doors!"

Syon nodded. "I know. I'll talk to Cid about it."

"I don't need you to fight my battles for me." Kate propped her hands on her hips. "I can tell Cid he's an asshole all by myself."

Ramsey snorted. "I believe her."

"I told you, Kate, privacy—"

"Yeah, is a casualty, but I was doing a fitting on you."

"What?" Ramsey looked up from a cell phone he'd

pulled out of his pocket. He pointed at the screen. "This look was missing from my fitting."

Ramsey turned the phone toward her, giving her a view of her bare torso, a saucy smile, and her own hands on her breasts.

"That's because she's my girlfriend," Syon said.

Kate snorted.

Syon swung his attention back to her, and his gaze had gone hard. "Take a hike, Rams."

"Later." Ramsey was gone, leaving her with Syon.

She was halfway into the dress, but Syon plucked it from her hands and pulled it off.

"My girlfriend," he repeated.

She stepped back, the warning in his tone chafing her. "I'm a little preoccupied with the issue on the table."

"I'll deal with Cid."

She moved around the bed and grabbed another dress that had landed on the floor sometime the night before. "I dealt with him before, and I'll—"

"Over what?" Syon asked pointedly.

Kate managed to get the dress on, but she didn't feel very secure.

Ha! Try hanging over an abyss...

Yeah, that was about the way she felt, but she wasn't going to admit it. Syon was distracting her as it was, slowly stalking her across the suite.

"Over what, Kate?"

He wasn't going to drop it, but the topic was at least a diversion from the idea of having to define their relationship status.

"I made something for Taz," she informed him.

"The Loki suit?"

She nodded. "Cid got in my face about it. Accused me of not being focused and understanding the terms of my contract, and helping Taz ignore his responsibilities."

Syon nodded. "And you did…what?"

She sent him a satisfied grin. "I quoted my contract and sent him a time sheet. I made the Loki suit on my own time. I like Taz."

"But you didn't tell me that Cid got in your face."

"That would have been unprofessional," she answered.

His lips rose into a menacing smile. "Because I'm your boyfriend."

She drew in a stiff breath, but a second later he had her crowded against the wall. He wasn't actually touching her but had his forearms braced on either side of her shoulders.

She shuddered anyway.

The scent of him filled her senses. He still smelled sexy. It was more potent than anything she'd ever experienced. The last month of excess should have worn the edge down, but the need swirling in her belly was still razor sharp.

He tilted his head, and his breath hit her ear. He captured her wrists and pulled her arms above her head, holding them there as he licked her earlobe.

"Boyfriend…"

His voice was raspy but full of demand. She shivered, excitement pulsing through her just about as fast as her uncertainty was growing. She was folding, losing all sense of boundaries, just letting him wipe them away.

"I'm not sure I can…"

He pulled his head back, locking stares with her. "Does it look like this is any easier for me?"

She searched his eyes, feeling exposed but needing to know if he felt the same.

"You scare me. The way you just sweep aside everything else." She wasn't sure why the words slipped out.

"I know the feeling."

He bit out the words and pressed his mouth down on top of hers to take shelter in passion. She kissed him back, relieved to have something familiar to focus on.

But it was hollow.

The kiss died. Syon pulled away and pressed his forehead to hers. That hollowness wouldn't dissipate. It felt like it was sitting inside her chest, carving out a hole—settling in for the long haul.

"Boyfriend," she said.

He stiffened, the grip on her wrist tightening. She leaned forward and kissed his jaw. "Boyfriend," she repeated softly. *"My boyfriend."*

"Why was that hard?" he asked.

He suddenly turned his back on her, leaving her leaning against the wall.

"Because everyone wants you." She felt like every fear she'd had about getting kicked to the curb was about to hit her. "How could I hold your attention for long?"

Her self-confidence was nothing but a puddle on the floor. It stung, and she stayed against the wall because she honestly wasn't sure if her knees would hold.

He turned around, letting her see the torment in his eyes. It knocked the breath out of her.

"They want the Marquis," he bit out. "That thing Cid gives them. It isn't me."

"Part of it is."

He shook his head, but she pushed away from the wall, suddenly feeling her confidence swell.

"Yes, it is. You have an allure that you aren't afraid to let people see. Cid is riding on your coattails because it's so powerful. I felt it the second I saw you. It was like a punch to the gut." She suddenly stopped, face-to-face with her own insecurities. "I'm not that brave. I can't let people see that part of me. You do. That's why they scream. You make it okay. It's that permission that they crave."

"It's a hunger," he said.

He took a step toward her, making her mouth go dry. "Yeah, it is," she said.

"A selfish one," he continued. "I need to be on that stage. The animal inside me needs to be out, to be seen."

She nodded. He reached for her, pulling her against him.

"And I need you to be here."

He pushed his hand through her hair, gripping it and holding her head still as he hovered over her lips. "Tell me you'll be here, for me."

She pushed her hand beneath his shirt, their skin connecting with that powerful jolt that thrilled her.

"I will."

His lips twitched just a tiny amount before they thinned with hunger. Sensation went speeding through her, shaking her down to her core. He caught the fabric of her dress and pulled it up and over her head. She made a soft sound of encouragement, her skin heating up.

She reached out, finding the buttons on his fly and forcing her fingers to work them loose. His cock sprang through, hard and ready the moment she finished. She stroked it, purring at the satin-smooth skin.

"I can't wait," Syon confessed.

He reached down and caught the backs of her thighs, picking her up and spreading her legs as he moved her back to the wall. He pushed her against it, his cock tunneling into her flesh, slipping deep because she was so wet.

"Mine," he grunted, pulling back and straining back toward her. "Mine... Mine... *Mine!*"

He punctuated every word with a hard thrust. Driving deep, touching that spot inside her that sent a current of pure rapture through her. It forced the breath from her, leaving her moaning.

"Yeah, baby... Let me hear you..."

There wasn't any real choice. But she didn't really want one. All she craved was the next connection between their flesh. She was suspended between time, falling through a crack in reality. There was only the two of them and the way they were satisfied only by each other. She was his; he was her addiction.

She craved him.

Would have done anything to keep him feeding her needs.

She dug her fingernails into his shoulders, trying to lift her hips toward him. He flattened her back against the wall, growling at her while he pumped against her, forcing her to let him set the pace.

"Mine."

It was more than a word.

It was an entire idea.

Her entire reality at that moment.

It shattered in a mind-numbing jolt of light, searing as it burned through her. She was caught in its grip, wrung by the power of it until she ended up as nothing but a pulsing lump clinging to Syon as he ground himself into her and let his passion explode. She purred as he emptied himself into her, the hot spurt of his seed intensifying the intimacy of the moment—binding them together with trust.

Everything was base, primal, and savage.

And the animal inside her wanted that last confirmation that she'd satisfied him.

Someone laid their fist on the suite door.

"We need to roll!"

Syon lifted his head and let her legs slide down. He cupped her chin and kissed her, a soft compression of his lips against hers that made her tremble with how tender it was.

—⁓—

"You don't need to turn in a time sheet again."

Kate looked up, catching a look from Syon as he took a final glance in the mirror. Everyone was amped up again, the arena full as Toxsin prepared to take the stage.

"You didn't need to get involved."

Syon turned away from the mirror, looking every inch the rock god he was: his makeup perfect, his skin hot and smelling like leather and man animal. The heavy eyeliner accentuated the slant of his eyes, making him once again into the Goblin King.

"You didn't ask me to get involved. But I needed to make sure things were clear. You're an artist."

He'd stopped in front of her. It might look like he was talking to her, but she knew him better than that. He was making a point of bringing up the subject during an

official moment. The makeup girls were listening, along
with at least eight of Cid's crew. Two private security
men were there, pigtailed ear devices on as they watched
everything from behind dark glasses. A sound guy was
trolling around, checking the small personal sound
systems attached to each of the band members. Two of
Cid's girls were there as well, but the road manager was
outside the performers' room, chatting up some VIPs.

Syon leaned down and kissed her. It was soft and
quick, but it felt like a brand.

"Time to get down into the seats." Cid had walked
into the doorway, his standard, happy-go-lucky grin
in place.

"Sure." Kate walked toward the door.

"Got to take that." Cid reached for the glass in her
hand. "Stadium rules. No booze in the stands."

Kate tossed back the last bit and relinquished the
glass. One of the polo-shirted guys guided her through
the backstage maze. Thick power cords ran along the
floor. There were barricades set up to form walkways
from the back of the stage to the performers' room. The
lights were already flashing, a preshow soundtrack playing over the speaker system.

The crowd was already filling the stadium with a dull
roar, like distant thunder. It was only going to grow in
intensity until Syon whipped them up into a storm of
spine-tingling climaxes.

She was pumped up for it, edging her way into the
crowd forcefully when people didn't want to let her get
to the seat reserved for her. The security guy made them
move aside. He reached out and snagged the "reserved"
sign off the seat and made sure she'd slid into it before

the crowd converged. Surrounding the catwalk and stage was the mosh pit. People had arrived hours earlier to fill it, and they were pressing up against the stage without mercy for anyone in their way. They were there to be in the crush; no one was interested in maintaining distance.

The crowd surged toward the stage as the performers entered. She felt it as much as saw it—a wave that seemed to lift the crowd off its feet and send it crashing into the music. Kate was carried along with it, giddy to be a part of the exuberance.

The concert went on and carried her deeper and deeper into the current. She lost track of what was happening, Syon the only fixed point in her world. Everything else blurred, until it was just a backsplash of colored smears that spun in a crazy circle. People pushed against her, dancing, well, maybe it was dancing. Maybe it was more of a primal straining.

Rubbing.

Groping.

She stopped, trying to push someone's hand off her butt. But concentration was impossible. In fact, holding her head up felt like too much effort. Her neck had lost all its strength; her eyelids felt heavy.

There were just hands everywhere. She felt them but didn't really understand what was happening. She was leaning on the catwalk but moved her hands to push the groping hands off her. When she did, she slid down, falling beneath the weight of the next wave of people surging toward the stage. They flooded in, filling the spot she'd occupied, stepping on her as Syon and Ramsey whipped them into the last frenzy of the show.

Pain tried to make it through the haze clouding her

thoughts, but at least the haze was thick enough to block most of it. It bore her into a tunnel of darkness that made the impact of feet insignificant.

Yeah…everything was insignificant.

———

"Can you tell me your name?"

Kate rolled away from the light being aimed into her eye.

"Do you know what's happening?"

Whoever it was, they lifted her eyelid and aimed the light right back in her eye. It felt like a needle being shoved down the center of her pupil. She tried to roll the other way, pulling her legs up to fend off the spinning.

"It's Kate Napier."

She turned over, lifting her eyelids a tiny bit. There was something about the sound of that voice that she knew, but the world beyond her eyelids was a swirling mess. She sank back down into the abyss of unconsciousness.

Syon fought to get close to Kate, but the medics were pushing him back. Cops were holding people back, the blue-and-red flash of their emergency vehicles casting an eerie glow over the scene. Ramsey was suddenly there, the only person who could pull him back.

"She needs a hospital."

———

"I'm going to fucking kill someone."

The security guard near the emergency-room door sent him a warning glance that Syon ignored.

"Let's watch what you say, mate. No need to say things you don't mean."

Cid tried to hook his arm, but Syon turned on him, curling his hand in Cid's shirt front. "Why the fuck wasn't someone watching her?"

He couldn't get to Kate's side, but he could sure as hell deal with his own people.

Cid covered his hand, smiling as the guard eyed them. He waited until the security guard looked away before answering. "Didn't know she needed babysitting."

Ramsey pulled him away, which likely saved Cid from getting his nose broken. Syon let Ramsey pull him across the waiting area before he shrugged free.

Beyond the doors behind the security guard, Kate was being treated. The local PD was struggling to keep the fans outside the emergency room as Syon and his bandmates paced the floor.

Two men finally came through the doors, heading toward him. "Syon Braden?"

"Yeah, I want to see her."

"This way."

"Just a minute." Cid slid in between them. "Where are you taking my friends?"

"Somewhere we can talk." One of the men held up a badge.

"Fine by me." Syon pushed past Cid, but Cid shoved him back.

"I think you can do that only with a lawyer present."

The detective turned and looked at Cid. "Since you've got something to hide, by all means, call your legal representative."

"What the hell?" Syon demanded. "I want to see my girlfriend."

"Your girlfriend—if she is your girlfriend—has

tested positive for gamma hydroxybutyrate," the cop said under his breath. "Now, maybe slipping girls roofies is normal in your world, but in my county, I won't let it slide. She could have been trampled to death beneath that crowd."

"Shit," Ramsey cussed.

The cop raked them with a cold stare. "She's under my protection, and I promise you, I'm going to do my best to get her to finger which one of you slipped her the spiked drink. So I can arrest you, celebrity or not."

"You're way off the mark," Syon warned.

"I don't think so," the cop answered. He dug a business card out of his shirt pocket and tossed it toward Cid. "Call your lawyer. I think he's going to be needed."

"Fuck this." Syon started toward the emergency-room doors, Ramsey on his heels.

"Yeah." Taz joined in.

A second later, they were all slammed against the wall, the herd of uniformed officers outside the doors swarming in to take them down. Cid was in the corner, frantically making a call on his cell phone as they were handcuffed and hauled into squad cars.

—◆◆◆—

"It's been a long time since we've been arrested," Drake observed. "Sucks that we're not even drunk or in a titty bar."

Syon lifted his hand and flipped him off. Ramsey mimicked the motion from where he sat on the other side of him. They were lined up in front of a pathetic television with the rest of the Saturday night jailbirds. Behind them, the booking officers were receiving the night's offerings of prostitutes, drug dealers, and public intoxication offenders. Those who were orderly ended up in the chairs to await bail, while the rest were hauled down the hallway and locked into cells to sober up or calm down.

Syon nearly ripped the sleeves from his jail-issued top, he gripped it so hard. Waiting for bail sucked and was driving him insane.

"Cid's falling down on the job. My little sister could have had us out of here by now," Taz complained. "My grandmother could have done it too, and she doesn't even speak very good English."

"They're stalling," Ramsey stated, "waiting for Kate to sober up enough to finger someone."

"Can't wait for her to do it," Syon said ominously.

Ramsey shared a look with him. They both returned their attention to the television in front of them, because the deputy assigned to watch the orderly crowd was doing his job. The choice was simple. Sit and watch television, or get locked into a cell with an added charge of resisting.

It left Syon sitting, which was a torment he was unprepared for. Kate was lying in a hospital, and he was stuck in a plastic chair.

Yeah, he was going to kill someone.

―⁂―

"Ms. Napier, I need you to help me protect other innocent women from becoming the victims of this sort of crime."

Kate drew in a deep breath. Her head was splitting, the light from the ceiling feeling like a laser beam carving up her brain.

"Who gave you the drink?"

"Deputy Jenson?" Forcing her brain to function took a lot. The cop nodded, doing his best to give her a winning grin.

Not a chance, mister. She could see the calculating look in his brown eyes. "I had one drink. Backstage."

"Who gave it to you?" he pressed.

The curtain suddenly moved aside. "You don't have to answer that question."

A man in a sharp black suit walked up to the foot of her bed and extended a business card to the deputy. "I'm here to represent Ms. Napier and ensure she has proper time to recover before making any statements. The attending doctor assures me she is in no condition to be questioned at this time, and any information you have obtained will be considered tainted by her condition."

The deputy slowly stood up. He took the card, his actions stiff. "Tell your clients I'm going to do everything in my power to lock them up. Maybe I can't keep their kind out of my county, but when they bring date rape drugs with them, I'm going to see them charged."

"Syon is my boyfriend. He doesn't have to drug me," Kate protested.

"Ms. Napier has nothing further to say at this time."

The newly arrived lawyer managed to get Deputy Jenson out of the room.

"Thanks. Where's Syon?"

"Being released from jail."

Kate blinked as that sank in.

"I'm Carl Pearson."

She lifted her hand to shake his but stopped when she spotted all the bruises on her hand. Two of her fingers were swollen black and blue, but at least they weren't broken.

"Maybe we shouldn't shake hands today," Carl said.

"Yeah. Can I get out of here?"

What she wanted was Syon. It was pathetic how much she wanted him near. She had no sense of time, and there wasn't a window in sight. A low rumble of hushed voices came from outside her room.

"I'm working on getting you discharged. The doctor was considering having you admitted for observation, but he seems satisfied with your CAT scan and the promise you'll seek medical attention if you have any vertigo or nausea."

"Guess that explains the headache."

Carl pulled his phone out of his pocket without a care for the "no cell phones" sign posted on the wall. He started texting someone as she took a moment to look at her hands and arms.

She was covered in bruises. Little ones from spike heels and larger ones that must have come from the guys in the audience. It was all still a haze, but considering how her arms looked, she decided she didn't need to remember being trampled.

"Kate, sweetie—"

Her eyes had started closing again when she heard Percy. Or at least thought she did. It was a nice dream.

"Holy Moses!"

Kate opened her eyes, recognizing Percy's brand of profanity.

Percy stood in the doorway, his eyes widening to the size of half dollars. "Oh my God! Someone needs to die."

"What are you doing here, Percy?" she asked.

Percy came in with his husband, Steve, on his heels. "I got on the first plane I could, of course. That hospital gown is criminal."

"You didn't need to do that," Kate protested, but Steve was carrying a duffel bag that he unzipped, pulling out a familiar-looking tunic. "I take it back. I really need people who understand me right now."

What you need is Syon...

She tried to ignore her pitiful thoughts and focused on getting dressed because it took her one step closer to escaping the hospital.

Her knees shook when she stood up, and her back ached, but she took a couple of steps and then a few more, until she'd escaped the room. Percy and Steve were right outside the door.

"I really need to get out of here."

She wasn't going to mince words about it. She was desperate. The hospital was pressing in on her.

Percy and Steve took over, bundling her into a car and filling a huge bag of prescriptions before Steve slid behind the wheel of the rental car, but he didn't start the engine.

"Now, Kate honey..."

She looked at Percy, recognizing his serious tone.

"We can go anywhere you want," Percy said gently. "Home?"

"I've got a contract to fulfill."

Percy made a little sound under his breath. "Cid spent a great deal of time making sure I recognized how much he understood your need to go home and recover."

"Cid is an asshole."

Steve flipped her a thumbs-up in agreement.

"He's also trying to shove me off his turf."

"While I agree with you," Percy said, "I do have to admit that you look a little rough around the edges. I'd be completely insensitive if I didn't offer to take you home."

"You'd also call me a wimp, and I am not a wimp."

Percy smiled at her. "Well...not out loud. At least not for a week or two."

Steve drove her back toward the hotel they'd been staying at. The two Toxsin coaches were pulled up along the side of the curb, a steady line of polo-shirted team members bringing luggage out and storing it in the compartments underneath.

Cid made a beeline for her the moment he realized she was heading toward one of the coaches.

"Kate, I thought your partner and I came to an understanding."

Steve started to come around the car, but Kate stepped up to deal with Cid. "An understanding would be great. I work here, and so do you. I don't quit."

Cid pushed his hands into his suit pockets and grinned at her. "Well...okay then."

It was easier than she'd thought it would be, and left her feeling guilty for thinking he was such an asshole. The guy was doing his job. He was dedicated; there was no missing that. She needed to see the glass as half full.

"This is very nice," Percy exclaimed as they made it up into the coach.

"I'd like to party here." Steve winked at Percy.

Kate sat down on the sofa, her strength suddenly spent.

"Here." Percy held out a glass of water and several pills. "You get some beauty rest and call me tomorrow."

Kate handed the glass back when she was done and sent him a grateful look. "Thanks, guys. I'm sorry you came all this way."

"Don't be silly," Percy said. "But I am going to have a little talk with that road manager for not having a release of liability on file for you. Where did he learn his job anyway? At least he flew us out here first-class."

"He better have."

She was getting sleepy and laid down on the sofa. There was a soft snap as Percy buckled one of the seat belts around her waist.

Relief went through her.

Okay, it was pitiful but true nonetheless. She was still there, still near Syon. The idea of being separated from the tour loomed over her like a thunderstorm as she drifted off to sleep.

But it wasn't a deep one.

She needed something.

Someone actually.

She ached for him, yearning for him as she drifted half in and out of sleep.

Syon…

~~~

"She's out." Cid caught Syon's arm as he launched himself at the steps of the coach. "Doc gave her a bag of prescription meds."

Syon stopped, uncertain.

"Oh, for God's sake!" Percy exclaimed from where he was still standing near the coach. "Get in there, you big, glorious bruiser. You'd better be glad I'm gay, because you don't know a thing about reading women."

Syon blinked. "Where did you come from?"

"Called them in to take care of Kate," Cid explained. "Seems we don't have a power of attorney for her."

"And you call yourself a manager," Percy said. "Kate and I exchanged papers years ago, because you never know."

"Had to make sure she would be taken care of," Cid finished. "Even if you weren't in the can, boyfriends can't sign treatment papers."

"I owe you, Cid."

He knew he needed to question something, but at that moment, there was nothing between him and Kate. He bounded up the steps and froze when he got a look at her.

Kate drew in a deeper breath and smiled when she caught Syon's scent. She almost didn't open her eyes, too afraid she was dreaming.

She wasn't.

He was there on a knee beside the sofa. She tried to smile but winced because her face was bruised. His expression tightened, rage flickering in his eyes.

"Don't." She reached out to smooth his jawline. "Smile… Just…stay here…for a bit…"

He reached out and pushed the button on the buckle of the seat belt. A second later he used both hands to pull the sofa out into a double bed. She smiled, scooting over to make room for him.

Now she could sleep.

Syon tucked Kate against his side and rested his chin on her head.

There was no fucking way he could smile.

But he could breathe at last.

Kate's scent filled his senses as the bus started to rumble. Ramsey opened the door and peeked in. Syon saw the look on his friend's face. A look of indecision. Ramsey let out a little huff and came up the steps. He stood there, his gaze sweeping Kate from head to toe before he turned around and opened one of the cabinets. Ramsey tossed a blanket over them before he disappeared down the steps.

The coach shifted into gear, and Syon cradled her close.

There was no fucking way he was letting her out of his sight.

There were hangovers, and then there were painkiller-induced hangovers.

Kate woke up staring at the ceiling of another hotel suite. The crown molding was perfect and painted a nice mellow shade of cream.

She groaned because she couldn't recall getting into the room. Her mouth was drier than the Sahara, and she was pretty sure it would be a whole lot simpler to list the parts of her body that didn't hurt versus the ones that did.

When she sat up, she caught sight of the bedside table. Neatly lined up on it were three prescription bottles and a folded card with her name on it. She picked it up and looked inside.

"Sound check rehearsal."

Three little words had never made her smile so easily. She read them a few more times before finding her way to the bathroom. An hour later, she'd decided she was going to live. She was dotted with bruises, but most of them were on her arms.

Sure better than losing an eye.

She wandered down the hallway to the room where her shop was.

Or at least was supposed to be.

The rolling racks were there, but none of her machines or boxes. One of Cid's guys came in a few seconds after her.

"No one thought you'd be up to working today. Afraid your gear is in the music coach, and it's at the arena."

"Oh. Okay. No problem."

She wandered back into the hallway, but she was anything but tired. It was sort of strange to get outside while the sun was shining. She'd been a nocturnal creature for the better part of two months.

Had it really been that long?

She opened the calendar on her phone and scrolled through the days, looking at the venues Toxsin had played, the states she'd been through. Hotels were blending together. The trees had their fall colors on now, and the hotel was situated in a beautiful location. She walked past neatly manicured greenways and several fountains. She turned her arms over, hoping to pick up a little bit of a tan to help blend the bruises. But honestly, it wasn't that bad. Now that the drugs were out of her system, her head felt like it wasn't going to split. Maybe it was time to go on the wagon for a spell. She'd obviously been undervaluing the lack of a hangover. She needed some grapefruit juice and a detox.

"Hey…Kate!"

She looked up, and a camera flash popped. She blinked, momentarily blinded.

"How did you get the bruises?"

There were another couple of flashes.

"Did Syon Braden use you as his sex slave?"

There was a live-action camera as well as the still ones in front of her. They crowded her, blocking the walkway.

"Excuse me." She tried to get through the wall of bodies.

"Come on, tell us about it."

"How about a look at those tits?"

She put her hands up. "Out of my way."

They only pressed her back. One of the fountains was behind her, bubbling away while the paparazzi tried to pull her in like a fresh kill. She turned around and walked right into the fountain, trudging through the knee-high water to the other side where the path wasn't blocked.

Hotel security was scrambling, trying to push the paparazzi back as someone slid up beside her. She turned her head and came face-to-face with Taz.

Only she'd never seen this side of him.

There was a hard look in his eyes as he glanced over her shoulder at the reporters. They instantly shut up, and she didn't blame them.

Taz looked ready to kill.

His black eyes were like obsidian, his expression tight, and she realized the little zip she'd heard was a set of ultralight nunchaku. He flipped them a few times in the air as he pushed her back behind him.

"We'd better get inside," he said softly, his English heavily accented. "I promised my mother I'd try not to get arrested again. Breaking my promise within twenty-four hours would be a little too hard to explain my way out of. She'd slap my ears good."

The hotel staff was swarming now, but they stayed

well away from Taz. He guided her back into the hotel before he pulled a cell phone from his pocket and held it up to his ear.

"Got her."

Once they were in the elevator, he transformed back into the happy-go-lucky guy she'd come to know him as.

"Aw…" was all she got out.

He shrugged. "Told you I was a bad guy." He swung the nunchaku through the air before they reached the top floor.

More like badass.

"You sort of freaked everyone out. I think Syon is going to kill Cid for letting you out of sight, today of all days. Why didn't you take your phone?"

"What? I just went for a walk."

Taz swung the nunchaku through the air again. "And how'd that work out?"

She suddenly recalled Syon's warning to her the first time the tour bus had stopped.

Fans can get a little crazy…

"I guess I didn't really think about it."

The elevator doors slid open, and she heard Syon's voice bouncing between the walls of the hallway.

"Security is your job, Cid. I don't want excuses."

Syon turned toward her, giving her a glimpse of Cid's furious face before she was swept inside one of the presidential suites.

"You're overreacting, Syon."

He slid his hands down her arms and captured her wrists. What made her gasp was the gentleness of his grip. He'd never hurt her before, he knew his strength, but now, he was handling her like glass stemware.

He pulled her into the bedroom and in front of the full-length mirror.

"Overreacting?" His voice was raspy with outrage. "Look at yourself, Kate. I want to put you in a fucking bubble!"

"Oh, please."

She turned on him and ripped his shirt open. "What's that?" She pointed at a three-inch area that was scratched and bruised. "Or that?" On his lower abs was a dark spot the size of a quarter.

He pulled back out of her reach. "I play rough."

"So do I."

He shook his head. "It's not the same thing."

"Bull crap."

She was shaking her head, but he flattened his hands on either side of her face, backing her up against the wall to control her.

It pissed her off, but it also sent a shiver down her spine.

"Someone tried to hurt you, Kate. That isn't the same thing. And it happened right under my fucking nose."

His tone froze her temper. She reached for him, smoothing her hands along his jawline. "You were on stage."

"But I told you to be there…for me."

His voice was full of self-loathing. He pulled away, looking like he was ripping himself apart.

"Don't you dare," she hissed.

He started to cross his arms over his chest, but she launched herself toward him and grabbed his wrist, pulling on it.

"Don't you dare pull away from me." She pushed right into his embrace. "You're my boyfriend, and you're not taking it back."

"Damn it, Kate." He picked her up by her biceps, driving home just how strong he was. "This is serious."

"It sure as hell is. You are not pushing me out of your life over a guilt trip."

Her feet touched the ground, but he held her away from him. His expression was raw. It ripped at her, stabbing into her with white-hot pain.

"It's fear," he said at last, his grip losing its strength. She pushed through his hands and was back against his chest as he shuddered. "A fucking lot worse than guilt. Worse than being jealous." He gripped her head, his fingers twisting in her hair as he fell back against the wall for support. "The only other person I've ever felt like that about is Ramsey."

Kate dug her fingers into his shirt, the thumping of his heart beneath her fingertips making her tremble. He was so close and yet still an eternity away.

He raised her head, locking gazes with her. "It's eating me alive, Kate. This thing between us."

"I know the feeling." They were finally close enough. Both of them laid bare, their feelings in the open.

"Maybe we should let it." Her voice was a raw whisper. She knew without a doubt she couldn't take rejection from him now. It would literally kill her. Forget crash and burn. This would be a soul-deep event.

She stretched up and kissed him. Words were just too hard to deal with. She wanted to feel. In the insane, intense way that only Syon made her feel.

He cupped her face, holding her back as he struggled to decide if he wanted to join her in sensory overload or continue trying to sort what they felt into logical thoughts.

"Maybe we have to see this through to the end. Boyfriend."

His lips thinned. "I don't want Rams to see you naked again."

It might have been a strange admission, unless she factored in everything she knew about him. Once she did that, it fit so amazingly well. He was pulling her closer, deeper into the private world where he hid his personal feelings, that fortress that kept him sane when the world around him demanded every last bit of his personality.

He fitted his mouth against hers, kissing her with a deep, hard motion. The way he moved his lips against hers sent her senses reeling. The touch of his tongue tipped the scales completely, so nothing remained but the need to fling herself into the swirling vortex.

She pulled at his clothing, unwilling to have anything between them. There was a rip as she tugged too hard. Syon pulled away from their kiss long enough for her to pull off his shirt, and before he got a chance to kiss her again, she was working on the fly of his pants.

"Oh yeah…" His cock sprang free. Hard. Hot. Ready.

But she wanted him to be on the edge. She sank down onto her knees as she stroked his length, enjoying the smooth texture of his skin and the hardness it covered.

"Why are you doing that, Kate?"

She cupped his balls and looked up, enjoying the sight of his bare body. Every ripple and ridge of hard male. His eyes were alive with a need that seared her.

"Because I want you to know who you need." She closed her hand around his cock, pumping up and down. "I'm going to suck you off."

And enjoy every second.

She leaned forward and took him inside her mouth. He arched forward, sucking air through his gritted teeth.

"I'm going to show you…why you can't stop thinking about me…"

He caught her head, threading his fingers through her hair as she worked her mouth up and down on his cock.

"Suck me… Oh yeah, use your tongue too…"

His words drove her crazy, pushing the heat up another few degrees. She pumped her hand along his length, moving her head forward and back as she sucked. His breathing became rough as he bowed back. His hips were thrusting toward her, his excitement peaking. She opened as wide as she could, enjoying the moment of having him on the edge while she was still able to think. Every sound coming from him delighted her, because she was pushing him past every limit, every polite boundary, and into that place where only instinct ruled.

"Kate…"

His voice was strained, and she clamped her mouth around his cock, rubbing the underside of the head with her tongue. He groaned and started giving up his load. It was thick and hot. He pumped against her mouth as he came. She sucked it down, and he let out a hoarse cry.

"That was selfish of me." He'd flattened his hands against the wall, his body shaking.

"Maybe it was selfish of me." She stood up, feeling a glow of accomplishment. It was a subtle shift in power between them. A moment when she felt like she had at least a smidgen of control. A time when he was hers.

He slowly grinned, the expression full of promise. "In that case…"

He scooped her up and took her across the suite. He kicked open a bedroom door and deposited her on a bed. That fast, the power shifted back. The bed hadn't even stopped rocking before he had her dress pushed up and her underwear down her legs.

"I'm going to enjoy proving myself to you, baby."

So was she…

Anticipation tingled down her body. He stroked her thighs, the feeling of his hands on her bare skin insanely good. She writhed, already on overload.

"I love seeing you spread out on a bed."

She looked up and caught him studying her. Pleasure tightened his features, a dangerous glint of possessiveness in his eyes. It stole her breath, making her insides churn. She shifted her thighs farther apart, feeling vulnerable, but there was something about the way he watched her that made her yank her dress completely off.

"Yeah…" he growled approvingly.

She fingered the front closure of her bra, unsnapping it and letting the elastic in it pull it off her breasts.

He nodded, reaching down to cup one breast. She stiffened, sensation flooding her. It was always so intense.

He reached farther down, trailing his fingers along her inner thigh. All her nerve endings were snapping with awareness. Her clit was pulsing, but he made her wait, teasing her inner thigh and then the sides of her slit. He pushed her back on the bed, shucking his pants and crawling up to join her.

She purred, savoring the feeling of his bare skin

against hers. He lodged his shoulder against her right leg and settled himself on one elbow.

"I want to play with you…"

He rimmed the opening of her pussy with a fingertip, sinking into the puddle waiting there as she arched with delight.

"Watch you come…"

Her mouth went dry. "Sounds…great."

It was almost impossible to keep her eyes open. But she watched him smile at her, flashing his teeth as something flickered in his eyes.

He was suddenly gone when she blinked. He disappeared into the bathroom as she sat up, frustration biting into her.

But he was back just as suddenly, pushing her onto her back and lodging his shoulder under her right leg so she was almost helpless again. He teased her belly, rubbing his hand up and down it.

"Let's have a threesome."

She stiffened. "What?"

He reached down and lifted something off the bed. She gasped as recognition set in.

"No."

He chuckled at her horror, holding her vibrator without a hint of squeamishness. "Oh yes."

"How did you even know where that was?"

Why had she even packed it?

He chuckled. "I'm obsessed with you. I notice every little detail."

"So you went through my bag?"

He waved the sex toy in the air. "Actually, I saw it when you opened the bag once because the team had hung up all your clothing. We need to get you a modesty bag for it." His expression changed. "But that's not what I want to do with it right now."

He pressed the power button, and the toy started to hum gently on its first setting. The rabbit part of it vibrating while the shaft turned. Syon looked down at her spread body. "I want to watch you come, Kate."

His tone was husky but full of demand. He turned the toy toward her, and she swallowed as her belly tightened unbearably. A little moan got past her lips before she sealed them tight enough. She was torn. Excited but feeling horribly exposed too. She worried her lower lip, and his caramel gaze honed in on the little telltale motion.

"Exciting…isn't it?"

He touched the tip of the vibrator to her, and she jumped, the soft vibration ultraintense.

"I want you to think about me…even when you're using B.O.B."

"I've been ignoring him since I met you."

Syon trailed the tip of the toy through her slit, pausing at the top and pressing it lightly against her clit. She gasped, shuddering as need yanked her away from conscious thought. She just wanted to let her eyes close and sink back into the storm of sensation.

But…she couldn't…really.

"Making a woman climax is a skill." He moved the toy down to the opening of her pussy. Teasing her with an inch of penetration. "I want to prove my worth to you. A lot of guys just get lucky because their partner is humping them back and it happens. I want to do more to you."

"You have," she rasped out. "You always make me…"

He raised an eyebrow when she had trouble getting the word out.

"This time, I'm going to watch, without any interference from my own body." He'd trailed the vibrator up to her clit again. "Isn't that what you just enjoyed doing when you sucked me off?"

She licked her dry lips, realizing she was unmasked. Hating how easily he read her, but at the same time, feeling like it was the most intimate thing she'd ever experienced. "It was."

He pressed the toy forward, giving her a full taste of the vibration against her clit. Her breath caught, a soft sound of delight coming from her.

"So now it's my turn."

She shivered, his words setting off a slow burn, like a fuse she knew was going to set off an explosion. He teased her clit, pushing against it to let her feel the vibration from the sex toy, and then trailing it down to the opening of her pussy. He'd give her an inch, never more, before moving it back up to her clit.

"You're so damned wet…"

She jerked, trying to move, but he had her pinned better than she'd realized. He had his left arm around her thigh and his hand flattened on her belly. She could move her left leg, but it wouldn't do her much good.

"But I want you wetter."

Syon's visage was hard. She could see the demanding side of his nature in control now. He teased her slit and pressed the function button on the vibrator so it started humming faster.

She cried out when he pressed it to her clit.

"Hmmm… I like that sound…"

She twitched; she was nearing that point where the sensation bordered on pain because it was so intense.

"Syon…"

"Not yet, baby." He soothed her, stroking across her belly with his fingers before plunging the vibrator deep into her.

"Oh Christ!"

She was so wet, she heard the sound of the toy sliding into her body. And when it hit her G-spot, she was sure she was going to explode, but he pulled it back before the rabbit portion of it touched her clit.

She snarled at him.

He shifted his attention to her face, locking gazes with her. He plunged the toy back in, watching her as it connected with her clit and G-spot at the same time. She gasped, her mouth open as she felt suspended between heartbeats. She was bucking up toward the toy, Syon working it with short, hard thrusts, watching her the entire time.

"That's the spot," he said softly, menacingly, as he kept thrusting the toy at the same place. "Right there… like that."

She was losing control, slipping into the vortex as the toy hummed. As he worked it. While he watched. She was on display, held down, and yet she didn't feel alone. He was there with her, and when climax claimed her, she watched his eyes narrow with victory.

It was the last thing she noticed for a while. Orgasm burst through her, laying waste to every last thought. There was only the intensity of the pleasure, the twisting and wringing of her muscles before she was dropped into a pile of quivering limbs all warmed in the glow of satisfaction.

When she opened her eyes, Syon had pulled her into his embrace, rolling over onto his back and pillowing her head on his chest.

It wasn't enough.

She needed more.

More something.

She lifted her head and sat up, locking gazes with him. Somehow, the rest of the world was being held outside the door. She could feel it waiting for them, just waiting to suck him away.

"You're mine right now."

He lifted an eyebrow at her statement. Kate swung over him. His cock was hard, jutting up from his lean abs. All she had to do was lower herself. He reached down, making sure her aim was true, thumbing her clit gently as she lowered herself.

"The rest of the damned world can stay the hell on the other side of that door."

"I like the sound of that." He grasped her hips, guiding her, helping her set the rhythm. "I like the feel of it even more."

She rode him, desire building slowly. They were bound together this time, their breathing increasing at the same rate. He sat up, and she twisted her legs around his waist.

"You want control."

He grasped her hair, sealing her lips beneath his in a hard, deep kiss. "With you, I crave it."

He turned her over, putting her on her back again. "I need to know"—his pace was increasing, the bed rocking as he pumped her harder—"need to know I do things to you that no one else ever has…or ever will…"

She gasped, moaning as words began to lose their meaning again. He ground himself deeply into her, their bodies straining toward each other.

"Or ever can."

"You do."

Her voice was only a hoarse rattle. Need had become a desperate thing, beating its wings inside her. They were covered in sweat, their bodies striving to feed their passions. It was a struggle, a hard meeting of flesh that reached a blinding pinnacle. She spun out of control, clinging to the only stable thing in her universe.

Him.

He wasn't just a person. He was the foundation of her existence. The center of her being.

And it scared the absolute shit out of her.

"Chow's here."

Kate was still rubbing her hair with a towel but poked her head out of the bathroom. Ramsey had shown up as usual, but today, he was tapping on some of the metal covers keeping the food warm. For the first time, two of her dresses were hanging on the back of the bathroom door. She took a moment to snap on a bra and underwear and pull on one of the dresses before she walked out into the suite. Taz and Drake were also there, rummaging through the spread room service had delivered. They all looked at her, their expressions set.

"I haven't had enough coffee for an ambush," she informed Syon. He was leaning against the breakfast bar.

Ramsey offered her a mug of coffee, along with a smirk that sent a warning through her.

"We like having you on the team, Kate," Ramsey began and offered her some half-and-half.

The members of Toxsin were spread out, making it impossible to keep an eye on all of them.

"Yeah, a lot," Drake said before shoveling steaming scrambled eggs covered in Tabasco sauce into his mouth.

"Great." Kate tried to shut them down.

"We can't watch you when we're performing," Syon said. "You need a bodyguard."

He said "bodyguard," but she heard "babysitter."

"No thanks."

"I have a cousin." Taz rolled right on without letting her denial land. "Taekwondo master. Total badass. He's not bad on a bass either."

"I said thanks but no thanks." She started to turn around.

"You say no, and you have to call Percy," Syon said.

Kate turned on Syon, trying to decide what he was up to, but he was holding out her cell phone like a challenge. "For what reason?"

Syon lifted his hands in mock surrender. "He made some very clear threats…and I think he means business. If we don't take better care of you, he's coming for us. Locked and loaded."

"Yeah, I'm…scared," Ramsey added. Kate shot him a "get real" look. He shrugged and poured syrup onto a mountain of pancakes.

"Good thing he's got a man, because I think Syon might be jealous. That dude has some serious passion for you," Drake added. "He threatened to kick all our asses if we let anything happen to you again."

"Somehow, I don't think that's what scared any of you," Kate replied. "You guys thrive on drama."

There was a flash of smiles before they closed ranks again.

"He did say he was taking the position himself if we didn't get someone for you," Ramsey admitted. "Besides, we don't know who doped you."

"So until we discover the source, you need a pair of eyes on you," Syon finished.

"I'll look out for myself, now that I know there is a problem." And that was going to be the end of it. She picked up a plate and started filling it. The topic changed, turning to something lighter as they teased one another. But suspicion tingled on her neck, because she caught glances among them from time to time.

"Are you tired?"

Kate looked up to find Syon leaning against the sliding glass door's frame. The door was open, letting the breeze in. The sun was starting to set.

"No."

He looked at her skeptically.

"My internal clock is flipped. Besides, I slept most of the day," she said. "I need my shop set up. I know you're behind the crew not doing it."

The crew had been holding her shop hostage, and none of the polo-shirted guys were willing to give her a straight answer when she asked to have it set up. Syon offered her only a shrug. "The doctor said rest."

"I'm full up on resting," she assured him. "We're talking stir-crazy time."

"Then get dressed. It's date night."

Kate sat up. "Really? Cid's going to have something to say about that."

Syon's expression hardened. "Yeah. We all sort of came to that conclusion too. Get dressed."

Kate disappeared into the bathroom, trying to decide what vibe was dancing through the air. She was no closer to pinpointing it when she finished dressing.

When she finished, Ramsey was lounging on the sofa, wearing a pair of black jeans for a change. He jumped up when she emerged.

Taz and Drake fell in with them on the way down the hall. Drake was grinning from ear to ear. "Pub night," he exclaimed. "I need to hear English spoken correctly." His voice had taken on a very British accent.

"Just to be clear," Ramsey said to Drake, "I am not putting anything into my mouth called 'spotted dick.'"

"This from the man who encouraged me to have octopus?" she asked.

Ramsey grinned at her as they started to pile into an SUV. "Octopus is good for you. Spotted dick, not so sure."

"It's custard," Drake stated like a schoolmaster. "And I've seen some of the things you put your mouth on."

"Only because you were behind me in line," Ramsey answered.

Taz hooted.

Syon sat beside Kate, massaging her nape as they wove through the streets. She could tell when they were nearing the section of town were the restaurants were. The sidewalks were better lit, and more people were about. Their driver edged up in front of a place that had a mock shake-shingle roof and a red police call box outside it. Their driver paid no mind to the red curb, but pulled right up to let them unload in front of the door.

The pub was darker inside than most restaurants. A huge wooden bar stretched along half of it and people were sitting up at it as well as occupying small, round tables.

"We've got to grab a spot. Trivia night is popular," Drake said. He dove into the section with the tables, managing to convince a pair of older guys to hop over a table so they could all sit together.

"Trivia night?" Kate asked.

Syon looked up from the beer menu and nodded. "Drake likes to think he's brighter than the rest of us."

"Sometimes, we even let him win," Ramsey added, "'cause we hate to see him pout."

A waitress with a Scottish accent came by, taking down their orders. A man stood up and got everyone's attention. Somehow, Kate had never realized that trivia could be such an intense competition. The air in the bar became thick with tension. Teams hunkered down over their answer sheets, guarding their knowledge. It seemed that bragging rights were indeed coveted. The topics ranged from science to mythology.

Ramsey threw his hands up in the air when they managed to pull off a tie with another team. He howled with the victory, until the waitress showed up with their prize.

"Spotted dick," Drake said with a smirk. "How sweet victory is."

Ramsey tossed a crumpled-up napkin at him.

"Oh…where's your sense of adventure?" Kate demanded. She picked up a spoon and dove into the dessert.

"Are you really going to eat dick right here in front of us?" Ramsey asked.

Kate choked on the custard, shooting Ramsey a killing look. But she pulled the spoon out of her mouth slowly, making Drake snicker.

It was a low-key sort of night, but she discovered that she cherished being part of the moment . They made it back to the hotel and found Cid waiting for them. The road manager had a smile on his lips, but there was something about his eyes that made Kate think he was forcing a professional look.

Tension tingled on her nape as the members of Toxsin stayed close to her, making their way to the elevators and on up to the penthouse floor. They all pounded each other's fists before breaking formation and going different directions in the hallway.

Syon had just closed the door to their suite when she asked, "What was that about?"

"Cid needs to be reminded that we're more than a wild bunch of animals." He captured one of her hands and raised it to his lips. "But I don't want to talk about Cid."

He lifted her hand and turned her around under her arm. Her skirt flared out as he did it a couple more times, twirling her across the suite until they were at the sliding glass door. He stopped and came up behind her, enclosing her in his embrace as they looked out on the balcony.

"I don't want to do anything except seduce you." His voice was a whisper next to her ear. "We've fucked, but we haven't made love…"

She shuddered.

"Like the sound of that?"

He moved her farther out the door. There was a private

Jacuzzi on the balcony. Several candles were set up around it, their lit wicks the only source of light, giving off a soft golden hue that heightened the sense of intimacy.

Syon kissed her neck, nuzzling against her sensitive skin. She leaned her head to the side as he gathered up her hair and pressed a row of tender kisses against her throat.

The candles had a soft jasmine scent, but she enjoyed the scent of Syon's skin more, his own personal musk. She turned and buried her nose in his shoulder, inhaling deeply as she stroked his chest.

"Fingertips are amazing things…aren't they?" he said. Syon leaned back and laid his fingers against her collarbone. "So sensitive…so simple…"

He traced her collarbone, and then down across the bare skin exposed by her neckline. He reached the fabric and slowly dove beneath it.

She was holding her breath, poised on the edge of sensation as she waited for him to touch her breast. He'd done it before, but tonight, anticipation was driving her slowly mad. He finally succeeded, his warm fingers cupping the tender mound, and she let out a contented little sigh.

"I want to stroke you," he said.

"Alright." Kate took a step back. It was a sweet torment, feeling his fingers slipping away from her flesh. But there was a reward in the look glittering in his eyes. In that moment, he was hers, devoted to her, fixated on her as she released the buttons holding her dress closed. The fabric sagged, and he reached out to ease it over her shoulders. It slithered down her body to puddle at her feet, leaving her in her underwear.

She reached behind her and unhooked her bra. With it undone, her breasts lowered.

"Perfect." Syon moved forward, cupping them, smoothing his thumbs over her nipples until they began to pull tight.

She worked the buttons on his shirt, opening it so she could touch him and flatten her hands on his chest. He made a soft sound of male enjoyment. His eyes slipped closed as she ran her fingertips through the crisp hair on his chest. He satisfied every type of sensation: touch, scent, and even those she hadn't really realized she had.

Like the need to have her desire for intimacy fulfilled.

He stepped back and stripped. The sound of his jeans and shirt being shucked drifted to her ears. He stepped forward again and caught the edges of her panties where they hugged her hips, slowly kneeling as he pulled them down. He left them at her ankles and buried his nose in her curls.

She fought the urge to step back, trying to find the courage to stand steady. He rose back up until he towered over her. Her insides were tightening, excitement prickling along her skin. He slid a hand into her hair and held her steady before sealing his lips over hers.

He took his time with the kiss, teasing her with soft compressions before deepening the touch. All the while, he kept her head prisoner to his whim.

She wanted more.

Kate rose onto her toes, seeking out a deeper kiss. Syon didn't disappoint her. He opened his mouth, pressing her lips apart and teasing her tongue with his.

She made a sound that was purely sensual. A moan, possibly a growl.

All she knew was he tasted good.

His arm came around her, securing her against his hard frame as they continued to kiss. His cock was pressed between them, feeling out of place. She wanted it inside her. She lifted her leg, leaving her panties on the floor. She hooked it around his hip, clearing a path to her throbbing center.

"Not yet," Syon warned her. He climbed up the steps to the spa, down into the bubbling water, and offered her his hand.

She took it and smiled as she stepped into the water. It wasn't too hot, making it easy to follow Syon down into it.

Her lover...

The term fit the moment. Syon pulled her gently into his lap, easing her onto his length. As she sank lower, the water bubbled up around her waist, teasing her skin, his cock satisfying the ache inside her.

"That's right where I want you, Kate."

His tone was full of demand. He cupped her hips, controlling their pace. She let him lead, let him take her through a pace that was slow and easy. Need was blistering her insides, but the tempo built the pleasure until it was glowing red-hot. Controlling it intensified it. Syon's jaw was tight, the muscles along his neck corded, but he didn't start hammering her.

She leaned forward and kissed his neck, continuing with the pace, slowly riding the rising wave. Their breathing accelerated, their gazes meeting as they neared the point of breaking. It broke with a rolling motion that churned through her. Not in a hard snap, but in a tumbling motion that lasted. She cried out, arching back to press herself against him. His grip tightened, his cock bursting as he pushed upward into her with sharp little thrusts.

He pressed her against his chest, still buried inside her as the rapture encased them. Slowly stroking her, petting her, cherishing her. If there was another person alive on the globe, she wasn't aware of them. In fact, she wasn't sure where Syon ended and she began. It felt like their heartbeats had fused. Just like their bodies.

It was by far the most intimate moment of her life.

———

"Stay in tonight."

Kate looked over at Syon, feeling like the breath had just left her lungs. He was watching her from beneath narrowed eyes.

"I thought you liked having me at the show."

Something crossed his face. "That was before you ended up getting hurt. I'll be fine."

It felt like he was cutting her from his life, and she didn't like it.

"It's not like I can't handle it. Someone slipped me a roofie."

He let out a sigh. "I know, and I'm not any closer to finding out who did it, so…"

"So what?" Kate came closer. "The vibe coming off you is curling my toes, and not in a good way."

"Don't be pissed, Kate. I can't back down when it comes to your safety."

She crossed her arms over her chest. "I'm going to be hurt if you tell me you don't want me to come tonight. Not pissed. This is personal, between us. Because you

want me there, I know you do, and I don't want to see
you cutting me from your life because we had some
bad luck. That's the difference between hooking up and
being in a relationship. Boyfriend."

He reached out and stroked her jaw, a hint of satisfaction flickering in his eyes. "Fine. We'll do it your way."

Suspicion tingled on her nape. The feeling that she'd
just stepped into a trap came over her.

He moved to the door and opened it. Standing in the
hallway was a lean-looking Asian man. He was dressed
in a dark suit, with only a half inch of spiky hair on his
head, and was at least six feet tall.

"Meet Yoon. Your bodyguard."

Syon offered the guy a nod before he shut the door.
Satisfaction was definitely glowing in his eyes now.

"Don't be so pigheaded," Kate argued. "I told you, I
don't need a bodyguard."

"And we all agreed that making sure you're taken
care of is a better way to go than the lot of us getting
thrown in jail."

Well, she had to concede that point. "That's a tad unfair."

"So is the way we react to each other. I lose my head;
you lose your head."

"I just won't drink," she offered, "until the show
is over."

"That won't solve the problem with the press."

"I'm a little new to this lifestyle. I'll get better at it,"
she said. "It should be my choice."

Syon shook his head. "No, it's not. It's mine, and the
rest of the guys agree."

He was halfway out of the door when she realized he
had every intention of leaving her with her escort.

"You can't just find me glorified pet sitters."

Syon flipped around and stepped up so they were nose to nose when she raised her chin.

"I have to concentrate, Kate, and I can't do that when I'm worried about you being in danger." He caught her shoulders. "Don't be difficult, or I swear I will promise him a fat bonus if he doesn't lose you the entire night. He'll stand outside the bathroom door."

"That is insane," she stated. "You're insane."

"Yeah, like I said, you make me insane."

He pressed a hard kiss against her mouth, absorbing her protest and working his lips against hers until she melted and kissed him back.

Damn him.

She couldn't think.

She never could when he touched her. The current was flowing between them, burning off everything else. Reality was just a puff of smoke.

He finished up with a last breath-stealing motion of his mouth before he was gone. Kate opened the door to go after him but ended up facing Yoon. He gave her a short, stiff bow. She slammed the door shut, feeling like she had just locked herself in a cage.

She cussed and went into the bedroom to get dressed.

⁓

Yoon stuck to her like a shadow. It was both eerie and impressive the way the guy was unshakable. He had one of the sharpest gazes she'd ever seen, and also had one of those pigtailed radio ear pieces. Kate gave a huff as she looked at her hair in the bathroom mirror.

You're hiding.

Yeah, so what?

You're hiding in the ladies' room.

Pathetic, but still, so what?

Back in the performers' room, Cid's team of makeup artists and sound techs were busy. The band members were warming up. Ramsey stopped fingering his guitar when she showed up and offered her a drink. He poured it from a bottle sitting on a table behind him with a rather burly security guy standing over the makeshift bar. The security guy looked bored off his rocker, but he stood there in front of the bottles without moving.

"I think I'm going on the wagon for a bit."

He nodded. "More for me." He took a swig from the drink before setting it down and starting in on his guitar again.

A soft hand landed on her nape. She didn't have to turn around to know it was Syon.

She knew his touch. Recognized it on a cellular level. He leaned close, setting off a ripple of awareness. "I'm glad you're here." It was a whisper, but one that eased some of the tension balled up inside her.

Her phone vibrated, and she looked at it out of habit. Seeing Percy's number made her swipe the screen and take the call.

"Sweetie…"

"Don't sweetie me, Percy." The instruments slowly died away as the band members looked at her. "I don't like ambushes."

"I don't like getting calls about you being taken to the emergency room," her partner informed her.

"So you help get me a bodyguard?"

Percy made a soft sound. "You need one, honey.

It's not my fault you and those hunks were slow on the uptake. There are crazy people out there."

"You're helping make me one of them," she groused.

"How much do you suffer with that man animal in your bed, darling?"

"Good night, Percy."

Her partner laughed before she hung up. But that left her facing the smug looks of four band members. They'd won the round and knew it.

"Percy sends lots of kisses to you all," she said sweetly.

Drake shuddered and took shelter behind his drums. Ramsey put his lips together and made kissing sounds.

"Does that mean you're not too pissed at me?" Taz asked. "'Cause I'm getting a craving for sushi again."

"We can do sushi," Kate decided. "But I think Yoon is coming."

Taz flashed her a smile.

Now two seats had reserved signs on them. Yoon parted the crowd easily and sat down next to her. It was an awkward moment, sitting there with the guy but not knowing him at all. They avoided each other's gazes for a bit before she decided to try and break the ice.

"How'd Taz get you involved in this?"

Yoon offered her a hesitant smile. "I was born in Korea. Good jobs are hard to come by, because everyone has a nephew or cousin they can hire. This was a good opportunity. I get to see the world." Anticipation edged his tone and shone in his eyes. "But don't worry. I won't let my guard down."

"You're likely going to do better than me," she said. "I've never had a bodyguard before. So sorry in advance for anything."

"You don't look like that much trouble." He eyed her. "I spent most of the plane flight over envisioning a Kardashian-type socialite."

He reached up and drew his hand across his forehead and gave her a look of relief. Kate laughed softly.

"Um…you might want to think about losing the suit."

He considered her for a moment. "My grandmother was proud I landed a job where I could wear a suit."

"Maybe Taz can help you with that."

"She was hoping I could talk some sense into him."

"Well, this is an opportunity."

Yoon grinned, looking ready to take on the world.

The stage lights started flashing, and the crowd roared. Over ten thousand people were screaming, but the members of the band still had the same problems as the rest of the world—pleasing their families.

It made her laugh.

But she also ached a little.

"You still mad at me?"

Kate forced her eyes open. "Depends."

Syon chuckled from where he was sprawled on his back next to her. The bed was in shambles, the sheets and pillows half on the floor. She was pretty sure she couldn't move. Her toes were still curled.

"On what?" Syon was merciless.

"I'm going to flat-out lie if you decide to prove anything else to me tonight."

He laughed and rolled over. At least he gave her the courtesy of groaning just a tiny bit before he propped himself on his elbow next to her. "I like proving things to you. Especially when it requires fucking the hell out of you."

He teased one of her nipples, stretching out his neck and catching it between his lips. "In fact, I think you should be mad at me at least twice a week."

"It's not funny, Syon. I think you're overreacting with Yoon."

He drew in a stiff breath. "I don't want to think about you having to deal with pricks who ask you if I use you as a sex slave. Everyone knows you're my girlfriend now. It's only going to get worse. You'll see. I'm going to have to get Yoon a partner, so there is a twenty-four-hour watch."

She groaned, feeling her privacy being shredded. What made it worse was the logical nature of Syon's demands. *Shit.*

"Can I win this argument?" she asked at last.

He shrugged and sat up. "Only if you want me to not worry about you."

"Ouch." She rolled over. "Kill the guilt trip. I get it. I don't like it, but I get it."

He kissed her bare shoulder. "Thank you."

It was a whisper, but she heard how important it was to him. She turned her head and found him watching her. For a moment, it felt like they were connected, in that soul-deep way only he was able to touch her. It scared her, but at the same time, she craved it. Wanted to just sink down and roll around in it until it coated her.

"You should tell Yoon to lose the suit on show night."

Surprise flashed across Syon's face before he laughed. "Bet that was interesting to see."

There was a squeal of a guitar from outside the patio door. The hotel faced a private pool area again.

"I promised the guys a look at what I've been writing."

Syon stood up and pulled on some jeans. He walked through the suite and opened the sliding door. The evening air came in as he greeted his bandmates. Kate pulled on a dress so she could move closer. The four members of Toxsin had their laptops out and were reading the music. They were every bit as raw playing for no one but themselves, pushing the music out of their souls and sending a ripple of awareness across her skin.

It was who they were. She was fascinated by it. Even if she was slightly intimidated too.

Tomorrow, it would be on to a new city. It was almost like they were too much to contain in one city for very long. She fell asleep listening to them.

———

"Sushi!"

Taz landed on the ground outside the music coach when they pulled into Memphis, and cupped his hands around his mouth.

"You promised, Kate!"

"I'm pretty sure we're having sushi tonight," Kate said to Yoon.

He flashed her a grin and reached up to button the top button of his dress shirt. Undoing that button was as far as he'd gone in "loosening up" his wardrobe.

Syon caught her up against him. "Are you making dates with my band bro?"

"Taz has needs," she explained.

Syon growled and nuzzled at her neck. "So do I."

"Hey, Mr. Lead Singer"—Taz was suddenly there, pulling Syon away from her—"you have an interview. You know, the one that only wants the Marquis? Give me my sushi date. You're busy." He captured Kate's wrist and started pulling her toward a waiting SUV. "Bye-bye, Mr. Lead Singer."

Syon flipped him a double bird, one on each hand. But Cid was closing in on him. The road manager had his customary happy-go-lucky smile on his face. A makeup girl was there, with her box slung over her shoulder. Another polo-shirted team member had several pairs of Syon's pants and leather vests on hangers. Syon gave in and walked toward another waiting SUV as the semitruck backed into the loading dock to begin prepping for the next concert.

Taz was fired up. He said a couple of things to Yoon in Korean as their driver took them through the business area of town. They ended up in Korea town, their SUV pulling up in front of a large restaurant.

There was only a single story to the place, but it was humming. There were tables with large burners set into them so you could cook your own Korean BBQ, with huge vents overhead to pull off the steam and smoke. But there was also a counter with sushi chefs behind it. Taz called out a greeting to them as they entered. Kate did her best impression of a bow before a pretty waitress guided them through the mass of people to one of the back tables.

Taz launched into a list of what he wanted.

And it was long. The waitress laughed at him before he finished, but she wrote it all down and bowed before leaving with a little wink for him. She was back within moments with the first tray sent over from the chefs.

"Syon hates it when he does solo interviews."

"Really?" Kate looked up from her plate. "Then why does he do them?"

Taz was chewing and had to finish before answering. "You know, Cid is new to us. He's got what he calls 'fresh ideas.' We're all trying to give his marketing a chance. But it's not good to split us up. Makes for friction. That could lead to trouble. I'm glad we went to the pub the other night. We need to be more than just party animals. I'm a serious musician."

"Cid seems to steamroll right over that point. I've mentioned it to Syon. The fans love you guys for more than your image."

Yoon nodded.

"You guys are tight," Kate said. "It's pretty awesome to see."

Taz stopped before putting something in his mouth. It was clutched between his chopsticks. "You think so?"

"I do."

"See, that's why you and Syon work. You get it." Taz looked at his plate and selected another piece of sushi. "So many chicks don't understand. They get jealous. Don't realize the…" He was searching for the right word.

"They don't realize that being in a relationship means accepting each other for who they are," she said. "Not trying to gain personal self-worth through getting you guys to split off from one another."

Taz's eyes widened. "Exactly. But that's a lot easier said than done for most people."

That was a solid truth. It was a balancing act, and it meant being flexible enough to deal with things like Ramsey walking through their bedroom from time to time.

It was all a part of Syon, and she'd be a liar if she said she wasn't fascinated by him. That meant all of him.

An hour later, Kate stared at Taz and Yoon in awe. "Where are you two putting it?"

They laughed at her and tried to feed her. She blew her cheeks out and shook her head. The restaurant was fuller now than it had been when they'd arrived, with parties of people waiting outside for a table to open up. Waiters were carrying food around while waitresses brought out the beverages and condiments. The tables were so close, anytime someone got up, the chairs bumped together. English was the odd language. Most everyone around them was chattering away in some Asian tongue. The table behind them finished, and within moments, it had been cleaned and reset.

Taz raised his hand to call the waiter over but suddenly stiffened. His good nature evaporated in a flash. Kate turned to see a woman standing in the walkway. She'd been on her way to sit at the table behind them. Her face was white, her mouth open in a little expression of astonishment.

They were both frozen, staring at each other. Someone behind the woman suddenly noticed. An older woman came up beside the young one, grabbing her shoulders and hissing at her in Korean.

Kate didn't have to understand the language to know when someone was cussing, or at the least being insulting.

Taz's expression tightened. But he watched the girl, waiting to see what she was going to do. The older woman was chattering away and even pointed at Kate.

The younger girl suddenly broke out of her trance, turning her back on Taz.

"Time to go," Taz said.

Taz pulled his wallet from the inside of his leather jacket pocket. He carelessly dropped three crisp one-hundred-dollar bills on the table and got up.

He was ten feet away before he turned, his face a tightly controlled mask of fury. He went up to the owner and passed the man several more hundred dollar bills. The owner looked back at the table where the girl was sitting with her family. She was looking at the tabletop as everyone seemed to be taking digs at her. She looked up, feeling Taz watching her. It seemed to be what he was waiting for. He raised his hand toward her, offering his open palm to her in a gesture that was overly gallant. He jerked his head toward the door when she only stared at his hand like she was really contemplating the offer.

She looked like she really wanted to take his hand. Taz hadn't moved; if anything, he looked like he was leaning toward her.

Her family noticed, and one of them stood up to block her view of Taz. His expression hardened. He looked back at the manager.

"Don't tell them until after they've eaten that I paid for their meal." He tossed another hundred dollar bill onto the counter and started for the street.

He was lost in thought on the way to the hotel. He pulled out of his thoughts only long enough to look at Kate.

"Thanks for dinner," he said.

He was gone a moment later, grabbing a key card from Cid's second in command and making his way to the elevators.

It sucked.

Ramsey had his family, and Taz seemed to have a girl who wouldn't cross her family to be with him.

Seriously sucked.

Kate made her way to her suite, realizing she was relieved to discover Syon's stuff set up inside it.

How long was it going to last?

Don't.

She needed to answer that question, but she couldn't. Doubt was a cruel little bitch, chewing on everything she thought she knew and twisting it. Time crept by. She checked her cell phone, but there was no text message from Syon.

She'd told Taz she got it. The lifestyle. The demands.

So she couldn't bug him when he was working. Instead, she slid into bed and told herself to let it go.

Which was another bit of good advice she completely ignored.

———

"The Marquis!"

Kate sat up. The space in the bed beside her was empty.

"You're so hot!"

"Come party with us!"

A round of giggles came from outside the suite door. Kate tripped as she fumbled to get some clothing on. By the time she opened the door, Syon was at the end of the hallway, surrounded by fangirls. Music was blaring, shaking the hallway. He plowed through the door, obviously eager to get inside the suite. It felt like the floor fell out from under her feet.

Members of Cid's team were still moving around. The early hours of the morning were just normal work time for them. A door suddenly opened, and Yoon popped into view, still shrugging into his suit jacket.

She retreated to the suite she shared with Syon, feeling like the bodyguard was a leash to keep her in her place.

Inside, it was dark, the candles unlit tonight. Her composure was crumbling, and there was no amount of willpower that could stop it. Her confidence was a puddle at her feet, even as she tried to go back to sleep.

You're overreacting.

Maybe.

A round of loud laughter made it through her closed door. She cringed, unable to fend off the feeling of loneliness.

Well, you can just go down there.

No. She wasn't going to chase him.

No matter how much she wanted to.

It was the final blow to her pride. The wound that left her without a plan of action, because she knew she'd defeated herself.

———

Someone was pounding on doors.

Kate rubbed her eyes. They burned as she blinked and realized she'd slept on the sofa. She stumbled into the bathroom but knew she was alone in the suite. It was well after two, and Cid's team was getting everyone off to the show. What had been exciting madness in the first few weeks was now a recognizable pattern.

Syon hadn't come back.

It crushed her. But she wiped her face and opened the suite door. She needed to be sure of her facts, not jump to conclusions.

"Okay, ladies…I need him back now." Cid was ushering a trio of half-dressed girls out of the suite at the end of the hallway. Their hair was mussed, their lipstick smeared, and one was still topless. Two of Cid's team members took over, herding them toward the elevators while enjoying the exhibition. No one gave her anything to cover up with.

Just a little more publicity.

It was nauseating.

"See you at the show!" one called before the doors slid shut and she was gone.

Kate's temper sizzled. Syon appeared in the suite doorway, drowsy, looking like he'd just crawled out of bed.

"What was that all about?" she demanded.

Cid was trying to cut her off, but she ducked around him.

"What?" Syon shrugged.

"Don't say 'what.'" Kate pointed at the elevator doors. "One of them was topless."

Syon's eyes narrowed. "We've been over this ground. You either trust me or you don't."

"Oh, like you had such complete faith in me when you pulled up to see me with Conan?"

"That's different."

She scoffed at him. "Different because it's you versus me."

"Boys and girls, we've got a concert to do." Cid

shouldered his way in front of her. "You know, that thing
we're all here to do? To bring in the money? You're
already running behind because of your late night."

Syon cussed but turned around and stormed toward the
elevators. Cid turned on her, blocking her path. "You've
been here long enough to know how it goes. He's not
going to play by the same rules as everyone else. Take it
or leave. As you see, there are plenty who will take it."

There was more than a little pleasure in his tone and
a glitter of victory in his eyes. She wanted to not see it.
Wanted to tell herself she was jumping to conclusions.

Kate turned away, unable to watch anymore. Tears
stung her eyes, completing the moment.

She shut herself behind the door of the suite and
curled into a ball, trying to contain the hurt.

It was impossible. It felt like she was being ripped
in two, the agony increasing as the hotel quieted down,
telling her that everyone was gone.

Yoon was waiting on her.

But that wasn't enough to make her get up.
Honestly, she didn't think she could manage to see
Syon. Not on stage with the hordes of fans willing to
do anything he wanted.

She wanted to think of him as being deeper.

Having more character.

*Yeah, right. He doesn't have to hold himself to
those standards.*

Your standards.

No, he didn't. And it hurt like hell to see him aban-
doning their relationship. Maybe he'd just been checking it out. Seeing what a good girl was like. Enjoying all
the offerings the buffet of life had for him.

She leaned her head back against the wall and felt the heat from the crash and burn.

She was pretty sure she could feel her skin blistering.

As well as her heart breaking.

———

Syon warned off his makeup girl with a finger. She stood poised with a blending sponge in her hand as she debated whether or not to heed him. Cid turned and gave her a sharp look. She flinched and started toward him again. Syon brushed her hand aside, irritated by the way Cid ran the crew. It was what he expected, but at the same time, there was something irritating about it tonight. Like he was a show monkey.

"Give me my phone, Cid," he demanded.

The road manager dropped the cell phone into his pocket. "You know how I feel, mate. It's concert time. All focus on the show. Toys later."

"I'm making an exception," Syon said.

Ramsey looked over at him from where he was warming up. There was already a thin film of perspiration on his chest, his features slightly tight as he let himself flow with the beat. Syon could feel the pull, but the way he'd left Kate was getting in the way. He couldn't drop it.

"I just need to touch base with Kate."

"Kiss-and-make-up time will have to wait," Cid said.

"Yeah," Ramsey added. "Kiss and make up when you have time to fuck out all the wrinkles."

"Watch your mouth, Rams."

Ramsey turned, still working his guitar, but his eyes were open now, his gaze keen as he tried to read Syon.

"Kate's not a fuck," Syon clarified.

Ramsey's lips slowly curved into a sensual smile. "That's what I'd be doing with her." But Ramsey shrugged, his gaze sharpening for a moment of seriousness. "I hear you."

At last, a tiny measure of satisfaction went through Syon. It wasn't enough though. He turned back to Cid.

"You're not even dressed." Cid took a pair of pants from one of his girls and held them out. "Ramsey's got a point. You might need a little more time with your girlfriend than a quick check-in."

It made sense.

Syon took the pants, still not happy with the circumstances. "One text. Then I'm all yours."

Cid handed over the phone. Syon flipped it open and typed in a line of text.

———

Kate stared at her phone, blinking as she read the message. I was a dick. Explain after the show.

You're in love.

Shit.

She was.

There was no other way to explain the rush of happiness, pure giddiness that went through her. Her fingers were trembling, for Christ's sake. She read the message once more and stood up.

Yeah, she might be in love, but there was no way she was going to let Syon steamroll over her. She marched into the bathroom and prepared for war.

Yoon was waiting for her. He checked his watch but didn't say anything about her late arrival. She was used to arriving with the band. Now, she was stuck in the traffic that was slowly being guided into the massive parking lots that surrounded the FedEx Forum. It was a line of brake lights following the hand signals of parking lot attendants. Traffic signals were turned off, blinking red because of the surge of cars trying to make it to the concert on time.

Darkness had descended, lending the perfect backdrop to the fans wearing more leather than cloth. They had spiked hair and piercings in every imaginable place. The parking lot lights shone down on them as they howled with growing excitement. They held up their cell phones to take selfies and pictures of one another.

"We'd better go into the seats," Yoon advised her after a quick look at his watch.

She nodded, filing in behind the fans holding tickets. Yoon flashed their VIP card. It raised a few eyebrows and earned him two winks from hopeful fangirls. Her escort never even blinked. He guided her through the seating, down to the floor, and up to the base of the catwalk.

One of Cid's security guys spotted them as they took over the two reserved seats. He reached up and pressed a button on his headset before saying something into the tiny microphone latched onto his polo-shirt collar.

She didn't have time to think about anything else as the huge spotlights over the stage began to fan out over the crowd and up to the ceiling. The fans roared with approval, thrusting their fists into the air as Drake leaped into view and took command of his drums. He started up with a beat that made her pulse. Taz joined in next, laying down the bass notes, looking like the cheers were soaking into him.

It was wild and raw.

Syon and Ramsey completed the descent into total sensory decadence, their music yanking her into its current like a flash flood. Her personal dilemmas melted away, overshadowed by the sheer abundance of emotion being stirred up. She was at the edge of the catwalk, moving with the beat as Syon moved toward her. By now, she knew the show, knew the spots he like to hit at certain cues.

Tonight he broke from the norm, strolling down the catwalk, prowling toward her. There were thousands of people around them, but all she saw was him. He had his hand curled around the mike with a strength and confidence that thrilled her. It was frankly breathtaking. She heard his soul in every word. He hit his knee, closing the distance between them and making her breath catch. For just a moment, he was inches from her. She caught a glimpse of his eyes, the intensity in them searing. She shuddered, feeling it shoot down her body. She reached up to touch him and watched his eyes widen with surprise.

He pushed back to his feet, shifting his body for a moment. It was the only outward sign he gave that something was off as the song began climbing to its climax. He had to lean back with it, tipping his head back as his body bowed out with the emotion.

Which gave her a glimpse at the open inseam along his thigh.

Her breath froze in her lungs, horror freezing her.

No way.

Just no fucking way!

Chapter 7

"YOUR WORK FUCKING FAILED."

Cid chucked the pants at her the second she made it into the backstage performers' room. She caught them and peered at the hole, her breath stuck in her chest. She was trapped in the moment. A horrible place where she was staring at a failure she was so sure couldn't have happened.

But something caught her eye. She blinked and drew in a breath.

"Like hell it did." She pulled the pants inside out to take a second glance at the garment in her hands, making sure she wasn't seeing what she wanted to see instead of what was there. She held them back up. "Someone pulled up the stitches...halfway down the inseam. They're cut with a ripping needle. You can see the indention from the point."

Cid rounded on her, his entourage backing him up. "So you did it on purpose? At least you admit it. That makes it a lot easier to deal with."

"I can't believe you think I'd compromise a performance."

"My lead singer's fucking pants opened up on stage!" Cid made a cutting gesture with his hand. "Which is why you're leaving. Got a car waiting for you now."

He had four crew members backing him up. He snapped his fingers, and they filed around him, starting toward her. But she was looking at Syon. He had that hard glitter of business in his eyes. His arms crossed over his chest as he leaned on the corner of a dressing table and studied her.

"I didn't pull those stitches up." She was talking to him and honestly didn't give a single fuck for anyone else in the room.

What she cared about was the way he remained silent.

"Get her out of here," Cid snapped.

She stood there, watching it happen in slow motion. She felt like something inside her was bleeding. Like a huge knife had been plunged deep into her heart. She couldn't draw breath. She was pretty sure she knew what it was like to be sucker punched, because her entire body felt like it was shaking and on the verge of collapse.

She'd known it was headed for an epic crash and burn.

Known it.

But it still hurt a thousand times worse than any mental anticipation had prepared her for.

The only thing she managed to do was look away, so Syon wouldn't see the pain in her eyes.

"Don't you fucking touch her."

Kate jerked her attention back up. Syon had slid between her and the crew members.

"I didn't tell you to do shit, Cid. We'll work this out."

The road manager didn't even blink. "My job is to manage this tour. She's disruptive and now sabotaging the operation. I'm just taking out the garbage. I don't wait for you to tell me my job. That's why I'm the best. Got the original artist on his way to the airport to join up with us."

Someone grabbed her bicep, and she jumped. Ramsey pulled her back and stepped in front of her.

"Kate isn't garbage," Ramsey stated.

She stood there with her mouth gaping. Syon turned to look at Ramsey. She witnessed the connection between them as he gave Ramsey a single nod.

"But someone has been sabotaging our show."

They all turned to look at Taz. He was standing near the rolling rack of pants. Two pairs had been tossed over his shoulder, and he had another pair turned halfway inside out. "Someone's been tampering with these. You can see where they nicked the leather with the ripping needle. All of these have been messed with too."

"I knew it. My work doesn't fail. And I am a professional." Kate charged over to him and grabbed the pants. The nicks were there, every third or fourth stitch broken. Syon was leaning over her shoulder, Ramsey on the other side.

"We've got a security problem," Ramsey muttered.

"Exactly, we've got a jilted-girlfriend issue," Cid said from across the room. "She's lashing out. Which is why she's got to go."

Cid was coming toward her. Syon stepped into his path, Ramsey right behind him. Taz gently tugged her back and joined his bandmates. Yoon was suddenly there, crowding her back.

Cid stopped. "I've seen it before." He faced off with them. "You hired me because I've got the experience. Trust me, the bitch is making trouble, and it affected the show." He stepped closer to Syon. "Let me do my job. You'll thank me tomorrow."

"Kate isn't jilted," Syon said softly. "We had a fight, that's all."

Cid laughed. "Is that why she was bawling her eyes out?" Cid shook his head. "Not a chance. She knows you spent the night somewhere else. With someone else. Not that I blame you. Those were some premium babes. Would have loved a taste myself."

Syon, Ramsey, and Taz all turned to look at her. She groaned, her face feeling like it was catching fire.

"I spent the night with Taz," Syon offered softly. "He was drunk and needed a wingman."

"The girls were with me and Drake," Ramsey told her. "Swear it."

"Yeah," Drake added. "Syon owed Taz, so we left him to it."

Relief poured through her, as well as a moment of surprise.

Of course! The girl in the restaurant flashed through her mind. The encounter had set Taz on his ear. Bad.

"It doesn't matter where you spent the night." Cid grabbed Syon by the shoulders and turned him back to face him. "You don't need a relationship to get laid. She's in the way. You guys are hot, and the fans love you. Relationships don't belong in rock. Why should you toe the line? You aren't men; you're gods! Live like it."

"Sounds like she's in your way." Syon shook off Cid's hold.

Cid wasn't willing to back down. His complexion darkened. "I know this business. You're the new kids, so better listen up." He pointed a finger at them. "You can fall just as fast as you've risen. The fans want to see you living the life they can't have. So you're going to be wild and fuck a lot. Because that's what the fans want. The whole package."

Syon smacked Cid's hand away. "You're employed to manage the tour. Not my dick."

Cid threw his head back and laughed. "It's part of the deal. You've got the music skills, but that won't cut it in today's market. You've got to have the image. As it is, you've already got one deadbeat on this team." Cid flung an open-handed gesture toward Taz. "You could both take some notes from Ramsey."

There was a blur of motion from the side. A hard smack, and Cid went stumbling across the suite. Drake stood there, his fist still in the air. "No one trashes my teammates or Kate."

The polo-shirted crew members had backed off. Cid made the mistake of looking toward them. His expression tightened when he realized they were sitting it out—waiting it out, actually. They were going with the winner. He jerked his suit jacket down and faced off with the members of Toxsin.

"I've worked with the *best*," he snarled. "Mega-superstars! And I know how to make sure they stay that way."

"Yeah, your résumé is impressive," Syon drawled. "Unless I consider the fact that none of those heavy hitters kept you."

"I'm getting a clue why that might be," Ramsey added.

"Do you have any clue what a bitch like that one can take from you?" Cid pointed at her. "She's going to want to play house. A divorce will cost you a bundle, even with a prenuptial."

"You're getting the cart in front of the horse," Kate interjected. She started toward Cid, but he sniffed at her, dismissing her.

But Syon had gone deadly still. "Did you have that roofie slipped to her?"

Cid paled. "Don't be ridiculous." But a trickle of sweat made its way down the side of his face, his poise suddenly faltering. Just a smidgen, but enough to outrage her. Kate took one step toward him, only to have Yoon slip an arm around her and pull her back.

Syon pulled his arm back and punched Cid straight on the jaw. Cid went down, unable to recover, and ended up sprawled on his butt.

"Anything to protect your meal ticket," Syon said in disgust. "She could have been killed."

"You can't accuse me of that." Cid was back on his feet.

"I just did," Syon said, cutting through Cid's argument. "You're the only one with an agenda that needs Kate out of my life. You had motive, opportunity, and as you're so fond of telling me, you can get anything."

Syon suddenly moved. He jerked one of bags out of the hand of one of Cid's entourage members. He opened it and dumped the contents onto the dressing-room table. He grabbed a small plastic ziplock bag that had a white pill in it.

"You forget, Cid, I'm not an idiot. I know what this is." He looked back at the table. "As well as a couple of those other mystery bags."

Cid pointed at the girl who was carrying the bag. "That wasn't in my pocket bag. I'll toss her out too."

The girl gasped, shocked to her core by the betrayal. Cid didn't even blink. "But you told me—"

"Oh, please." Cid cut her a hard look. "I'm a professional. I wouldn't have told any team member to bring drugs into a performance area."

"You did!" The girl insisted, looking toward Syon. "He wanted to scare her, make her think you were the one who liked to party hard. He'd heard about her rules. Thought she'd leave if there were drugs here."

"Shut up!" Cid snapped. "You're just trying to deflect. The dope was in your purse. I have managed mega—"

"You are full of shit," Syon snarled. "No wonder you were looking for a new band. What did you do? Get a gag order to shut up your last client? Is that why the background check came back clean?"

"You fucking asshole," Ramsey hissed. "We don't drug our women."

"You need your ass kicked," Taz added.

"And how." Drake had lost every last bit of his British composure.

Cid's complexion turned gray. He looked around again, but no one was coming to his rescue. The girl was sobbing, babbling about how he'd told her to buy the drugs. The tension in the air was twisting tighter, Syon and his bandmates looking like they were getting ready to spring.

Kate didn't have an ounce of pity for him. He suddenly stiffened, some of his confidence returning.

"Go on," Cid said smugly. "In a court of law, I'll win over the four of you any day. All I need is a hospital report." He cast a glance at Kate. "A bitch who has pictures of her tits all over the Internet sure isn't going to generate much sympathy as the reason for an assault. No one is going to believe she didn't take the dope herself, or that one of you didn't give it to her so she'd go for double time. It won't be hard to get pictures of the three of you on that dance floor groping each other. Drunk or high, it looks the same to a jury."

Syon pulled his arm back, but Ramsey stopped him. "He isn't worth it."

Syon was fighting. She could see him battling the urge to tear Cid apart. Part of her needed to see it, needed the balm for her wounded pride.

But the rational side of Kate's brain couldn't let Syon put himself at risk either. "He's an opportunist prick. Don't give him the evidence for a lawsuit and a gag order. Just can his ass and enjoy knowing you can tell the truth to the next people he tries to work for."

Cid snorted at her. "Good luck. My contract is iron-clad. It will cost you a bundle to get rid of me without hard evidence, which you don't have."

Cid went skidding across the performers' room floor, a hard hit on the jaw from Syon sending him reeling.

"Don't ever insult my fiancée."

"My friend," Ramsey added as he popped his knuckles.

"Mine too," Taz said.

"Definitely," Drake chimed in.

"Let me remind you what else is in your contract." Syon stood over Cid. "A no-tolerance clause for drugs, which includes any personal assistant you have. She"—he pointed at the girl—"is your personal assistant. She has dope in her possession. I've got plenty of witnesses, and if you're smart, you'll get out of here before I call up Deputy Jenson."

Syon looked at the girl. "Will you testify against him?"

She'd stopped crying, realizing it was a lost cause. Syon's question made her eyes brighten. "You bet your ass I will."

"Still, her word against mine," Cid insisted.

"No it isn't," the girl said. She grabbed her cell phone off the table where the contents of her purse were still lying. She held it out toward Ramsey. "There were text messages. He erased them, but you hack phones all the time. Can you get them back?"

The phone went crashing to the floor. Cid had moved up while everyone's attention was on the girl. He went to smash the phone with his foot, but Yoon spun around and sent him into the wall with a back kick that landed in Cid's midsection.

Ramsey scooped up the phone. "You bet I can retrieve them."

Cid was struggling to his feet, clutching his midsection. "I'll countersue for assault."

"You just don't know when to quit, do you, mate?" Drake was suddenly across the room, sending his fist into Cid's jaw. The road manager went stumbling, Drake following him. "Sue me. I dare you. Your career will be finished."

Ramsey pulled Drake back, scuffling with his bandmate as Cid leaned against the wall, blood seeping down his chin from a split lip.

"You can have your severance," Syon said, "and you'll sign a gag order, or I'll call Deputy Jenson and let him know we've got new developments in the case."

"Full severance," Cid snapped, "and a gag order on your side too."

"Full severance only. Take it or leave it," Syon said.

"Better than you deserve," Ramsey added.

"Let me take it out of his hide," Drake insisted.

"Deal!" Cid said, sending a cutting look at the girl. Taz stepped between them, the nunchakus back in his hand.

"Just so you know," Taz said as he swung the weapon, "if she ever calls me, with say, even a small concern that you're making grief for her…or her family…or… her dentist"—the nunchakus made a wicked sound as he twirled them in the air—"there's going to be trouble."

Syon looked at the team of polo-shirted crew. "Get him out of here, and keep him out of my sight if you all want your jobs."

The team that had always hopped to Cid's commands now jumped to haul him off the floor and out of the performers' room. The members of his entourage stood frozen, like a pack of deer attempting to decide who was going to be the dominate buck. Syon pointed them toward the door. They went with a click of their spike heels, the one girl taking the time to scoop the contents of her purse off the table before she stood there, looking lost.

"The guy wanted us partying, because it covered his own love of the sport," Ramsey said at last. "I swear one of those skirts is a dude."

Kate's emotions felt wrung out.

What just happened?

She needed to sort out her thoughts, but she was stuck on the admission Syon had made. He turned and looked at her, stirring up all the hurt that had been burning inside her for the last day.

Only a day? It had felt so much longer.

"When did we establish that I'm your fiancée?"

Ramsey groaned. He tossed his hands into the air and turned away. "Later." But he cut her a wink before he disappeared into the hallway.

"On your six," Drake said as he hurried to catch up.

"Don't leave me behind," Taz called after them. "You better come too, Yoon. They're about to get lovey-dovey."

Her bodyguard deserted her in a flash, taking only a moment to encourage Cid's ex-entourage girl to join them.

Kate stood there for a moment, feeling like she'd been tossed up on the beach by a gigantic wave. She choked on a laugh. Syon. Only Syon affected her that way.

He raised an eyebrow. But she shook her head, suddenly completely unsure of him.

Okay, of herself.

Of them.

"Sorry about last night," he said, trying his hand at explaining. "I should have told you where I was. It's sort of hardwired in me to put the team first."

She shrugged. "I was temperamental this morning."

He flashed her a grin. "I loved it."

"You did not," she scoffed.

He nodded. "I did. Even if I owe you an apology for it. I just can't help that I like knowing you cared enough to come after me, looking to tear a strip off my ass."

"Well…I'd say you have it coming, but I saw the look on Taz's face last night when we ran into that girl. I think she likes him."

"She loves him." Syon's expression hardened. "And he's got it bad for her."

There was a hard certainty in his voice that made her ache for Taz.

"Looked like her family had big problems with that."

"Major ones," he confirmed.

Syon fell silent. But she could see his thoughts buzzing in his caramel eyes.

"It kills me to know I made you cry."

She wanted to shrug it off. She started to, but he was suddenly there, clasping her in his embrace, and she lost her grip on everything except how she felt about him.

"I should have gotten rid of Cid sooner."

She stiffened, trying to regain her composure. Syon pressed her back into his chest. "That was a dick move he pulled with the pictures. I should have let him have it."

"You should have."

He tipped up her head so he could lock gazes with her. "Percy might have threatened to bikini wax me over it."

"I'd be disappointed if he didn't."

She felt like she was drowning. There was so much security in his embrace. It had the power to seal the entire world outside the circle of his arms.

"Does this mean Percy is going to be your maid of honor at our wedding?"

"We haven't known each other long enough to get married." The words were out of her mouth before she thought about what she was saying. She backed up, escaping a few feet as she scrambled to think.

"We haven't been able to keep our hands off each other since we met." He took a step toward her. She retreated, knowing she was going to lose all grasp on logic if he touched her.

"You didn't ask me to marry you."

He slowly shook his head, stalking closer to her. "It just happened, Kate. I'm as surprised by it as you are. I don't need to hear you say you love me. I see it in your eyes. Tell me you don't see how much of a slave I am to you? You saw it onstage. I felt the connection."

She wanted to smile like a simpleton.

But she shook her head instead. Syon edged closer, his eyes glittering with mischief. She looked at him suspiciously, trying to gauge what he was planning, when he snagged her wrist. He stopped her train of thought, and a moment later, he bent over and she tumbled over his shoulder. He straightened up and smacked her butt with a satisfied grunt.

"Since I just fired Cid, no one will be paying off the paparazzi tonight."

He carried her through the doors and backstage.

"Syon!"

He chuckled at her plea, walking out of the building with her on his shoulder. She lifted her head and ended up blinded by the camera flashes going off.

"Nice catch!"

"Me next!"

"Great ass!"

He carried her down to a waiting SUV and let her slide off his shoulder onto the seat. Syon paused in the doorway of the vehicle, maintaining his hold on her. He had an arm around her waist, and she'd ended up on her knees on the seat. He cupped her head, holding her steady as his eyes glittered with victory.

"'Kiss me, Kate, we will be married o' Sunday.'"

She laughed as the line from *The Taming of the Shrew* rolled off his lips a second before he claimed her lips in a hard kiss. The crowd cheered, cameras snapped pictures, and Syon kissed her senseless.

Yeah, completely senseless.

Love?

It was that too.

———————

"Really?" Kate demanded. "*Roadkill* is getting first shot at our wedding pictures?"

The three cameramen were pulling on their suits, obviously ill at ease in formal clothing. Around their necks were the very coveted press passes into her wedding. They were happily dashing around the perfectly manicured lawn of the church grounds, getting shots of the celebrities in attendance. Spring was just coming to England, making the two-hundred-year-old church look majestic.

It had a bell tower with massive bells, flying buttresses holding up the ceiling, and stained-glass windows. The pews looked ancient but were gleaming from recent polish. Just stepping inside felt like a time-travel moment. She was sure she could feel the centuries of joy the building had played host to. The minister had put them through the wringer too, demanding three visits and premarital classes. But today, it was all worth it as he stood in his starched white vestment, ready to marry them.

Everything she'd ever wanted from a fairy-tale wedding. Which just happened to fit in with the European tour dates.

Syon started to turn to face her. She hissed at him through the open window of the bride's dressing room. "Don't peek! It's bad luck to see the bride before the ceremony."

"You insisted I come over here," he growled, but he leaned against the stone wall, looking away from her.

"Because I want to know why *Roadkill* is here!" She felt like she was explaining something to a three-year-old.

"Had to give them a horse trade," Syon explained. "Some pictures more valuable than the ones they had of you."

"Oh." Surprise held her silent for a moment.

Syon took that moment to flip around and press a kiss against her lips. She squealed and slapped him on his shoulder.

"Behave," she scolded. But her tone lacked any true reprimand. She was so touched to hear he was championing her modesty.

He flashed his teeth at her. "Never." He backed up with his hands in the air. "I can promise you anything but that, sweet Kate."

Even dressed in a tux, he looked uncivilized.

Just the way you like him…

"What are you doing?" Percy exclaimed from inside the bride's room. There was a huff and heavy footfalls as he charged toward the window.

"You can't see the bride before the wedding!"

Syon grinned, unrepentant, as Ramsey came into sight. The rocker was wearing more clothing than Kate had ever seen him in.

And he made it look good.

But he was still rebelling, his dress shirt unbuttoned halfway down his chest.

"Looking fine, Kate!"

"Don't make me come through this window," Percy threatened in a tone that was way too playful. "I take my matron-of-honor duties seriously."

"Stop screeching like a scalded cat," Steve said from across the room.

Percy turned to look at his husband. "Does that mean I make good on my threats?"

"No." Steve picked up Kate's veil. "He's about to become a married man. So hands off."

"The other one isn't." Percy purred as he took a look at Ramsey.

"But you are," Steve said. "Now get over here and finish dressing the bride. That's your job."

Percy smiled at her. "Oh, *sweetie*…you look divine, if I do say so myself."

Percy started to fuss, making sure the dress he'd made for her was perfect. His deep teal suit matched Steve's perfectly. She was wearing antique lace that suited the church. A small demi-train, and a skirt that was just loose enough to flow when she walked. The silk Percy had chosen was a perfect complement to her red hair.

"Well, if you have to get married to a man, at least you have a matron of honor I approve of."

Her mother was decked out in a gypsy-style skirt and tunic top. She'd kicked off her shoes by the door and was walking around barefoot, sporting a new pedicure for the occasion.

"She's not marrying a man; she is marrying *the man*,"

Percy exclaimed. Steve reached over and slapped him on the shoulder.

"Well, *the man* of those who aren't taken," Percy said warmly.

Steve beamed at his husband.

The church bells began to toll. Steve fluttered over to set her veil on her head as Kate sat down on a stool. Every butterfly in Great Britain was clearly in her belly. Her fingers began to tremble, and she was pretty sure she could feel the color draining from her face. There was a round of chuckles around her.

"She's ready," Steve announced.

Percy leaned over and giggled at the look on her face. "Oh yes, she's ready."

Actually, she was.

Kate stood up, feeling her insides clench with anticipation. Yup, that was exactly the way Syon had always affected her. Excitement was running through her like a live current, warming her from head to toe. She felt like she was making that climb to the crest of a roller coaster, the first drop just coming into view as she was led into the foyer where two altar boys waited to open the massive doors leading to the sanctuary. High above her head, the bells rang. The pipe organ was playing, and the hinges groaned as the doors were pulled open to let her see her groom waiting for her at the end of the aisle.

Her mother had found her shoes and hat. She offered Kate her arm. "Ready?"

"I sure am."

Her belly clenched as she took the plunge.

Epic.

Just epic.

Read on for a sneak peek at book two in
Dawn Ryder's sizzling new Rock Band series

Rock Steady

THE FOG HAD COME IN TO SETTLE OVER THE CITY OF SAN Francisco. The locals put on their coats and stayed on the streets, casting off the chains of the workweek with excess. The local bars and clubs were in full swing even two full hours after midnight.

"Where in the hell did you go?" Kate Braden propped her hands on to her hips and sent Ramsey a seething glare. "We've been shaking the trees for you."

Ramsey offered her a smile that was a shot of pure sin. He curled a hand around Kate's hip and pulled her against his hard body while taking a moment to enjoy the display her corset top pushed her breasts into. "Would have surfaced sooner if I'd known you wanted me."

He purred out the word "wanted."

Ramsey looped an arm around her shoulders. A faint scent of scotch surrounded him, but it was a fine grade and only added to his dark-as-sin persona. He was wearing leather pants and a vest, as usual, but he fit with the crowd on the sidewalks of San Francisco. At least the crowd that was out at three thirty in the morning.

He started to nuzzle her neck.

"Hands off my wife there, Rams."

Syon Braden appeared, neatly lifting Ramsey's hand

off her hip. Syon slid in and took possession of her as Ramsey grinned.

"What happened to Tia?" Syon asked his bandmate.

Ramsey frowned. For a moment, his rocker image cracked, showing the very sharp mind of the man who lurked inside the Toxsin band member. It was only a momentary glimpse before Ramsey shrugged and offered them a bored expression, retreating into his bad-boy persona.

"Guess she's gone." He kept his tone nonchalant. If Kate didn't know him, she never would have guessed he cared at all about the girl in question. He shrugged again, his leather vest opening to display a peek at his six-pack abs.

But it also showed her a flash of something else.

Kate reached forward for the waistband of the leather pants he wore.

"She might be your wife, but she can't keep her hands off me…" Ramsey taunted Syon.

Kate's husband shifted, trying to decide what she was doing. She moved the leather down just an inch and gasped.

Syon cussed.

The other two members of Toxsin found them and joined Syon.

Kate moved the waistband a little more to get a better look at the new tattoo on Ramsey's lower abdomen. "They're…cherry blossoms…" Her voice was a horrified whisper.

Ramsey frowned and looked down. He was sobering up quick, his expression turning deadly. "That bitch."

"Damn it, Ramsey…" Syon snapped. "You can't slip

the leash like that." He peered at the delicate, blush-pink blossoms.

"I wasn't drunk when I went off with Tia," Ramsey said.

"Damned straight you weren't," Taz said. "I would have stayed on your butt if you were."

Ramsey was struggling to remember how he'd ended up with a tattoo. "I didn't have that much." His forehead was furrowed as he tried to concentrate. He popped open the button on his waistband and looked down.

"Oh shit…" Drake said, his British accent emerging.

"That's bad," Taz agreed.

"We've got to do something," Syon confirmed.

Clearly tattooed on the singer's body were two sprigs of pink cherry blossoms. They conflicted so badly with Ramsey's dark, bad-boy persona, his bandmates stared at him for long moments as shock held them silent. It was a serious crash-and-burn moment.

Kate pulled him closer to a street lamp, hoping the light might show it to be a temporary tattoo.

No such luck.

"You're screwed." Kate detected the faint red marks from the needle. There was a faint gloss from Vaseline, too.

"We're screwed," Syon added. "We've got a show in forty-eight hours."

The members of Toxsin stuck together. Ramsey and Syon were tighter than most married couples. Kate had learned that firsthand when she'd met Syon and spent a season on tour with the band as their costumer.

"It's Toxsin!" someone yelled from across the street. There was a blare of a horn as the fangirls stepped right into traffic in their quest to connect with their music idols.

Kate reached out and refashioned Ramsey's pants to hide the tattoo.

"I dreamed about this differently," Ramsey drawled. "You took my pants *off* in my dreams. I remember that detail perfectly."

"Right now, they need to stay on." She fastened up his vest while she was at it, but the garment wasn't going to hide the top half of the second blossom.

"We've got to get this fixed. Now," Syon said. "That is going to show onstage, big time."

They might have been sporting long hair and leather, but all of them were dead serious as they recognized the potential for disaster the little feminine tattoo posed.

As in…epic disaster.

The tabloids would have a field day if even one fuzzy picture surfaced. Toxsin had just hit the Bay Area and had two days until show night. Ramsey was known for his guitar solos, and his lack of a shirt made sure his abs were on display.

"I don't think cover-up is going to do the job on that one," Drake offered.

"One little rub from the waistband of your pants and it would be all over cyberspace," Kate added.

"We need tattoo rescue. Like, now," Taz added as he dug his phone out of his pocket and started searching the Internet. "The paparazzi gets a shot of that and we're never going to live it down."

———

"What do you think you're going to prove?"

Jewel tapped her fingers against the countertop and bit her lower lip. Her mom was just getting started.

"Don't you appreciate the education your father and I paid for?"

"I do, Mom." Jewel managed to keep her tone even and sweet. Really, it didn't take much effort. At this point, she was well acquainted with her mother's disdain for her current employment choice.

But her skin wasn't as thick as she'd like to think. The tone of her mother's voice cut deep, slicing into the dream she was trying to live with the sharp blade of reality.

Don't hate the messenger...

"Well, you wouldn't know it by the way you're playing around in that tattoo shop like some sort of orphan who didn't have the benefit of a university education," her mom said.

"Are you open?"

Jewel looked up and fumbled her phone. She was pretty sure her mouth was hanging open, but wasn't completely sure because her brain decided to fry, leaving her staring at the decadent man prowling across the shop toward her.

"Tell your mom you'll call back. I need you right now."

Okay, *fried* wasn't nearly hot enough a word to describe the sensation going through her. The guy in front of her was a god. Six and a quarter feet of raw muscle, with black eyes that looked like they'd been carved out of a moonless midnight sky. His shoulder-length hair was spiky and screamed nonconformity. But it was the flash of arrogance in his eyes that drove home just how raw he was.

This guy took what he wanted and never apologized for any of his desires.

It should have raised her hackles. Instead, it made her wet. And she wasn't sure she liked it.

Scratch that. She was sure she didn't like it, because it felt like she was losing control.

"Mom, I've…got someone in the shop."

Her voice had become raspy. She blinked, trying to scrape together some poise. The god grinned at her, sending a bolt of heat straight into her clit.

Shit.

The guy was sex-on-a-stick. And his leather pants made it clear he had quite a stick.

"How can I help you?" she asked.

"So, you're open?" She realized the god had companions. One was an Asian man with short, spiky hair, black as a raven's wing, with a flash of blue fire that made it look amazing; the other one's blond hair fell to his shoulders.

"Oh…sorry. I was talking to my mom…" Her tongue felt like it had gone lame. "When you walked in, that is. We're always open."

And her night was suddenly looking up. "I'm Jewel. What are you gents looking for?"

"Do you do tattoo rescue?" The blond one was talking now.

"You can only go darker. So if it's already black, your options are limited. But sure, I do rescues."

"Wait," the Asian guy insisted. "Do you have a portfolio?"

"Of course." Jewel pulled a large book from underneath the counter.

She was used to seeing leather and brawn in the shop, but there was a level of detail on all three of these guys that spoke of money. If those pants weren't all custom-made, she'd pack it in and start sending out marketing résumés like her parents advised. She knew the difference between wannabes and genuine badasses.

"I mean, nothing personal, but we can't have this done by an amateur," the Asian continued as he started flipping through the pages of her work.

"Speak for yourself, Taz…" The dark-eyed one was leaning farther across the counter, making the air between them sizzle. "I'd like to get very personal with you."

His voice was like black velvet. It would be super easy to just let it rub all over her. She got the feeling she'd end up purring. There was a flash of something in his eyes, sending a tingle of apprehension through her.

He knew exactly what sort of effect he was having on her.

She bit her lower lip. His dark gaze dropped to the little nervous motion, his lips curving rakishly in response as he leaned on the counter, moving closer to her. He was too damned smooth, pushing on her comfort zone with an ease that was annoying but that she admired at the same time. He was arrogant but with a solid core of confidence that sent a shiver down her spine; part of her really wanted to put him to the test.

Which wouldn't help her pay the rent. She dug deep, trying to get a grip on her professionalism.

"You might want to see these too." She lifted another album from beneath the counter and handed it over. "These are my awards, and the back half is rescues, before and after shots."

The blond took it in a flash, leaving her once again staring at the dark-eyed god.

"Maybe you should let me in on the…problem?"

His grin grew into a huge smile that showed off gleaming white teeth. "Thought you'd never ask…"

He straightened up, giving her another glimpse of just how tall he was before he popped the button on his pants. She was actually holding her breath as he worked the buttons on his fly.

One…

Two…

Oh hell, the guy was chiseled.

But the delicate pink blossoms hit her like a bucket of ice water. "Oh, that is just wrong."

Jewel came around the counter, her attention fixed on his lower belly. She sank to her knee to get eye level with the cheery tattoo. It was a sacrilege, like putting pink ribbons on the ears of a panther.

"Hmmm…" The dark god made a soft sound under his breath and reached for her head. For a moment, she was caught in that second, waiting for his fingers to land on her.

"Don't be an idiot, Ramsey." Taz smacked the hand away. "These pictures are good. We don't need her getting pissed off because you get touchy."

"Looked to me like she wouldn't mind me…touching." There was challenge in his voice.

Jewel straightened up, forcing herself to take a reality check. "Pissed off your girlfriend?" she asked pointedly.

About the Author

Dawn Ryder is the erotic romance pen name of a best-selling author of historical romances. She has been publishing her stories for over eight years to a growing and appreciative audience. She is commercially published in mass market and trade paper, and digi-first published with trade paper releases. She is hugely committed to her career as an author, as well as to other authors and to her readership. She resides in Southern California.